DOUBLE TAKE

DOUBLE TAKE

ALMA J. YATES

Copyright © 1999

All Rights Reserved.

No part of this book may be reproduced in any form whatsoever, whether by graphic, visual, electronic, filming, microfilming, tape recording, or any other means, without prior written permission of the author, except in the case of brief passages embodied in critical reviews and articles.

ISBN: 1-55517-416-7

v2

Published by: **Bonneville Books**

Distributed by:
925 North Main, Springville, UT 84663 • 801/489-4084

CFI Distribution • CFI Books • Council Press • Bonneville Books

Cover design by Corinne A. Bischoff and Sheila Mortimer
Printed in the United States of America

To my wife
Nicki

CHAPTER ONE

The early May sun perched warmly above the pine-covered mountains on the western slopes of the Huntsville Valley as I climbed from my faded orange Volkswagen Bug, my only real possession from my pre-mission days. During high school the Bug had been a teen novelty, something my brother and I had purchased, preened and protected. We had been ecstatic to have anything to drive; now, a bit more mature and a whole lot more sensitive, I longed for something that implied more affluence, but post-mission poverty prevented little more than indulgent pondering.

Slamming the Bug's door, I looked toward the red brick house with white trim, set back from the street amid an imposing stand of tall poplar trees. A faint afternoon breeze breathed through the branches causing a soft whisper among the million poplar leaves. I glanced at the number scribbled on the scrap of paper in my hand—325. It matched the black block numbers on the right side of the front door.

I headed up the narrow, cracked walk that cut across a patch of thin lawn. Climbing the front steps and stepping onto the porch, I gently rapped on the wooden frame screen door. I heard someone moving about inside; then an older woman's voice called, "I'm coming. I'm coming. I'll be right with you." The voice changed to a soft hum as slow footsteps approached. "Yes, young man, how may I help you?"

I smiled through the screen, looking down on a short, compact woman in her seventies. Her hair was completely white, and her skin was smooth but lined with smile wrinkles about her small mouth and dark eyes. "Hello," I greeted, nodding my head once. "You must be Virginia Pritt." The lady smiled and nodded. "I'm Jacob Matthews. I was…"

"Oh, you're JB's brother," she gushed, pushing open the screen door. She shook her head, took my arm and pulled me into her modest living room. "I should have known it was you. You're twins, for goodness sakes. Identical JB said. I can see that now." She chortled as she studied me a moment with her head cocked to one side. "But of course, even being twins, you're different. JB's hair's longer." She laughed and patted me on the arm. "Lots longer. I've got daughters with shorter hair than his.

"He doesn't always shave." A twinkle sparkled in her eyes. "But he's found that razor more and more. It's that girl Camille's influence on him. I've always liked her. My youngest daughter used to baby-sit her and her sister. If someone can get your brother to clip his hair and straighten up, Camille would make a dandy wife."

She became serious. "I will have to tell you that I detest that horrid thing he wears so proudly in his ear. I know I'm from another time," she lamented, "but every time I see it, I want to yank it out. And take his ear with it. When I was growing up, a young man never wore an earring." She studied my ears.

I laughed. "Don't worry, I'm not big on earrings either."

"JB said you're back from a mission in Mexico."

"About two weeks ago. I'm just learning to speak English again."

"My third son served in Mexico. Almost twenty years back, though. Veracruz, I believe."

"I was in Culiacán. Not at all close to Veracruz."

"I can understand why you're so tanned and handsome with your short hair and clean-cut look. Without the horrid earring." She grimaced and shuddered noticeably. "JB better watch out or Camille will take one look at you and drop him flat. Tell him to throw the ghastly thing away." She leaned toward me and whispered. "But I think it's rather expensive. He told me himself it was a real diamond. Can you imagine? He ought to put it in a ring and give it to a nice girl."

I laughed. "Actually, I think..."

"Don't get me wrong," she went on. "JB's a nice young man. He checks on me occasionally. He'll help me in the yard. He doesn't have to. He just likes helping folks out."

I got the distinct impression that Virginia Pritt rarely closed her mouth and just as rarely opened her ears. She was going to talk my leg off before I could get a word in edgewise. I decided I was better off just nodding my head rather than trying to keep up to her.

"JB needs a good roommate." She patted my arm. "He's excited to have you here. He brags on you a lot."

"James brags on me?" I questioned, laughing and using his given name. During my mission I'd grown accustomed to thinking of him as James again because that was how Mom had referred to him in her letters. His full name was James Bradley Matthews, but since junior high practically everyone had taken to calling him JB. Mom refused to be swayed, though. She loved the name James because her dad was James Jacob Johnson. That's how James and I got our names.

"He was sure proud you were a missionary. Do you call him James or JB? Everybody around here knows him as JB."

I laughed. "I used to call him JB all the time, but my mom's trying to break me of the habit. She hates the initials."

"I always liked James as a name. I have a brother named James. But we always called him Howdy." Suddenly her mouth dropped open and she touched my arm, mortified. "But I'm just babbling, Jacob. Let me get your key. I can't guarantee how your brother looks after his apartment. It might need a good cleaning." She continued talking as she stepped to a hutch across the room, opened a drawer and extracted a key. "You look like you'll be more particular." She handed me the key. "The stairs are just around the corner. It's not big, but for a basement apartment it's not too bad. A man and woman and their four kids lived down there for…"

"Thanks for the key," I managed to squeeze in before she launched into another monologue. I grinned, backed out of her house and hurried down the front steps.

"Now if you need anything, Jacob, you just give a little holler."

I heaved a sigh as I disappeared around the corner of the house and spotted the concrete steps descending to a wood-frame screen door. The steps were a bit dirty and littered with wind-blown scraps of paper and brown poplar leaves. The screen door's white paint was chipped and covered with greasy smudge marks around the door handle.

I pulled the screen door open. It creaked a protest and the

metal spring twanged softly above. I put the key in the lock, turned and pushed the door open. The mixed smell of stale pizza, soiled laundry and overripe apples accosted my nose.

Stepping in, I looked around. I was standing in a small kitchen, the only light coming from the open door and a narrow window at ground level just above the old-fashioned porcelain sink. The faded green tile floor not only begged to be swept, but it obviously had not seen a mop in weeks. A crumb-covered card table with three gray folding chairs served as the dining area. A fridge, looking like a tenacious hold-over from the '50s, hummed softly next to the sink. The sink and sideboard were littered with unwashed dishes as well as discarded paper plates, crumpled napkins and bits of pizza crust and dried and partly eaten sandwiches. A small gas stove with an oven was scrunched in the corner next to the fridge.

Taking a couple of steps into the kitchen, my shoes crunched on dried crumbs. Behind the door and to the right, the area opened into a miniature living room. The only dividing line was where the green tile ended and a matted, soiled olive-green carpet began. Against the far wall, under another narrow, ground-level window was a brown couch, its misshapen cushions stacked haphazardly at one end. There were also two overstuffed chairs, neither one matching the other. In the middle of the room, serving a desperate attempt as a coffee table, were two wooden crates turned upside down and draped with a colorful beach towel.

Heaving a sigh, I muttered with a wan smile, "Home sweet home, James. Mom would flat out faint walking in here."

Leaving the front door open, hoping for some fresh air, I stepped to both windows and pushed them open; then I wandered down the dark hall leading from the kitchen. There was a bedroom on either side, both doors open. The bed in one was unmade, piled with wrinkled clothes. A stack of dirty laundry clogged one corner and part of the closet. A four-drawer dresser was just inside the door with two of the drawers open. The top of the dresser was covered with bottles of cologne, aftershave, hand lotion, and a mixture of discarded coins, loose screws and sundry junk.

The other room was no less appealing but it was clean. Dingy gray curtains covered the window, leaving the room dimly lit and a bit dreary. There was a twin-size box springs and mattress mounted on a half dozen cinder blocks. The bed was actually made with two brand new sheets. Two new quilts, still in their plastic covers, were at the foot of the bed. There was a battered dresser next to the closet and a plastic bucket for a garbage can just inside the door. The rest of the room was empty.

The bathroom was at the end of the hall, across from the furnace room. There was a tiny wall sink under a white, rusting metal medicine cabinet with a cracked mirror. The toilet was next to the sink. On the opposite wall was a large empty towel rack with three crumpled towels under it. The frosted shower door was ajar and the shower head was leaking loudly, making the air dank and humid. I peered inside. "I'd dare bet that in the two months James has been here this hasn't been cleaned," I muttered disapprovingly, looking at the dark, dirty corners and the flourishing mildew on the tile walls.

I wandered back to the kitchen. Pushing my hands into my pockets, I looked around me. "Well, James, you didn't exactly invite me to a nobleman's royal manor," I joked out loud, "but I suppose I'll survive. As long as I don't contract some strange disease in the shower," I added wryly.

I glanced at my watch. It was ten minutes to five. James had said he would be off work by four-thirty. I thought of bringing my things in from the car just to occupy my time, but I reconsidered, not wanting James to think I was crowding him.

This construction job offer in Huntsville hadn't been my only chance to work after my mission. I had received a similar work opportunity from a family friend in Brigham City. That way I could have lived with my parents and family on our farm outside of Brigham. But when James wrote to me a month before my release and told me there was an opening on his crew in Huntsville, I wrote right back and accepted, sensing that this was my last chance with James. That didn't mean that I had no apprehensions about coming, though.

I pulled out one of the folding chairs and sat down, leaving the front door open and the lights off. A breeze rustled a discarded Snickers wrapper and a half dozen leaves at the bottom of the basement steps. Looking about these cramped quarters, I tried to get a better impression of the guy who lived here. I knew it was James. And yet, he was a different James.

I placed my forearm on the corner of the card table but quickly removed it when it pressed against a moist, sticky surface. I wiped my arm on my shirt, pushed the chair from the table and began to pace. I wanted to find something of James here, something that would remind me of another place, another time, another relationship.

Whistling softly to myself, I left the kitchen and wandered down the hall again, stopping at James's room. Growing up, James had been the one to hound me about having everything orderly and clean, exasperated with me for leaving dirty socks on the floor or pants flung over the back of a chair. Now his whole apartment was unkempt and chaotic.

I stepped into the room and looked around, reflecting on our first and only meeting since my return from Mexico. My three older sisters and their families along with Mom and Dad and my two younger brothers and little sister had greeted me at the airport. James was noticeably absent. Work was his excuse. I knew a 2 p.m. arrival time was not conducive to a work schedule, but I had still hoped he would show. It was three days later, a Sunday, the day I gave my missionary report in sacrament meeting, that I saw him.

He drove down the gravel driveway in his black Firebird a few minutes before we left for church. I sensed he wanted to impress me with his car. We had always talked about being rich one day and going out and each buying a black Firebird. But that was supposed to happen after our missions.

"What do you think?" he questioned hopefully.

"It's nice." I tried to seem pleased. "You left the Bug for me?"

"It still runs. I always liked the Bug."

"We could always trade, straight across, James."

"JB," he corrected me. "Mom's the only one who calls me James any more, and I can't break her of the habit." He shook his head and laughed. "I'll stick with the Firebird." He ran his finger across the black fender.

I glanced at my watch. "Well, we better get going. Sacrament meeting starts in twenty minutes. Are you going to change?"

James looked down at his white Levis Silvertabs and the red-button sport shirt open at the neck. His long reddish-brown hair was tied in a short ponytail in back. "You don't think they'll let me in unless I come in a coat and tie?" He grinned.

I laughed. "You look fine," I hedged.

The short drive from our farm to the stake center in Brigham City took only a few minutes, but our conversation was stilted by mere small talk. I could have had the same conversation with a complete stranger.

James returned to the house after our meetings and had dinner with the family, but he left early, something about another obligation, but I suspected that his leaving had more to do with his comfort level than prior engagements. With so many family members there, he and I didn't have a chance to sit down and talk. There was never the right moment, and neither one of us knew how or where to begin.

I glanced toward James's cluttered dresser top. Amid the chaos I spotted something familiar, not what I had expected, not anything I had anticipated. In fact, when I first noticed it, I wondered if it was a mistaken illusion. Reaching out, I picked up the small gold picture frame holding a Polaroid snap shot, one of James in a white tuxedo and his junior prom date in a very short black formal with a titillating slit on the left side, revealing the lower part of her thigh. I had taken that picture. James and I had doubled to the prom that year. I had been surprised, even shocked, that James had decided to go with Leticia Trujillo.

I sat down on the edge of James's bed and studied the picture in the dim light of the basement bedroom, trying to sort through the memories, unravel the puzzle. I always suspected Leticia lie at the center, but how?

James and I hadn't ever done anything without the other one, or at least without consulting the other one. We could discuss anything. Many things we didn't have to discuss; we just knew, through some sixth sense, what the other one was thinking and feeling. Leticia Trujillo—everybody called her Leti—changed that.

Being shy and more involved in sports and school work, James had never dated much before Leti. Then at the middle of our junior year, when she was only a sophomore, James met her at lunch in the library working on a research paper. She asked him to help her locate a resource book. They talked most of the noon hour. One noon-hour session led to another and another until those sessions spilled over into after school visits. The junior prom was James's first date with Leti.

I knew why James was attracted to her. She was beautiful with her long dark hair, jet black eyes and light creamy skin. She wasn't painted up and gaudy like some girls. Outside a movie or a magazine, I had never seen anyone as beautiful as Leti Trujillo. She was carefree, daring, likeable. And wild! She hadn't actually established herself as part of the wild crowd. Her beauty and charm allowed her to walk a delicate line between them and the popular crowd, but I suspected that she would eventually gravitate toward the wild element.

I wasn't ever sure why James fell for her. Or why she fell for him. Not that there was anything wrong with him. He was handsome enough, at least that's what people told us. He was more serious than I and always determined to do everything right by the book. But going with Leti Trujillo wasn't even in the book. She was completely out of the mainstream for someone like James. She was already serious with a guy, Marcus Roper, six years older than she. He worked full time and drove a black Nissan truck with dark tinted glass, wide chrome wheels and a megabuck stereo system crammed in it. Marcus was Leti's type. He fit her mold. But not James!

I suspect Leti was attracted to James's innocence. And his unlimited capacity to like and care for people. James wasn't one to pass judgment on anybody. James accepted people as they were, regardless of where or what they were. Racial, economic, social or political prejudice was unfathomable to him. I'm convinced that was how Leti unsuspectingly wormed her way into his conscience and then into his heart.

After the junior prom and James's subsequent increased interest in Leti, I tried to tell him Leti wasn't his type. She wasn't LDS. Her parents were divorced. She lived with her mother, who worked as a waitress at a truck stop. Her dad had run off years before. For all her beauty and charm Leti had a reputation. I was confident that she was the type who would make a low social splash, attracting the hungry hormonal attention of the guys, and then she'd fizzle into bitter oblivion.

But I think Leti relished stepping away from that hard life, which, unknown to her, was destined for despondency. As much as she liked the hard, fast lane she was recklessly cruising, she was intrigued by James. James was a diversion, another adventure, tamer than what she had grown accustomed to, but enough of a twist to keep her attention for a while.

Had her circumstances been different, Leti might have succeeded. Had she grown up in a stable home with different parents, she could have been anything she dreamed of. But circumstances weren't different. Even before she met James, the doors of opportunity had already begun to swing closed. Nothing James was going to do would change that.

As we were growing up, James and I had argued occasionally, but not like we did over Leti Trujillo. At first I thought he was only succumbing to a bit of flattery by a very pretty girl, but I realized, long before Mom and Dad picked up on it, that a bond had developed between Leti and James. But the bond was lopsided. Leti didn't give up Marcus Roper. James was a breath of fresh air in her sultry social slum. I told James that she was using him. He refused to believe me. He said they talked about good things, about college, his mission, the Church, about her changing her life.

"And what does she discuss with Marcus Roper?" I asked pointedly one evening. "Do you think he's discussing the scriptures when he takes her riding up the canyon?"

Once in frustrated desperation I asked him if in his wildest dreams he thought he could ever marry somebody like Leti Trujillo. He didn't even hesitate. He just looked at me and answered in all seriousness, "Jacob, you don't know how many times I've thought of that. Some things would have to change, of course. But…" He shook his head and looked away. "You don't know Leti like I do. All you see is the reputation. There's more to Leti than that. She knows about her reputation. She wants to change. I want to help her. I might be the only one who can."

I wanted to reach out and shake him, wake him up. But he actually believed everything he was telling me.

There were only two times in my life that James and I went to blows. Both times were during the summer between our junior and senior years, both fights over Leti. The last one happened while we were working in the barn a couple of weeks before school started. I had been trying to talk sense into his head. I'd tried patience, reasoning, kidding. Nothing worked.

Finally we dropped the subject altogether and worked in silence. James was the first to speak. "Jacob," he asked hesitantly, "I need to talk to you. I mean really talk to you."

I faced him. "We can always talk. That's what we're good at."

"I need your help. But," he added quickly, "I don't want you preaching or saying anything about Leti."

"All right."

He was uncomfortable, not sure of what to say but bursting with the need to say something. "What would happen if I married Leti?"

"What?" The question caught me off guard. I couldn't help myself, responding with disbelief and disgust.

"Just give me a chance, Jacob. Don't go judging me until I've at least had a chance to explain some things."

I shook my head in utter puzzlement. "Do you mean marry her after Marcus Roper dumps her, or do you figure you'll wait a while? Or do you figure you'll pull this whole thing off behind Roper's back?"

"I mean now."

"Now?" I started to laugh and turned away. "Like today, tomorrow, next week? What do you mean by *now?*"

"Never mind," he suddenly muttered. "I thought maybe you'd understand. You don't. And you don't care either."

"That's where you're wrong, JB," I flared. "I do care. That's why I've been trying to talk some sense into that thick head of yours. JB," I burst out angrily, "you're caught up with a pretty face. But if you just opened your eyes two seconds, you'd see past Leti's good looks and see that she's nothing. And it doesn't matter how hard you try to make her something, she'll always be a sleaze-bag tramp with a cute face."

James came at me with his fists, his eyes boiling anger. I don't know how long we would have fought if James hadn't wrenched his ankle and knee when he tripped on the straw-strewn floor. For a while he couldn't even stand up. He just lay there, moaning and groaning and threatening me through clenched teeth. Our knuckles were bruised and scraped, and we were both bleeding from the nose. I felt sick. Even then I knew that during those few hot seconds we had killed something between us, something that we'd never call back.

Three days later Leti Trujillo was killed when her car, traveling sixty miles per hour down Sardine Canyon above Brigham City, missed a curve and smashed into a rock embankment. There weren't even skid marks.

I know it's a morbid, heartless thing to say, but I was relieved because I thought James was finally rid of Leti. She wouldn't be around to mess with his mind and his infatuated emotions.

I went with James to the funeral, but he walked out halfway through. For over a week it was like he was lost in a daze. He wouldn't talk; he wouldn't laugh. Then gradually he came out of it. He didn't talk about Leti. It was as though she were erased from his life, but she'd left a vacuum.

After Leti's death, I knew James was hurting. I could feel the pain myself, but he locked me out, and we became strangers. We didn't ever fight again. We didn't even argue much. We just went different ways. He lost interest in the Church, going on a mission, attending college, all the things we had dreamed of doing together as we grew up.

Three days after graduation he left Brigham City and traveled to Phoenix, Arizona, to work construction with Uncle Fred, one of Mom's brothers. The day he left home I went up to the room while he was finishing his packing. As he closed his suitcase and set it on the floor, he said, "I wish things had been different, Jacob." He didn't look at me.

"Hey, you're just leaving for a few months," I tried to joke. "We still have a lot of things to do. We need to be thinking of those mission papers."

"You better do that one without me," he said softly, trying to smile.

"Sure," I laughed disbelievingly. "You're the one that's been keeping me on the old mission trail, having a royal cow every time I even looked like I was going to stumble. Now you're telling me I've got to do this one on my own? Come on, JB, get real."

"You'll be a good missionary, Jacob."

"We'll *both* be good missionaries."

He smiled but didn't argue.

When we turned nineteen in September, I didn't send my mission papers in. I had suspected that James was going to need some extra time to get things straight in his mind and in his life, so I had enrolled at Weber State with plans of going fall semester. I waited, hoping James would come around. By Christmas I knew it wasn't going to happen so I entered the MTC in April. Without James.

Once in Phoenix James didn't write and rarely called. Even when I left on my mission, he didn't bother to see me off. When I flew to Mexico, I stopped for a couple of hours in Phoenix. Mom had given him my flight plans. I looked for him, but he never showed. I wrote to him a few times, but all I received in return was one Christmas card signed "JB." Then a month before my release, he wrote and said some friend of his found him a job with a Roger Franco in Huntsville. He said he could get me on with the same outfit if I was interested.

All during my mission I had thought of James, feeling guilty that I was out sharing the gospel with complete strangers while my own twin brother drifted away from me and the Church. Working with James in Huntsville was my chance to repair our fractured fraternity.

I stared down at the snapshot in my hand, wondering why James even had it here. What kind of hold did Leti Trujillo still have on him? He was dating this Camille girl Mrs. Pritt had mentioned, so why keep this picture of Leti?"

I set the picture back on the dresser and left the room. As I looked about the kitchen again, I noticed the note stuck to the fridge door with a jagged piece of duct tape. I had been vaguely aware that it was there, but I hadn't paid enough attention to it to realize that it was for me: "Jacob, I might be running a little late. If I'm not here by five, go over to the Hardaways. They're only a couple blocks from here. There's a map on the back of this note. I'll see you there. Get there by five."

I looked at my watch. I was already late. Pulling the note off the fridge door, I studied the map. I wasn't exactly excited about charging over to a stranger's place without James, but this seemed important to him. I didn't want to disappoint him. Not on our first day together. Heaving a sigh, I left the apartment and strolled to the car.

CHAPTER TWO

I pulled up to a large two-story frame home with white siding and black decorative shutters and trim. I checked the map again and double checked the house number. I hadn't expected James to send me to a place like this. It was huge. There was a two-car garage with both doors open revealing a Buick LeSaber and a Suburban. Parked in the driveway was a red Toyota truck. The lawn, shrubbery and flowers were well manicured. There were three small blue spruce along the edge of the lawn opposite from the driveway and a medium-size willow tree in the corner closest to the driveway.

James's Firebird wasn't in sight so I was tempted to put the Bug in gear and return to the apartment. I debated a moment longer and then shut the engine off, not because I wanted to be here but because James did.

Stepping from the Bug with a deliberate slowness reflective of my reluctance, I walked up the narrow walk to a heavy wooden white door with a prominent brass knocker at eye level. I reached for the door bell and then changed my mind and used the brass knocker.

Before I could take my hand from the knocker, I heard a young girl call out, "I'll get it," and then there was the soft pad of feet. The door swung open, and I stood looking down at a girl about eleven years old wearing white knee-length shorts and a loose fitting red knit blouse. Her hair was sandy brown and falling down about her shoulders. Her face was cute, innocent but inquiring.

"Good gosh!" she gasped. She took a step back and looked me up and down, her mouth dropping open. "I don't believe it," she muttered, barely above a whisper, her dark brown eyes wide with wonder.

"I don't know if I'm at the right place," I stammered awkwardly, feeling the warm color of embarrassment flush my cheeks, "but James told me to come here, and I..."

"Millie," the girl blared without taking her eyes off me, "you better get down here. Now! This'll blow you away." She laughed. "I'd have never believed it!"

I heard and saw someone coming down a flight of carpeted stairs behind the girl. "What is it, Teresa?"

The second girl stopped three-quarters of the way down the stairs and studied me in shocked silence. She was eighteen or nineteen and not very tall, perhaps five foot five. She was well proportioned. And very good looking! Her blond curled hair was past shoulder length and her eyes were the most striking color of blue that I had ever seen. Her nose and mouth were small and her face was more round than long. She was wearing a pair of designer blue jeans and a men's long sleeve cotton shirt with the sleeves rolled to her elbows and the tails hanging down to mid-thigh.

I was smitten by a sudden shyness, not exactly sure whom to address, Teresa, who had opened the door, or Millie, the girl on the stairs. I cleared my throat self-consciously, shifted my weight from one leg to the other and then blurted out, gesturing involuntarily with my hands, "I'm not sure if you were expecting me." I coughed. "This might be a bit of a surprise for you, but I..."

A quick, disarming smile burst across Millie's face; then without warning she charged the rest of the way down the stairs, across the entry way and through the front door. She took me completely off guard, throwing herself against me, wrapping her arms around my neck in a tight, hungry squeeze and pressed her lips to mine in a heart-pounding kiss.

I had always been a little shy around girls, but complicating that reluctance was the fact that I had just finished two years in the mission field where girls had always been at arm's length, and now this very beautiful girl was engaging me in the most passionate kiss that I had ever experienced in my life. And I didn't have the faintest idea who she was. I might have been able to enjoy the experience had I had a moment to brace myself for it, and had I not had an intrigued, gasping audience in the form of Teresa.

I stumbled backward and would have fallen off the steps if Millie hadn't clung to me so tightly and helped me maintain my balance. Without releasing her embrace about my neck, she interrupted her kiss and looked into my eyes, her face no more than six inches from mine. "You've done it," she whispered, her voice trembling slightly with emotion. "I used to think of this happening. But I didn't dare think it would come so soon." She caressed my hair and then my face.

"I'm not sure…" I tried to explain, still baffled and attempting to catch my breath while I unscrambled my brain, but I was positively sluggish, somewhat intoxicated by this exhilarating moment.

Millie didn't allow me to finish. She kissed me again, this time reaching up and holding my face with her hands.

Everything happened so quickly. For a fleeting second I wondered if this was a set-up for an unsuspecting returned missionary and that James would pop out of somewhere, laughing at my embarrassing predicament. And yet, in spite of the sudden unexpectedness of Millie's demonstrated affection, it was not an entirely unpleasant experience. In fact, I distinctly remember thinking that if this was what people meant by love at first sight, I could convince myself to believe in it.

As suddenly as Millie had fallen into my embrace, she separated, stepped back and looked me up and down as though she couldn't believe what she was seeing. There was a mist in her blue, engaging eyes. Her lower lip quivered and she bit down on it. This was no put-on. Genuinely blinking back tears, she smiled. "I've even prayed for this, JB."

She could have punched me in the stomach and not knocked my wind away as quickly as she did with those words. Still staggered by the effects of her quick, unexpected passion, I felt suddenly dishonest and just a little immoral having shared something with this stranger that wasn't meant for me.

"When you said you had a surprise for me," she said laughing and wiping at her eyes with the tips of her fingers, "I was expecting some…" She shook her head. "I don't know what I was expecting, but it wasn't *this*." She pointed at me with two outstretched arms. "JB, I always knew that deep down inside there was something so…"

"I'm not JB," I burst out, taking a step back and shaking my head. "I'm Jacob, James's brother." I wet my lips.

"James? James who?"

"James Matthews. I guess you know him by JB." I gulped. "He told me to meet him here." I tried to smile. "He didn't warn me about the welcoming committee." I touched my lips.

Millie looked at me, her smile frozen, but there was no humor there, only startled disbelief. "What?" she finally rasped, recovering only slightly.

"I'm Jacob Matthews, James's...I mean, JB's twin brother."

"JB's brother?" She was incredulous, her mouth dropping open and her whole person seeming to deflate. "JB has a twin?"

"I'm sorry if I confused you. James..." I stopped and shook my head and smiled. "I used to call him JB all the time. I got out of practice. I'll have to start calling him JB again." I coughed. "JB just left me a note in the apartment." I held up the note. "He told me to come here before five. I didn't know what to expect." I forced a sheepish grin and shook my head. "I wasn't expecting this, though. Do you suppose either one of us needs to make a confession to the bishop or something? I think we can both plead ignorance or temporary insanity?" I said, attempting a bit of humor. "Our ignorance of the facts makes us pretty innocent, but..."

Millie reached up and touched her lips. "Ohhhh," she whispered slowly. Taking a deep breath, she straightened her shoulders and stepped back away from me, rapidly composing herself. "I'm sorry," she blushed, looking around, afraid someone had seen her gushing mistake. She spotted Teresa still holding the front door open and struggling to squelch a grin behind the hand covering her mouth.

"That was better than those movie scenes. Why don't you try it again just in case I missed something the first time."

"Teresa, would you please run on," Millie ordered. "And don't you dare blab this to anybody."

"Me, blab?" Teresa questioned, pretending to be shocked. Then a grin exploded across her face. "When JB comes, you don't ever kiss him like that. He'll be jealous."

"Teresa!" Millie warned.

Giggling, Teresa turned and charged into the house, her giggle expanding into a full laugh before she disappeared down the hall. Millie turned back to me, the bright pink of embarrassment still evident on her cheeks. At first she attempted a serious demeanor, but she was a failure in suppressing a grin that burst across her charming, lovely face. Quickly she ducked her head and laughed into the back of her hand that she pressed to her mouth. "You must think I am one *crazy* girl," she said, looking at me.

"Dang," I joined in her laughter, "you were too quick for me. I didn't have time to think much of anything." I rubbed my chin. "But, I can tell you right now, I've never been kissed like that by anyone. At least, if I have been I don't remember." I shook my head. "Of course, we could try it again just to make sure. There's no sense in leaving any doubts."

Millie continued to laugh, leaning her head back and looking upward. "You might not believe this," she went on, shaking her head and looking down at her hands clasped in front of her, but I've never kissed *anybody* like that." She peeked up at me. "I haven't even kissed JB like that."

"Well, actually, I'm glad you decided to practice on me. I think it would have been wasted on James." I shook my head. "I don't think he gets into things like that. Absolutely no sense of appreciation."

"You're going to tell him, aren't you?"

I grinned and then forced a somber look onto my face. "I don't think you have to worry about anything. I think he's two-timing you anyway. Let him have the other one."

"What?"

I cringed. "Well, there's this girl named Camille who…"

"Camille? I'm Camille."

"You?" I pointed down the hall where Teresa had disappeared. "She called you Millie."

"My dad used to call me Millie Camillie. Sometimes different ones in the family call me Millie just to be crazy."

"Oh, I'm sorry," I blushed. "If she had called you Camille, I would have known and could have stopped you in time." I smiled. "I think we can safely say this is all your little sister's fault."

"So you're not going to tell your brother."

"I've already forgotten everything."

"You have?"

I burst out laughing again and shaking my head. "No, I lied. I haven't forgotten it. Dang, my heart's still pounding," I said, pressing my hand to my chest, "and I can hardly breath, but I'll be the last guy to tell James."

"You mean JB?" I nodded. "Once a long time ago he told me his name was James something."

"James Bradley."

She nodded. "But I've always known him as JB. He said he had a surprise for me," she tried to explain. "When I saw you, I just assumed he had…" She shrugged and blushed. "Well, you're what I assumed he had done to himself."

"Well, I'm not going to tell him what kind of reception I received or he'll be down to the barbershop in nothing flat. Then I think *I'd* be jealous. I think we've already developed a relationship here, and you can probably just forget all about James."

Camille laughed and walked backwards into the house. "Well, don't just stand out there on the front step." She waved me in and pointed to a huge sofa in the living room. "JB will be here any time. He should have been the one to introduce us." She held out her hand. "I'm Camille Hardaway. Most people just call me Cami."

I took her hand and shook it. "I think I prefer the other greeting."

"You said you'd forgotten."

I held up my hands in surrender. "It must have been a flashback. It's gone now. I don't remember a thing."

I stepped into the entry way. To my left was a massive living room with rich carpet and elegant furnishings. To my right was a carpeted dining area with a long, oval oak table with eight high back chairs. In the center of the table was a huge dry flower arrangement.

Still feeling a bit awkward in this luxurious home, I followed Cami Hardaway into the living room. She sat in a soft overstuffed chair while I dropped onto the sofa. For a moment we were quiet, Cami looking at me while I looked about the room self-consciously. I noticed three paintings on three different walls. Although they were well done, I wondered if they were original work.

"Is someone here a painter?" I inquired, attempting a conversation.

She pointed to a lake and mountain scene to the right of me. "Mom painted that a few weeks before she died."

"Oh, I'm sorry."

She shook her head. "It's been almost eight years."

There was another brief silence. "JB told me he had a younger brother," she remarked.

My gaze left the painting on the wall and moved to Cami, who snuggled in the chair with one leg drawn up in front of her and her forearm resting on the raised knee. "I take it he didn't mention his younger brother was two minutes younger than he was."

She pursed her lips. "He talked a lot about your family, but…" She smiled and shook her head. "Nothing about having a twin. At least if he did it didn't bump. He talked a lot about you, though," she quickly added. "You've been on a mission in Mexico."

"Did he mention that he got me a job up here in Huntsville?"

"Working construction with him?" She sounded surprised.

I nodded. "How long have you known James?"

She thought a moment. "Last fall I went to school at Arizona State. The first night I was in Tempe, I had a flat. I was with my roommate. We were both from Huntsville and scared out of our minds to have a flat between Tempe and Mesa at ten minutes to midnight. The last thing Dad had told me before I drove to Arizona was don't ever be out alone after ten o'clock. I kept thinking to myself, `Cami, it's almost midnight, and you're all alone.' Jessica wasn't any help. She had already made up her mind that we were going to end up strangled and dumped in some ditch. I was driving our Geo Metro. I didn't even know where the spare was even if I had dared get out of the car in the first place. If I had known, I wouldn't have known how to get to it. Do you know where they squeeze that little donut?"

I shrugged. "Probably tucked underneath somewhere."

"How was I supposed to know that?" She rolled her eyes. "JB happened along about then. We freaked out. " She heaved a sigh. "With his long hair and beard and tough guy look and…"

"James had a beard?"

"Back then. He's shaved since. He kept the mustache, though. Well, anyway, he was quite a sight for two helpless Huntsville girls stranded on a big city street. We locked the doors and started looking for weapons. All we found were a couple of Bic pens and a plastic picnic fork."

"So you decided not to fight him off?"

"He got a real kick out of our hysteria. He told us through the rolled up window that we could stay in the car with the doors locked and he'd change the tire for us. He told us he'd already beaten up his quota of helpless girls for the day and didn't need any more till the next night so we were safe." She heaved a sigh and rolled her eyes. "We calmed down after a couple of minutes and before long ventured out of the car. When we found out he was from Brigham City, Utah, we were sure he was a long-haired guardian angel. He was quite handsome, even with his beard."

"Obviously you saw him again after he changed your tire."

"The donut was flat. He took it over to a 24-hour service station to inflate it. Jessica and I went with him. In his Firebird. He said he was hungry so we stopped for something to eat." She smiled. "After he fed us, we were no longer just impressed."

She smiled, remembering. "There was something about JB." She pondered silently. "He just pulled me in. Not to mention Jessica. At first glance, he really isn't my type. You know, the long hair, the beard, the earring, the rough life. But something in my brain keeps pestering me, telling me that JB isn't what he seems. I'm right, aren't I?"

"What do you mean?"

"You know him better than I."

I stared at the smooth, thick carpet and crossed my legs, considering the question. "James and I haven't had much to do with each other for a while." I shook my head. "I've seen him only once since I returned from Mexico. Actually, you probably know him better now than I do. I know the old James

Matthews. You know JB."

"I always had the impression that you and JB were close."

"We were."

"And?"

I didn't answer right away. "Things just changed."

"He said your dad was the bishop for a long time. Was he the infamous bishop's son? The wild one in the family?"

I shook my head. "Neither of us was wild. I guess if you wanted to say one of us was straighter than the other one, it would have been James. He was a genuine straight arrow. No gray with James, all black and white. If he couldn't do something right down the line, he didn't want to do it at all. That's just the way he was.

"Then he decided there was a gray area after all. It was quite sudden. I really don't know how he feels anymore. I find it hard to think that he's given up on everything he believed. His beliefs weren't a put-on. They were genuine. I suspect they're still there."

"I'm listening."

"You'd be safer to get the story from James. All I've got are suspicions. I don't know what really happened. And we've been apart for almost three years."

"I'm interested in people's opinions."

I pondered a moment, tempted to talk but not knowing how much to say or even what to say. "Well, at one time there…"

The phone rang, cutting into my explanation. Cami pulled herself from the chair and moaned, "Excuse me." She crossed the living room and picked up an old-fashioned decorative phone on a small table in the corner. "Hello. JB!" she called out, turning to me and grinning. "I thought you said you'd be here a little before five. Why didn't you call? Well, never mind. Come over. Where are you anyway?" There was a brief pause. She laughed. "Yes, Jacob is here. He's feeling lonely." She listened a moment and then cleared her throat ceremoniously. "Yes, I think you could say that we've introduced ourselves." Smiling guiltily at me, she winked and then cringed for my benefit. "You didn't tell me Jacob was your twin. When you said younger brother, I always just assumed he was younger than just two minutes. Now that you mention it, JB, my first impression was that Jacob was you. Yes, I was a bit surprised, but I think I'm over that now. Yes, we're going to wait for you. What? You're taking us both to dinner? We'll be here. Good-bye."

Slowly she returned the phone to the receiver. For a brief moment she stared down at the phone without taking her hand from it. She faced me, serious and pensive. "I guess we wait a little longer," she commented quietly. "He got tied up at work. One of his buddies was supposed to call but apparently didn't," she spoke as she strolled back to her chair and sank into it with a sigh. "He's at the apartment now. He just climbed out of the shower. When he didn't see your things there, he got to wondering if you'd even showed up. He's taking us out for something to eat. Are you hungry?"

I grinned. "If he's paying, I'm starved. If I'm paying, then I'll probably go pretty light. Technically I'm still unemployed."

Cami smiled and ran her thumb nail along her upper teeth. "We'll talk JB into paying. After all he invited us." Suddenly she pushed herself from the chair. "I better change into something else before JB shows up. Make yourself at home. I could call Teresa in to keep you company." She laughed. "Of course, she'd talk your leg off, and by the time she was finished with you, you wouldn't have any secrets. Nor would any of the Hardaways."

"Cami, you're talking about me," a voice called from down the hall.

"And you're eavesdropping," Cami called back.

"Not either. I'm just here reading a book."

Cami looked at me and shook her head. "Watch her," she whispered. "She's only eleven but her IQ's about 210. And she's dying to know everything about everybody."

I laughed. "I think I'll just sit here by myself and catch my breath. I'm still panting from something that happened a while back. I don't remember what it was," I quickly added, "but it certainly took my breath away."

"On second thought, you and Teresa might hit it off really well." She glared at me playfully and left the room.

CHAPTER THREE

Alone in the Hardaways' spacious living room, I reached for a month old issue of *Reader's Digest* lying on the glass-topped coffee table and began thumbing through it. I heard a car pull into the driveway, but from where I sat I couldn't see it. I hoped it was James. A car door opened and closed. A moment later someone pushed open the front door.

I looked up from the *Reader's Digest* just as another girl, older than Cami, stepped through the door and started for the stairs. She hadn't taken more than three or four steps when she spotted me sitting on the sofa. She froze in mid-stride. A strange awkwardness stirred in me. She obviously lived here, and I just as obviously didn't, but I was sitting in her living room appearing calm and comfortable.

Both of us waited for the other one to speak, which we didn't for several seconds, which to me seemed like several minutes. She was at least my age or older with short light brown hair. She had brown eyes and a smooth olive complexion accentuated by a hint of eye shadow and lipstick. She was quite different from Cami, but there was enough family resemblance that I was confident she was Cami's older sister. She was taller than Cami, probably close to five foot nine. She had a slender figure with long legs and a commanding aura about her. Although she wasn't as strikingly pretty as her younger sister, she was nice looking in a serious, professional kind of way. She wore a loose-fitting, cream-colored silk blouse that fit about her neck. She also wore brown dress slacks and low heeled sandals with hose.

"Hello," she greeted guardedly. "This is a surprise. Where's Cami?"

Setting the *Reader's Digest* down, I pointed to the stairs and pushed myself to my feet. "She went to change. We were going out to dinner."

She looked me over carefully. Nodding, she asked, "I guess it's celebration time." Her voice was a deeper soprano than her sister's, but it had a pleasing quality to it. I deduced immediately that she was more serious than her sister and not nearly as warm.

"Celebrating?" I questioned.

She smiled suspiciously, showing even white teeth. Her smile was wide, but devoid of genuine friendliness. "Cami must be very impressed."

I grinned. "You must be Cami's sister."

Her eyes narrowed slightly. "What?"

"Hi, Susan," Cami suddenly appeared at the top of the stairs in a white blouse, casual vest, slacks and bare feet. As she bounced lightly down the stairs carrying her shoes, she smiled and remarked, "I see you've both met. He looks a lot like JB, doesn't he?"

"What?" Susan questioned incredulously, turning to Cami.

"In fact, I thought he was JB when I first saw him." She laughed and winked over at me. Sucking in a quick breath through rounded mouth, she added, "Boy, did I ever think he was JB."

"This isn't JB?" Susan asked, enunciating each word for emphasis.

"So you *haven't* been introduced?" Cami laughed. She looked at me with raised eyebrows. "You're lucky I came down when I did. Susan's not crazy about your brother. Of course, she really hasn't had much of an opportunity to get to know him very well. She just returned from her mission in Chile three weeks ago."

"Oh. I was kind of expecting another warm welcome."

Cami laughed and wagged her finger at me. "Not hardly. Not from Susan." Turning to her sister, Cami said, "Susan, this is Jacob Matthews, JB's younger brother, by two whole minutes. Jacob, this is Susan, my older sister. By three whole years."

"You and JB are twins?" I nodded. She considered that bit of information. "You didn't ever say anything about JB having a twin," Susan accused Cami.

"I didn't know until just a few minutes ago when I found

myself..." She blushed and grinned. "We won't go into that again."

"Nice to meet you, Susan," I said, holding out my hand to shake hers. She hesitated a moment and then gave me her hand. Her handshake was firm. I liked the feel of her warm, soft, slender hand in mine, but there was no friendliness exchanged, neither in the grip nor in her probing gaze. In fact, she was noticeably guarded and cool towards me.

"Susan's been trying to adjust to the real world since returning from Chile. She still believes that all guys should look and act like missionaries. You can understand why she hasn't been terribly impressed with JB." Turning to Susan, she added, "Jacob just returned from a mission in Mexico. He just barely took off his white shirt and tie. You two could speak Spanish to each other if you wanted to."

"I guess we could," Susan replied, sharing her unfriendly smile. "Maybe another time." She turned and started for the stairs. "Nice to have met you, Jacob," she said perfunctorily. "Maybe we'll run into each other again." Without saying anything else, she disappeared up the stairs.

Cami watched her go. Turning back to me, she explained, "Susan can be nice when and if she wants to."

"I take it she didn't want to today."

"She and JB don't..." She grimaced. "Let's just say Susan isn't a fanatical admirer of your *older* brother."

"She's just being protective."

Cami threw her head back and laughed. "That's an understatement. Most of the time I don't know if I should treat her like my sister or my mother. She's played both roles ever since Mom died. But she likes the mother role best. I thought being away from home for eighteen months would change all that, but one look at JB and all of her motherly protectiveness kicked into high gear." She smiled. "She thinks I'm getting serious."

"Could she be right?"

"We're just good friends."

I recalled the unexpected greeting she had given me. "Well, if you greet James like you did me, I can understand how Susan might get the impression that you're serious."

She blushed, shook her head and looked up the stairs. "Susan is…Well, you see, Mom died when I was eleven. Dad didn't remarry. Oh, he made sure we had everything we needed, but having a housekeeper and someone to do meals occasionally wasn't the same thing. Susan was fourteen and felt responsible. She still plays mom with me occasionally. Out of habit, I guess. I think she's afraid I'm going to run off and get married. Actually, I'm really pretty level-headed. At least that's my unbiased perception." She grinned. "I'll admit I'm a bit daring, willing to try something new."

"You don't worry about running off and marrying just anyone?" I found Cami intriguing. Her casual, warm, open manner was appealing. Unlike her sister Susan, she exuded a boundless friendliness. I hardly knew her, and yet I felt that I could speak openly with her. Even joke with her about rather personal things. I'd never met a girl like that. I could easily understand why James had liked her after changing her flat tire.

Cami studied me. "JB's kind and gentle and unassuming, not stuck on himself. But," she laughed, "a long time ago I made up my mind about the kind of guy I wanted to marry and how and where I'd get married. JB knows that."

"Maybe if he changed, you might…" I started dubiously.

She considered my unfinished question. "He hasn't changed, though."

Feeling boldly humorous, I smiled and remarked, "Dang, I'm the same model as James, but maybe without some of the baggage. Perhaps we could work something out. After all, we've had a pretty good start today. There's no sense in letting that warm welcome go to waste."

She laughed and pointed her finger at me. "You promised me that you had forgotten. That was all a great big mistake, and you know it."

"I like to think of it as a subtle premonition."

"And I'd like you to start forgetting it like you promised."

I heard a car pull up in front. I glanced out the window and spotted the hood of the black Firebird. "Looks like he's here," I announced, turning back to Cami. "I can break the news to him when he comes in."

"I'm going to break your arm if you keep this up," she threatened lightly, standing up and starting for the door. A bell chimed. Cami was at the door and opened it as soon as the chimes started to play. "Sorry I'm late," James said.

"What's my surprise?" Cami asked, feigning sternness and standing in the doorway to block James's entrance.

"Surprise?" He hesitated. "Oh, the surprise!" He laughed. "Jacob. Jacob was the surprise."

"Oh," Cami sighed, stepping aside so James could enter. "I suppose then that I demonstrated a generous amount of appreciation for your surprise."

I found it strange that I felt a greater nervousness in meeting James than I had in meeting Cami a few minutes earlier when I wasn't a bit sure whom I was going to face at the door. James was dressed in a tan pair of Docker slacks and a bright blue, red and yellow cotton shirt that was open wide at the neck exposing a V-shaped portion of his tanned neck and upper chest. He wore a pair of soft leather loafers without socks. His face was a deep tan with a reddish hue to it. His deeply set green eyes sparkled with excitement as he saw me. His light brown hair, touched with a hint of red, was clipped short about his ears but thick, curly and long on top and in back where it hung over his collar and brushed along the top of his back.

"Well, how's it going, Jacob?" he greeted me, approaching me with his hand out and his familiar crooked grin under his thick reddish brown mustache. The rest of his face sported the light shadow of a one day's growth of whiskers.

"Hello, James."

He shook his head. "JB, Jacob. I go by JB," he said firmly but not unkindly. "I'm not James any more."

"Mom got me out of the habit," I apologized.

"Nobody'll know who you're talking about if you call me James."

"I like *James*," Cami spoke up. "It sounds distinguished and…"

"I'll stick with JB. It fits me better."

"All right, JB," I smiled. "We'll try it your way." I took his hand. His grip was firm, his hand hard and strong. I could see that he was thicker and more muscular through the chest than

I. The day he attended sacrament meeting with my family he had mentioned that he had been working out regularly. Lifting weights as well as the physical demands of his construction job had built his strength and his physique. We faced each other, both of us smiling. Even though I made a conscious effort not to, I found myself staring at the diamond stud in his right ear.

"I'm sorry I wasn't here to introduce you to everybody," he apologized, shrugging, "but Cami's good about making people feel welcome."

I laughed. "She definitely gave me the royal treatment."

Turning to face Cami, JB remarked, "We really don't look all that much alike. I mean, Jacob here has been plucked straight from the mission field and I'm a genuine gentile."

Cami reached up and tugged on James's long hair. "Give me a pair of scissors and I think I can do a little something about your gentile appearance. Did I ever tell you that I used to cut my brothers' and dad's hair? I was really pretty good. It will only take me about ten minutes."

JB pulled away and shook his head, grinning. "Now don't get any wild ideas. My hair keeps the sun off the back of my neck."

"Look at your brother," she kidded. "Doesn't he look nice with his hair cut?"

"It suits him. He's a returned missionary. I'm not. Never will be."

Cami smiled, but I detected a hint of sadness in her eyes. She turned away as though she were looking for something, but I was certain that her action was an attempt to hide her disappointment.

JB slapped me on the shoulder. "Well, Bro, are you hungry?"

"I won't turn down good food."

"How about the Black Angus?" Before I could proclaim my poverty, he quickly added, "And I'm paying. We're going to put some meat on you or you'll never last framing houses."

"So my eyes really weren't playing tricks on me."

We all turned as Susan came down the stairs in her bare feet wearing a blue denim, loose-fitting dress that hit her mid-calf. She looked relaxed but she hadn't warmed up at all. "For a while there I thought you had reformed, JB," she stated. "You looked like you were ready for your mission."

He smiled, but as he did a deep red embarrassment flushed his tanned face. "You didn't think I'd do anything radical like that, did you?" he tried to joke. "If the bishop heard a rumor like that, he'd fall over dead."

"I know what you mean. I almost did myself when I saw your brother. I was encouraged, though. For a moment there I was very hopeful."

"You figure I ought to look like Jacob?" he asked, attempting to joke.

Susan considered the question, her smile slowly disappearing. "That could be a start." She walked toward the kitchen while the three of us watched her, all of us feeling a little awkward.

"Shall we go?" Cami asked cheerily, trying to dispel the residue of coolness Susan had left.

"Susan," JB called out unexpectedly, "do you want to come with us? We're going out to dinner. It would give Jacob somebody to talk to."

Susan poked her head around the corner and smiled. "Thank you, JB, but I think I'll stay here and have a sandwich."

"Well, Jacob," he said, turning back to me, "you can't say I didn't try to get you lined up with someone."

"Why don't you let me do the choosing?" I grinned.

We left the house and climbed into JB's Firebird, Cami and JB up front and me in the back straddling the hump with my knees just under my chin.

Huntsville is in a little valley about a twenty-minute drive from Ogden. In the southwest corner of the valley is Pine View Reservoir, a beautiful blue man-made lake. We drove around the south end of the reservoir and then headed down Ogden Canyon toward the city.

We found a Black Angus restaurant and feasted on steak. JB was generous, sparing no expense. I had worried about things being awkward with him, but it was almost like old times. He was relaxed and happy with Cami. I saw the old spark in his eyes, the enthusiasm for living that had been so characteristic of him at an earlier time. I could see and feel from the start that he liked Cami, but I sensed a cautiousness on Cami's part; however, she was friendly and warm toward me, willing to joke and talk as though we were seasoned friends.

Before the evening was over, I learned that Cami liked living at home again, although she considered it temporary. In her ward she was teaching the Mia Maid girls. She was a great athlete, having been presented the outstanding girls athlete award at Weber High her senior year, lettering in volleyball, basketball, and softball. She had also managed to run on the 400-meter relay team, which placed third in state. Her dad, Denton Hardaway, owned a successful furniture and home appliance store in South Ogden, which explained why their home looked like something out of *Better Homes and Gardens*. That was where Cami now worked, handling orders and supplies.

I also learned of Cami's college experience at Arizona State. The latter part of February, she became disenchanted with life in Tempe, Arizona, and withdrew. That was when she talked JB into returning with her to Huntsville to work for Roger Franco, who was an old friend of Denton Hardaway. Although she withdrew before completing her second semester, she had managed to keep her grades up and was planning to go to BYU in the fall where she had originally been accepted before charging off to Tempe on what she described as "a wild, wonderful whim."

"Wasn't that a rather expensive whim?" I asked. "You know all that tuition, book money, etc. What did your dad say when he found out you were leaving ASU? And leaving all of his hard-earned money behind."

Cami ducked her head. "I did feel kind of stupid calling him. I was afraid he was going to tell me to stick it out, but he was really quite understanding. Besides, he said he didn't like having me that far away. And I told him I wanted to be home when Susan got off her mission."

I glanced at JB, who raised his eyebrows and shrugged. "Are you always so capricious?" I questioned, fighting back a grin.

"I think dingey is a better word," JB kidded, quickly ducking away from Cami's playful retaliation.

"Don't you ever get a sudden urge to do something

crazy?" she asked me, smiling but serious.

"Sure, but they have to be in my price range."

"I think Jacob's a little too practical for you, Cami," JB chuckled. "Everything has to fit nicely into a neat little package or he doesn't want anything to do with it."

"Oh, come on," I protested. "Now, it wasn't very long ago that I remember you as being the totally practical one, James."

"It's JB, Jacob," he reminded me again. "I've loosened up a little bit."

"I think Jacob would be a good match for Susan," Cami said, pretending to be thoughtful. "What do you think, JB?"

"Hey, don't look at me," JB answered, raising his hands. "I tried to line him up with Susan this evening, but he was too practical for her."

The bantering continued throughout the evening, and when it was over I was more than a little impressed with Cami Hardaway. She was so free, willing to make the most mundane activity an adventure. After eating we went window shopping along Washington Boulevard, insisting that JB and I escort her together, one on either side of her. JB and I actually enjoyed our first window shopping jaunt. We strolled up the hill to the big Catholic church east of Washington and caught the tail end of an evening Mass because it was something Cami had never done. She talked us into stopping at the Ben Lomond High School track to have a sprint by moonlight. Cami won because she tripped both JB and me as we bolted from our starting positions.

All evening the thought kept hammering in my brain that if JB weren't dating Cami, I'd snatch her in a moment. I hadn't done a lot of thinking about what I considered to be the ideal girl, but after this crazy evening, I was willing to seriously consider Cami Hardaway

"What do you think of her?" JB asked me after we had dropped Cami off and had driven back to the apartment.

I laughed as JB helped me haul my stuff from the Bug to my room. "I can see why you fell for her. What I can't see is why she fell for you." I playfully drove my shoulder into James's chest as I packed two suitcases up the driveway toward the basement stairs.

"She was looking for a real man," JB came back. He paused, holding a cardboard box and doing a quick flex. "How could she resist this?"

"Tell that to her sister Susan."

"I'm not interested in Susan. She's your department."

"I'll pick my own girl. And Susan Hardaway isn't on my tentative list."

"If Susan loosened up a bit instead of playing the queen spinster, she might not be too bad. In fact, if she were really honest, she'd admit that she's got the hots for me too. She's just jealous Cami got to me first. But under the circumstances, she might be willing to settle for a close second so don't lose hope, Jacob."

"Your boundless humility is overwhelming." I laughed as we went down the stairs and entered the apartment. "The next time she slips out of the social deep freeze," I kidded, "I'll mention that little observation to her. I'm sure she'll appreciate knowing that she's got the hots for you and that I can rescue her from spinsterhood."

JB set the box down in the middle of the kitchen floor. He went to the sink, turned the water on, bent over and took a long drink out of his cupped hand. Turning off the water and straightening up, he remarked, "I had most of the family convinced they liked me, even Denton Hardaway; then Susan waltzed in from her mission. She made up her mind the minute she saw that I didn't look like some fresh-from-the-field missionary. She thinks I ought to cut my hair, get rid of the mustache and run around in a white shirt and tie."

"Maybe she's right," I laughed, punching at him.

"Don't you start on me." He became serious. "Take a good look, Jacob. This is what I am."

"Maybe," I replied, shrugging. "Everybody can change, though. And if Susan holds the key to your success, do a little changing. Cut your hair, chuck the earring. Cami's worth it."

"Nobody said Susan Hardaway holds the key to anything. Besides, I already shaved my beard and trimmed my hair. You should have seen me before. And do you know how much I paid for this stud?" He tugged on his right ear lobe.

I studied the stud and smiled. "Probably a couple hundred more than it was worth."

"It cost me two hundred and five bucks."

"Like I said, a couple hundred more than it was worth."

He chuckled. "Actually, I bought it in Phoenix from one of the guys at work who was behind on his child-support payments. The court was breathing down his neck, and I was trying to help him out. Once I had it," he added, "I had to wear it. You're just jealous you don't have the guts to wear one."

"That's all I've been dreaming about for the last two years, how to hammer a stud earring into my ear."

We carried my things into the bedroom and set them on the bed. "The place isn't very clean," JB observed, looking around. "I tried to do a little work in here. The rest of the place could use a good touch up." He seemed embarrassed.

"Well, I'll have to admit it's not the way Mom keeps things at home. You used to keep a pretty clean room yourself."

JB nodded slowly, sadly. "Yeah. Well, that was a long time ago. Things have changed." He left the room and returned to the kitchen.

Without Cami around, I recognized in JB some of the old foreboding bitterness that used to cling to him like a blemish. I heaved a sigh and looked about the room. Then I heard the water in the kitchen sink running. I wandered out to find JB attacking the dirty dishes in the sink and strewn along the sideboard. "What time do we go to work?" I questioned.

"Starting time is seven, but Roger asked me to be there a bit early to get things ready for the crew. Are you ready to wear off some flab and tone up your muscles?"

"You're not going to have to worry about me keeping up." I thought a moment. "How much do I owe for rent?"

"It's three fifty a month, but it's paid up through May. You can chip in your share for June."

I pulled out my wallet and counted out a hundred and seventy-five dollars. I set the money on the sideboard where JB could see it. "I'm not a charity case," I laughed. "There's my half."

JB looked over at my money. "I thought you were broke."

"I had a little money in savings. I don't want you to throw me out in the street if I ever get on your nerves."

"You don't have to worry about that. Unless you start messing with my girl." He faked a threatening frown and then grinned.

A worm of guilt pushed its way into my mind. "Actually, she did fall for me," I remarked, attempting a careless air of humor. "Who wouldn't?" JB looked over at me while he continued to scrub a plate with a sudsy dish cloth. I folded my arms across my chest and leaned against the fridge. "Oh, being as good looking as I am, how could you expect anyone to resist me?" JB stared at me, smiling. "Cami took one look at me, and she couldn't help herself. Before I knew it she had her arms around me and was laying a kiss on me like..." I paused. "Come to think of it, nobody's ever kissed me like she did." I touched my chest. "My heart's still pounding."

"You're so full of it," he muttered, grinning and shaking his head.

"I'm not kidding. Actually, there were two or three of them, but they were so long and intense they could have been a dozen or more." I was starting to get into my joke and was enjoying it. "She didn't even let me come up for air." I looked at him. "You don't believe me, do you? Ask Teresa. She was there and saw the whole thing. She got a real education. Dang! Come to think of it, I got an education too."

JB stopped washing, turned from the sink and stared at me while his wet, soapy hands dripped on the floor. "What did happen over there? Cami acted a little strange when I talked to her on the phone."

"She was still recovering from her encounter with me."

"Did she...*kiss you?*"

My eyes narrowed and I looked down at the floor, pretending to be deep in thought but having a difficult time remaining serious. "I'm not sure I'd call it a kiss. There was too much there to be a mere kiss. Perhaps embrace would..." I shook my head. "No, it was more than that. It was everything wrapped up into one. Wow!"

"I know you're lying."

I threw up my hands. "I tried to tell you, but you wouldn't listen."

"What happened back there?" He was still smiling but there was an uneasy suspicion in his eyes. "Did you try to tell her you were me?"

I laughed. "Now you're getting close." I returned his stare and became serious. "I can tell you one thing, she likes you. A lot!" I held up my hands. "Now don't get mad when I tell you this. She claims she's never kissed you like she kissed me."

"What?"

"But that's not the good part. She figured I was you. That's why she did it. I haven't had anybody kiss me like that. Not even close. I've never even known anybody well enough to get kissed like that. She definitely likes you, and she's worth anything you have to do to keep her."

"You mean cut my hair and mustache and get rid of my earring so I can look like you?" He was still smiling but there was an accusing edge to his question. "She was so passionate all of a sudden because she figured I'd made a turnaround."

"JB, it's a compliment to you," I argued.

He shook his head. "No, it's a compliment to you. It's a kick in the head to me." His smile was gone.

"Hey, I'm just saying that if she likes you with your hair short and without the earring, why not go for it? I don't even know Cami, not really, but if she's as good as she seems to me, you're crazy to let someone else steal her from you."

"Especially my own brother." He turned back to the sink and started scrubbing plates.

"Hey, come on, I was just razzing you a little." JB didn't answer. "JB, I don't have anything going with Cami. Was I impressed with her? Sure. Everything between her and me was a big mistake. And part of it's your fault. You never told her about me. Not that I was your twin. How was she to know? Were you afraid to tell her about me?"

"It didn't exactly come up," JB came back warmly. "Do you expect me to drag you into every conversation I have in my life?"

"I guess not." I was quiet for a moment, leaning against the kitchen counter with my arms folded across my chest. "Well, there's one thing for sure—she's got Leti Trujillo beat."

JB turned on me like I'd poked him with a hot stick. "What do you know about Leti Trujillo?" he questioned in a low hoarse voice.

I attempted a smile and shrugged. "I remember you liked her." He turned back to his dishes. "Do you ever think about her much?" I asked, remembering the snapshot on JB's dresser.

"Every day."

"What?" There was no masking my shock.

"You wouldn't understand. You never did."

"But she's been gone for three years."

"Four years in August."

"What kind of a hold does she have on you?" I said it as though I were kidding, but there was something in JB's reaction to the mention of Leti's name that troubled me.

"I don't want to talk about it," he replied quietly. "She's gone and there's nothing I can do about it. So let's just drop it."

CHAPTER FOUR

I woke up to scrambled eggs, bacon, fried potatoes and cold milk. JB was at the stove cooking when I came into the kitchen. "Now just because I'm a soft touch your first day on the job," he warned me, jabbing a fork in my direction as I looked down at the table setting, "don't get the idea that this is going to happen every morning. It's a one-time deal."

"Wow!" I grinned. "And I thought I was going to miss Mom's cooking."

"I'm not Mom, but I can keep you from starving. And I don't want you fainting the first day on the job."

"I'm not going to embarrass you, JB. In fact, the boss is probably going to give me your job before the end of next week."

We joked through breakfast and then headed out the door, leaving the unwashed dishes in the sink. "You better take your car," he told me, "because I might have to stay late. I've got some things to catch up on."

JB didn't exaggerate the difficulty of the job. After meeting the big boss, Roger Franco, and the rest of the guys on the crew, it was straight work. James was good at what he did; I was definitely the apprentice and the "gopher" man. Although everybody was patient with me until I learned the ropes, they expected me to work and pull my share of the load.

All the guys liked JB. He was friendly and helpful. Several times I saw different ones on the crew struggling or needing a word of encouragement. JB was the first one to step in. It was his nature. That's the way he had always been.

Roger Franco had four different construction crews going in Huntsville and Ogden. He had a contract to put up a dozen condos and a half dozen homes. There was plenty of work for everyone.

By five-thirty, after having worked close to a ten-hour day, I was stiff, sore and exhausted. JB still had an hour or more to do before knocking off for the day, so I climbed into the Bug and headed for the apartment. The only thing I wanted to do was have a long hot shower and crash into bed, but after JB had kidded me about being soft and out of shape, I knew there was no way I was going to do that.

I stopped and picked up a sandwich and chocolate milk at a convenience store and then headed home. By the time I showered and dressed, JB came rushing into the apartment. "I'm heading over to Cami's," he announced as he started pulling his clothes off and heading for the shower. He grinned at me. "You're not tired, are you, tough guy?"

"I discovered some new muscles today," I admitted lightly.

"Do you want to come with me?" He shrugged. "We can see if Susan has warmed up at all."

Twenty minutes later I was alone in the apartment and it was only seven-thirty. I felt restless and was envious of JB. I found myself thinking of Cami, wondering if something could develop between us.

"Wake up!" I growled at myself. "JB's off with his date and you're hoping things will fall apart so you can cut in." I pushed up from the lumpy coach where I'd been resting. Looking around the apartment, I muttered, "This place stinks."

My cleaning the apartment was as much an attempt to take my mind off Cami Hardaway as it was to erase the filth and grunginess of my immediate surroundings. My first intent was to merely clean out the sink and sweep the crumbs from the kitchen floor, but as I eliminated one source of dirt and grime, I was pressured to move on to another.

I borrowed the vacuum and a mop and bucket from Mrs. Pritt upstairs. I found a bottle of PineSol and a can of cleanser. I became so engrossed in my work and the slow transformation of the apartment that I didn't notice the passage of time.

Although there was a feeling of satisfaction in cleaning the apartment, I discovered I was irritated with JB for allowing this place to sink into such a disgusting condition. I resented having to clean up his messes; however, my cleaning was selective—only those parts of the apartment I had to live in, just enough for me to survive.

I was finishing up the shower when I heard voices and footsteps coming down the steps to the front door.

"What happened in here?" I heard Cami call out in surprise. "I don't recognize the place."

"Jacob," JB called to me, "you here?"

Wiping my brow with the back of my forearm, I walked down the hall with a scouring pad in one hand and a plastic mop bucket in the other.

"Now I know why JB wanted you to stay with him," Cami greeted me with a smile. She looked around. "This place hasn't ever been this clean."

I shrugged. "I didn't have anything else to do." I smiled at JB, who seemed a little embarrassed. "I tried to get JB to line me up with someone, but he refused."

"He's lying," JB laughed. "I tried to line him up with Susan again."

Cami smiled, shaking her head. "It's good Jacob decided to clean this place. Susan had a date with one of her old missionary companions."

"Old missionary companion?" I pulled the corners of my mouth down and set the mop bucket and scouring pad by the fridge. "They must do things differently in Chile than they do in Mexico."

Slapping at me and laughing, she said, "Just one of the elders she knew in Chile. He's been home about a year."

"I think they went off and gave each other the first missionary discussion," JB commented.

Cami jabbed JB with an elbow and looked about the apartment again. "Things do look nice." She studied the floor. "The floor's even mopped." She looked at me. "But the real test is the shower. Did you have the courage to touch the shower?"

I chuckled. "I didn't have the courage to shower in it until it was cleaned, burned or soaked in acid. I think there were a half dozen new deseases in there. I cleaned it for my own preservation."

"This I've got to see."

The three of us wandered down to the bathroom where Cami inspected my work. "This isn't the same place. Maybe you can come over to our place. We'll even furnish the bucket and PineSol." She jabbed me with an elbow. "You free tomorrow night? I'll even throw in dinner."

I laughed and glanced at JB, who was smiling but wasn't amused with this unexpected invitation. "I don't know about the bucket of PineSol, but dinner sounds fine."

"I have a feeling that some girl out there is really going to get a good deal when she finds you. Where'd you learn to clean like this?"

I blushed. "Mom was pretty particular. She figured boys ought to learn to clean as well as the girls."

Cami nudged JB playfully. "Did any of this rub off on you?"

"Actually," I spoke up, "Mom always said nobody could clean like JB. He was the one who made sure our room passed Mom's inspections."

Cami raised her eyebrows. "What happened since then?"

"I'm just keeping my talents hidden," JB remarked.

"Hidden? The way this place looked the last time I saw it I'd say you didn't just hide them. You buried them. Really deep."

"I figured you'd be in bed, Jacob," JB commented as we all returned to the living room. "It's almost eleven."

"I lost track of time, and I was having so much fun I couldn't stop."

"I'm glad you did," Cami laughed. "We were going for a drink and maybe a bite to eat, but JB discovered he'd left his wallet here. I think it was intentional," she whispered loudly to me.

JB went down the hall to his room and Cami dropped onto the lumpy couch. She patted the cushion and remarked, "I helped JB pick this out. In fact, I helped him pick out most of these unique furnishings."

"Oh, so that's the kind of furniture store your dad runs."

"No," she shot back, narrowing her eyes. She smiled. "We had to hit every yard sale in the Valley to find these things."

"Yard sales?" I questioned. "Are you sure you didn't just pick this stuff up along the curbs on garbage collection day?"

"You're not even funny, Jacob Matthews." She paused. "Perceptive, but not at all funny."

JB rejoined us in the living room. He pulled Cami up from the couch and started for the door. Maybe Jacob wants to go with us," Cami offered, turning back to me. "You're welcome to come. Now that JB has his wallet we're all set."

I was definitely hungry and thirsty, but I suspected that JB wasn't interested in a tag-along. I shook my head without looking at him. "Something tells me if I don't get into bed in the next few minutes, I'm not going to wake up in the morning. I'd hate to get fired my second day."

As I heard JB's Firebird pull away, I dropped onto the couch where Cami had been a moment earlier. Cami Hardaway affected me in a way that I'd never experienced. Heaving a tired sigh, I shook my head, pushed up from the couch, quickly finished putting my cleaning things away and started getting ready for bed. Fifteen minutes later as I strode into the kitchen to switch off the lights, JB stepped through the front door carrying an unopened bottle of Ocean Spray grape juice. He set the juice on the card table.

"That was quick," I called out.

"Cami decided it was getting late," he grumbled. He nodded toward the juice. "She figured you needed that."

I smiled, pleased. "She's looking out for me."

"I noticed." He headed down the hall to the bathroom without answering. I flipped off the lights and went to my room and sat on the edge of my bed until JB returned from the bathroom, still wiping his hands on a towel. "Is anything wrong?" I asked.

JB paused in the doorway to his bedroom with his back to me. For a moment he didn't say anything. "Everything's fine," he sighed. "You're a regular sensation."

"Did I do something wrong?"

He turned and glanced in my direction. "No. You did everything right. Cami was impressed. And I'm supposed to feel grateful to have you around to take care of me. Are you sure that misplaced kiss yesterday was really a mistake?"

"What's that supposed to mean?"

"I'm not you, Jacob!" he flared suddenly. "This is what I am." He pointed to himself with both his thumbs. "Maybe other people don't like the long hair, the mustache and the earring. But those things aren't me. I'm me, under the hair, the mustache and the earring. And if people can't accept me the way I am, then they can take a walk. That includes you."

"JB, I knew what you were like before I ever came to Huntsville."

He shook his head. "You don't know me, Jacob. I've wished you did. But you only want to see the things you like. You want to change everything else." He gestured toward the apartment. "It wasn't good enough for you the way it was."

"That's what's bothering you? Cami didn't seem to mind."

"Did you do it for her?" he accused.

"Do we have to live in a garbage heap?"

"Maybe that's the way I like it."

"Maybe you should have posted a `Do not clean' sign on the front door then." I shrugged. "You used to like things clean. I just figured you hadn't had time to get around to cleaning it. I had some time so I was trying to do us both a favor. You fixed me breakfast this morning. I was just returning a favor." That was a stretch of the truth, but it sounded better than that I was sick of sitting around in the mess.

"Maybe I liked it just the way it was."

My anger smoldered inside me. "I guess I prefer to be able to walk across the kitchen floor without my shoes getting stuck. I prefer not to slop through mildew when I take a shower. I'll keep it clean. It'll be my contribution to our humble home."

He forced a humorless grin. "Maybe Susan Hardaway is your type. The two of you might get along fine. But just remember, Jacob, I don't need another mother." He turned and entered the bedroom, slamming the door behind him.

CHAPTER FIVE

Friday afternoon when I finished work, I climbed into the Bug and decided to take the long ride home, going out through Liberty, cutting back around the reservoir and driving over the dam before returning to the apartment in Huntsville.

I was enchanted by the Huntsville valley, isolated so peacefully from the rest of the world, surrounded by gorgeous hills and filled with small farms, grazing sheep, horses and cows. Its beautiful, serene quaintness beckoned to me.

As I drove slowly down the narrow winding road, I left the car window down, inviting the fresh air to wash over me. I relaxed and reflected on my five days in the valley. After our tenuous, shaky beginning, JB and I had settled in with each other. The warmth that characterized our relationship during our growing up years was absent, but I hoped with time even that would return.

As I drove slowly across the dam, I stopped momentarily and gazed out over the placid blue waters. Several motor boats criss-crossed the water. I put the Bug in gear and proceeded across the dam. As I headed back to town along the road that wound along the south side of the reservoir, sandwiched between the hills and the shoreline, I spotted a blue Metro off the side of the road. I didn't pay much attention to it until I was passing it and recognized Susan Hardaway standing by the passenger side.

Pulling off the road, I flipped a quick U-turn and drove back. Susan was dressed in a beige skirt and white blouse. She was wearing hose and heels. Leaning out the window, I called across the road, "Are you just taking in the view or is there some other reason you're stopped?"

She recognized me and her cheeks colored as she rolled her eyes and threw up her arms in frustration. Looking up and down the road, she crossed the highway and stepped over to the Bug. "I feel stupid," she grumbled, avoiding my eyes. "I think I'm out of gas."

I pushed open the door and climbed out. "Let's take a look."

Susan walked ahead of me as we crossed the highway. I took a good look at her. She was tall and lithe with a graceful, self-assured, pleasing figure. In her heels she was only a couple of inches shorter than I. Even though she was frustrated and suddenly dependent—a situation I was convinced she detested—she was prettier than I had remembered her.

"I'm not a mechanic or anything," Susan said, turning when we reached the Metro, "but I'm pretty sure I'm out of gas. I usually don't even drive this car," she complained, obviously upset with herself, "but Cami wanted to take the Buick. She said it was almost out of gas, but she thought it would get me to Ogden and back."

I opened the door and looked at the gas gauge, which registered empty. "Did the gas light come on?"

"It's been on the whole time. Dad always said you could drive this forever and never run out of gas."

I laughed. "When he said you could drive forever, what he really meant was that you could drive fifty miles or so after the gas light flashes. Forever ended right here."

"What now?" she asked, sounding somewhat forlorn and helpless.

Although she was relieved to have someone stop, I sensed that she wished I had been someone else. The impression irritated me. As a result a shade of orneriness stirred within me. I wanted Susan Hardaway to sample a touch of humility, figuring it would do her good to actually ask for help.

Susan looked up and down the road, disgustedly studied the Metro, glanced out at the reservoir and heaved a couple of tired sighs, but she wouldn't look at me or ask for my help. "I guess I'll need to get back into town," she finally said. "I don't know if we even have a gas can. Maybe I ought to have Dad or my brother come out and get the car."

I chuckled. "That certainly seems fair. You run the gas out of it and then send your dad out here to bring it in."

"It's not my fault. I hardly ever drive this car. Cami should be the one stranded here."

"For my sake, I wish she were," I thought to myself.

Finally in frustration, she burst out, "Are you going to help me?"

I laughed. "Do you want my help?"

She turned a withering glare my way and her frustration surfaced in full view. "I thought that was obvious."

I scratched the back of my neck and shook my head. "Well, I turned around and came back with intentions to give you a hand, but I don't know if you want my help unless you tell me."

"And why wouldn't I need help?"

I took a deep breath and watched a boat zip across the smooth surface of the reservoir. "Well, your sister told me that the first time she met JB she was broken down in this car. He came along and gave her a hand. That's how they got together." I didn't say any more for a moment.

I could feel her eyes studying me. "And what's that supposed to mean?" she demanded.

"You didn't seem all that thrilled to see me when I stopped. I was just wondering if you were hoping for someone else."

She turned, opened the Metro's door, grabbed her purse off the seat, locked the doors and started down the road in her heels.

"Now that's one proud lady," I muttered, watching her go. "Are you always so stubborn?" I shouted after her.

She stopped and turned. "Are you always so rude and unhelpful?"

"I stopped to help," I called back, my own anger rising. "I could have driven right by."

"Maybe you should have done. I wasn't trying to be picked up. And if I were, I would have been more selective." She turned and started walking.

"No wonder she puts JB on edge," I growled, stomping across the road to the Bug. I climbed in, revved the engine, put it in gear and spun out in the loose gravel on the shoulder of the road. I made another U-turn and headed back toward Huntsville.

I drove past Susan, fully intending to leave her stranded,

but as irritated as she had made me and in spite of the fact that I really didn't care what she thought of me or JB, I really couldn't bring myself to drive past her and leave her to the uncertain mercy of some other motorist. Especially since she was Cami's sister. I didn't want to leave a negative impression with Cami.

Slamming on the brakes, I pushed the gear shift into reverse and backed up to where she was walking while three cars zipped past, one of them hitting the horn. Getting out of the car, I stomped around to the passenger side and opened the door as she came walking up. "Get in," I growled. "I'll give you a ride."

"I'll walk, thank you," she snapped, trying to push past me.

I stood in her way, looking back toward town. "How long do you think you're going to last wobbling down the highway in those heels?"

"I'll take them off. Someone will probably give me a ride."

"Man, you don't give an inch, do you?"

"I don't appreciate being treated rudely."

"Is it too much to expect that you could say, `Hey, I'm in trouble. Can you give me a hand?'" I swallowed. "Do you expect everybody to beg for the privilege of helping you out, or is that just reserved for me?"

She continued to glower at me. She was breathing hard, and although it was early May and late in the afternoon, it was still warm. She had little beads of perspiration on her nose and forehead. "I don't want your help unless you really want to give it to me. I don't want to put you out."

"Lady, get real! Anybody that stops is going to be put out. People don't stop to lend a hand only if they won't be put out. Maybe the only thing they expect is a little gratitude."

"Is that what you want?"

"No, I don't want anything. I just want you to get in the car so I can drive out of here without being plagued with a guilty conscience. I gave up on this being a sincere act of charitable service several minutes ago."

"Is that right?"

"Right now I just want to get this whole thing over with and you back home. Then we won't have to run into each other ever again. This was all a mistake. If I'd just taken my regular route home, I wouldn't have even passed you, and you'd be having this ridiculous conversation with some other poor, hapless soul."

For another moment we just stared at each other, neither one of us willing to give in. "Maybe I'd better just take my chances with somebody else," she said, her tone softening for the first time.

"Why don't you bend just a little bit? Get in the car and give me a break." She didn't move. "What do you have against me any way. I was the one who tried to be nice, and I get kicked in the teeth."

I don't ever remember being so aggravated with a girl, and I hardly knew her. And at that moment I didn't care if I ever got to know her better. But as we glared at each other standing along the side of the road, Susan's steady brown eyes began to mist up. At first I wasn't sure I was seeing it, but when she started blinking and dabbing at her eyes with the tip of her fingers, I knew she was on the verge of tears. Then I did feel like a jerk! As exasperating as she had been, the last thing I wanted to do was to stand there while she bawled.

"Susan, would you just get in the car?" I asked, suddenly gentle and solicitous. "I'll stop my growling. I won't even say anything to you. I'll just drive you into town. JB probably has a gas can at our place. We'll fill it up and come back and get your car going."

"Will I need to come back?"

As patiently as I could I answered, "Once we get gas in the Metro, which car do you suggest we leave out here on the road, yours or mine?"

She stared at me a moment and the first traces of a smile brushed across her lips. "Am I acting really stupid? Don't answer that," she quickly added as she stepped to the Bug and dropped down on the passenger side. Heaving a sigh, I closed the door. For the first couple of minutes we didn't say anything. I was bound and determined to get this disastrous act of volunteer service behind me with as little pain and hassle as possible. I told myself I would never again take the long way home.

"I guess I was a little ornery back there," Susan spoke after a moment, offering a veiled apology. I didn't say anything. "It did surprise me when you were the one who pulled up." She heaved a sigh. "I know this sounds crazy, but I was rather hoping someone I didn't know would help me. I felt stupid running out of gas this close to home."

"So you figured you'd bite my head off for not being a stranger."

"Maybe it's your brother I have a problem with," she spoke honestly. "When I see you, I see him. I'm sorry." I turned, taken back by the unsolicited apology. Susan was looking out the side window. "I've had kind of a lousy day."

"So you wanted to make sure everybody else had a lousy one too," I thought to myself, but I used my better judgment and kept my mouth shut.

"I'm sorry I wasn't more…grateful for your kindness."

"Neither one of us would have won any awards for our gracious tact today," I conceded. "Shall we make a truce?"

She laughed. "Has JB given you a negative impression of me?"

"Actually, JB hasn't said much at all. Except that you're not crazy about him."

"You probably don't understand that," she said quietly.

"Oh, I don't know. If Cami was my daughter or my sister, I don't know that I would want someone like JB taking her out." Susan looked over at me, surprised. "On the other hand," I added, "I know some things about JB that most people don't see. There's a good side to him."

"I've misjudged you."

I chuckled. "I had that distinct impression."

"I'm sorry."

We drove to my apartment, and Mrs. Pritt let me use her gas can. After stopping to fill up with gas, we headed back to the Metro. Once I got the gas in the tank and started the engine, Susan held out her hand and smiled, "Thanks, Jacob. Do we leave as friends?"

I wanted to say, "Let's just leave, as quickly and as quietly as possible." I resisted the temptation, though. I took her hand and shook it. "I'll have to admit that the next time I see you on the side of the road, I might look the other way."

"I don't blame you. I hope there isn't a next time, but if there is, I promise to be nicer. But," she added with the touch of a rebuke in her voice, "I certainly don't like the insinuation that I park on the side of the road waiting for eligible guys to pick me up."

"I wondered if that might have been the comment that raised your temperature."

"It was." She was serious again. Folding her arms, she gazed out toward the reservoir. The sun was slipping behind the hills west of us. "For a good part of Cami's growing up years I was the only mother she had. I still love her like a sister, but there's a little bit of motherly protectiveness there too. Cami's always been the undaunted champion of the underdog. It didn't matter if it was a stray cat, an outsider at school or some complete stranger who seemed to need her help. Cami always wants to be there to lend a hand."

"Is that bad?"

"Usually not."

"Unless it's some guy like JB who comes along and she falls in love."

"I don't know if she's fallen in love with JB."

"Maybe not. But he's fallen for her."

Susan turned to me and studied my face. "Are you sure?" The question was full of worry.

I nodded. "That's not all bad from my perspective. He's my brother. I want him to have a chance. There's that good side I told you about. Maybe he should look for someone like he is, but if he does, that good side is going to stay buried. Maybe disappear altogether. Someone like Cami might help him out. Of course, Cami takes a chance. If JB won't change and she falls for him, where does that leave her?"

I opened the Metro door so Susan could slip inside. "I'll follow you back. And I'd suggest that before you do anything else, you put some more gas in this thing."

"I'll do that."

I was about to close the door. I hesitated. "It's past my dinner time. Is there anyplace around here we could grab something to eat?" What I had meant to say was someplace where *I* could grab something to eat. The *we* just sort of slipped out.

"There's a little cafe in town."

"I'll buy you something."

"Thanks." She smiled up at me. "I think everybody's expecting me to fix dinner."

"Are you the only one at the Hardaway home who knows how to put a sandwich on the table?"

She smiled wanly. "Sometimes I wonder. I've got another appointment later on too."

"Appointment or date?" I kidded her.

"A date."

"So I wasn't the first to pick you up?" I joked, laughing.

"He's an old friend from before my mission."

"Well, tell him to fill up his gas tank before you charge off this evening. I won't be out cruising the highways tonight."

"I'll tell him. Thanks again, Jacob. I'm sorry for being less than pleasant. And," she added, "I'll think about what you said about JB."

I laughed. "Actually, I'd just as soon Cami dropped him."

Susan looked puzzled. "Why?"

I smiled and looked away. "Then I'd probably ask her out myself."

CHAPTER SIX

My alarm went off a little before seven Sunday morning. I had planned to return to Brigham City and attend church with my family, but JB and I were both called in to work Saturday. We didn't get off till late so I decided to spend Sunday in Huntsville.

I shaved, showered and got dressed. JB's door was ajar, and he hadn't stirred, even with all the racket I made. At eight-thirty I rapped softly on his door. Nothing. I knocked. He still didn't move. Finally I banged on his door and called to him.

"What's wrong?" he finally demanded groggily, turning over and staring at me bleary eyed.

"It's Sunday morning," I answered cheerily.

"What?" He pushed himself up on his elbow and squinted toward his clock radio on the dresser.

"Church is going to start in about thirty minutes." I grinned. "I don't want you to be late. I was kind of hoping you'd introduce me to the people in the ward."

JB glared at me and then a crooked smile cracked his hard, rough features. "I hope this isn't a Sunday morning ritual, Bro." He punched at his pillow to fluff it up. "Sundays are my day of rest. I rest. Until I get good and ready to get up. You'll have to introduce yourself today. Cami'll be there. She'll show you around."

"You trust me with her?" I teased.

He considered that. "Probably not. So keep your mind on church." He dropped back on his pillow.

"Won't you even get up to see Cami?" I cajoled.

"She invited me to dinner. I'll see her then."

"She'd like to see you in church."

"Jacob, give up. You're not going to send me on a guilt trip. Not over missing church this morning. I've missed too many mornings already. One more isn't going to make any difference." He grinned and wagged a finger at me. "However, you might make me mad if you keep bugging me, but you won't get me to church. You have a good one, Bro. But you have it without me." He closed his eyes and turned over.

I wasn't ready to give up. "Do you mind if I tell you one more thing?"

"Something tells me that it won't make a bit of difference if I mind or not," he growled sleepily. "Get it over with and close the door."

"You like Cami, don't you?"

His answer was a deep sigh but no further acknowledgment.

"You'd probably marry her if you figured she was willing."

"I haven't said anything about marriage. In fact, she's the one who's brought it up, telling me what kind of guy she's going to marry. If I ever meet that guy, I'm going to personally saint him. He's probably out walking on water right now. Either that or out moving mountains or something."

"She won't take you the way you are," I said quickly. "You know that."

"Are you going to preach to me?" Turning on his back and opening his eyes, he studied me as I stood in the doorway.

"I'll make it quick. She won't have you unless you come up to her standard. And you wouldn't want her if she went down to yours. You like her because she's different. She's someone you can admire and look up to. You pull her down to your level, and not only will no one else want her, but you won't even want her. So if this relationship is going anyplace, *you've* got to change. It doesn't take a brain surgeon to figure that out."

"I get the impression that if I don't go to church," JB remarked tiredly, "you're going to bring the church to me. I'm going to get more preaching lying here in bed than you're going to get sitting in church. I might as well get up and go with you."

"I already invited you."

"What difference does all this make to you?"

"If you're not going to do what it takes to keep Cami, you ought to let her go. She deserves that much."

"Let her go so you can have her? I suspect you're worrying more about you than you are about Cami. Am I right?"

I didn't answer immediately. "I've thought of her." I shrugged. "I've thought a lot about her. I'm a little envious. Maybe a whole lot."

"Are you warning me so that you can cut in with a clear conscience?" The question held a biting accusation.

I shook my head. "Come to church with me," I said, smiling, "and you won't have to worry about me horning in on your girl behind your back."

"You won't shed any tears if she dumps me, will you?"

"JB, I'd like to see Cami get a fair shake. It's okay with me if you're the one who gives it to her."

"I'd like that myself," he said softly, the angry crispness gone.

"It won't happen if you lie in bed every Sunday morning."

"And it's not going to happen just because I go to church either." He was quiet a moment. "Jacob, there are a lot of things you don't know about me. It's just as well." He stopped and shook his head. "I'd like to be in your shoes, Jacob. I really would. I'd walk up to Cami right now and propose to her. Maybe if you knew everything and weren't so quick to pass judgment, you'd understand why I stay at home. Church isn't going to help me any."

"There was a time you didn't believe that."

"I believe it now." He turned over and closed his eyes. "You'd better get out of here or we'll both miss the meetings. And, Jacob, keep your mind on church. Let me worry about Cami."

I didn't understand JB. We had had the same home and strong gospel upbringing, but it was as though he had closed his eyes to things that he knew were true, closed them and hoped that by ignoring the truth, that truth would somehow disappear.

I remembered the first time I realized JB was no longer saying his evening prayers at home. "Aren't you going to pray," I asked him as he climbed into bed.

He hesitated, tossing the covers off. For a moment I thought he was going to climb out of bed and drop to his knees. Slowly he pulled the covers back over him. "It's just so many words," he muttered, "and none of them are going to help me much."

"What do you mean?" I wasn't sure if he were kidding.

"My prayers don't even get off the floor."

I watched him more closely after that to see if he ever prayed. He didn't. He'd say the family prayer if Dad called on him, but I couldn't help feeling he was just going through the motions.

There were times, however, when I'd get up from my prayers and reach to turn off the light, and I'd see him lying on his pillow with his hands behind his head staring up at the ceiling, deep in thought. There was some battle going on in his mind, but he didn't share it with me.

It was a gorgeous Sunday morning, and the church was only three blocks away so I walked. As I was strolling across the parking lot, Susan, Cami and Teresa pulled in behind me and whipped neatly into a vacant parking slot. I stopped and waited for them.

"Are we late?" I called to them as they piled out of the car.

"Depends on whose time you're using," Cami answered, smiling. "According to Hardaway time, we're probably about ten minutes early."

"According to real people's time," Susan sighed impatiently, "we've got about thirty seconds to get into sacrament meeting."

"I think I prefer Hardaway time," I said, laughing.

"So does everybody in our family," Susan came back.

"How's your little Metro?"

"The tank's full. No thanks to Cami here."

Cami giggled and winked at me. "Susan told me about her little...adventure. By the time she got home she said she realized why she was trying to bite your head off."

I raised my eyebrows with interest. "I'd like to hear that one."

"She was really mad at me for getting her stuck out there on the highway. And having JB's brother stop to lend a hand didn't help her attitude any."

"I am sorry," Susan said to me. "I'll make it up to you sometime."

"Just don't run out of gas again."

"You didn't bring your brother?" Susan said as we started up the walk to the front doors, Susan and Cami on either side of me and Teresa staying a couple of steps ahead.

"He was in very deep meditation when I left; however, I did extend an invitation."

"Was he snoring?" Teresa flung over her shoulder.

"Not that I could hear." I heaved an exasperated sigh. "I did attempt to preach a little to him. He wasn't terribly receptive."

Cami smiled and shook her head. "I thought you had more influence on him than that. I expected him to march in here this morning in a dark suit with a big Bible under his arm."

I opened the door for the three girls and we all stepped into the foyer. "We're not as late as I thought," Cami grinned. "The hall and foyer are still full of people. The meeting probably won't start for another fifteen seconds." She poked me playfully with an elbow.

I hadn't taken three steps inside before I was surrounded by brethren pumping my hand, slapping me on the back and welcoming me. "Great to see you this morning, Brother Matthews. You give these lovely ladies just the right balance."

Cami smiled broadly. "That was Bishop Harrison," she whispered, nodding to a man in his early forties dressed in a navy blue suit.

With everybody shaking my hand and introducing themselves to me in quick succession as we made our way into the chapel, my head was spinning by the time we reached the bench where the rest of the Hardaways were seated. I sat on the end of the bench next to Cami.

"This is a very friendly ward," I whispered. "I wish I had some investigators. This is unreal. They act like they really care about me."

Cami pressed the back of her hand against her mouth, struggling to stifle a laugh.

"What's so funny?"

"I don't want to burst your bubble," she finally managed to whisper, "but they think you're JB. They think you *are* an investigator. The same day Dad met JB and thought I might be getting a little serious with him, he went to Bishop Harrison, hoping he could do something to get JB activated. I suspect that the bishop has the whole Ward Council involved in this activation project. Bishop Harrison has been good to JB. He checks up on him all the time. And believe it or not, JB really likes the bishop."

"Oh," I muttered, deflated. I looked around at the smiling faces.

"They think you've cut your hair, shaved, turned over a new leaf, become a new person. You know, all the wonderful things you hope will happen to wayward people. You're their Sunday morning miracle. Do everybody a favor and just introduce yourself as *Brother Matthews*."

"So I'm the success story showcased in next stake conference. You could have gone all day without telling me that," I said out of the corner of my mouth. "For a while there I was expecting them to ask me to speak in sacrament meeting and share my infinite wisdom. Or sustain me as bishop."

"I suspected as much. Your pride had reached a critical level." She nudged me with her shoulder, still shaking a little as she chuckled. "You needed a humility check."

"So this is a little like *our* first meeting. Except they're shaking my hand instead of kissing me." I sighed. "You know, JB's starting to give me a complex. It's a bummer to be the wrong twin."

"Do you want me to tell everybody you're not JB?"

"Heck no!" I retorted. "Nobody would speak to me then. I like this celebrity status."

After sacrament meeting, Cami and I headed to the Sunday School gospel doctrine class. Cami led the way as people continued to shake my hand and smile. Understanding what was occurring, it was difficult to keep from laughing outright. Cami and I shared knowing glances and winks.

When we stepped into the Relief Society room where the gospel doctrine class was held, Susan was up front preparing to teach. "*She's* the teacher?" I asked, surprised.

"She was called her first Sunday back. This is her third week. She's really quite good. Nobody likes to teach the gospel doctrine class because there's this guy, Frank Norman, who thinks he knows everything. For years he has disrupted the class. The first week Susan taught the lesson, he tried to drag her off onto some gospel tangent. She didn't let him. And she knew what she was talking about. She took control from the first day. It was like she was home bossing all of us around. She's pretty good at that. Frank hasn't been brave enough to launch a second attack."

"You sound impressed."

She turned to me, very serious. "I am. Susan's talented. In more ways than one. She doesn't put on the dog about it. A lot of people think she's stuck on herself because she's self-confident. Her self-confidence comes from knowing what she's doing."

I hadn't paid much attention to Susan as we entered the church. My attention had been drawn to Cami, but as Susan stood in front of the class and took charge, I studied her more closely. She was wearing a burgundy two-piece suit with a small pink rose on the lapel. Her tanned face and dark brown eyes were accentuated by lips with a trace of lipstick. For a moment I wondered if I had a case of temporary blindness because she was beautiful. In fact, I found her beauty crowding past Cami's good looks, which had been my standard, and evolving into a mature beauty of its own. Her smile was pleasant and engaging, and she had a definite grace as she walked back and forth at the front of the class.

I was captivated by Susan until she turned unexpectedly to me and asked me to stand up. Wrenched from my quiet admiration, I realized that she was going to introduce me to the rest of the class. "This is Jacob Matthews, twin brother of JB Matthews, whom some of you know. Jacob just recently returned from a mission in Mexico. Jacob," she said to me, "I hope you will feel free to participate with us this morning."

"Well, there goes the charade," I muttered to Cami as I sat down. "Did you hear that loud sigh of regret when she said `JB's twin brother'?"

The lesson moved smoothly. I spotted Frank Norman early, but just as Cami had indicated, Susan maintained control. She was a natural teacher. Soon I was as caught up in her lesson as I had earlier been by her looks.

Once again she caught me off guard, though. She made reference to her being stranded on the highway Friday. She didn't refer to me by name, but she wove the experience into her lesson in an entertaining and enlightening manner, pointing out how her pride and prejudice had created conflict and hurt feelings. Several times during her account her eyes caught mine, and before she finished, she extended to me another veiled apology for what had happened.

"Did something else happen between you and Susan last Friday?" Cami whispered, leaning toward me.

"I rescued her," I said, feigning smugness. "Now she's probably eternally grateful."

"Really?"

I inflated my chest playfully.

She studied me out of the corner of her eye. "It might not hurt to try another humility check, Jacob Matthews, not his more prominent brother."

I shook my head. "You really know how to punch a guy while he's down."

"You can live a long time on humility. You get malnourished on pride."

By the time meetings were over, I understood even more why JB had become so attracted to Cami Hardaway. She was so casual, so unpretentious and non-judgmental, so overtly friendly and caring. "Do you have someplace to go for dinner?" she asked me as we were leaving the church.

"Well, I think there are some things at the apartment—lunch meat, peanut butter, mayonnaise, bread and…"

"Sounds like you'll have a banquet! Want something more appetizing?"

"What did you have in mind?"

"I invited JB to dinner."

"Great. I won't have to share the peanut butter."

She laughed. "We have plenty at our place."

"Is that an invitation?"

"One o'clock."

"Will JB mind?"

"He's not cooking. But I suppose if he's bothered too much by the arrangement, he can stay at the apartment and feast on peanut butter. Don't worry, he'll be there, regardless of who we invite."

"I guess you've twisted my arm and forced me into submission."

"What did you think of Susan's lesson?"

"She's good."

"Just good?"

"Really good."

"Do you think you'd ever ask her out?"

I choked ostensibly. "You're not very subtle, are you?"

"I like to get to the point."

"I've considered taking her sister out," I came back, suddenly bold and daring, but not to the point of looking her in the eyes.

"Oh, Teresa's too young," was her quick comeback. "Dad wouldn't consider letting you take her, even though you are a returned missionary. If you're still available in five or six years, I'll let her know you asked."

Having been so bold already and seeing that Cami was in a joking mood, I pressed. "I was really thinking of her other sister." I shrugged and looked down the street. "I keep remembering that first greeting. I can't help thinking that at least a little of that was meant for me."

"Humility check." She smiled and pushed me.

"Don't you ever think about it?"

"Occasionally, and I get terribly embarrassed. I can feel my cheeks burn right now."

We walked in silence for a half block. "I think you would like Susan."

"She's impressive." I pondered a moment. "Perhaps too impressive for me." I quickly added. "I'm not sure I'm up to her level."

"But you think I'm fine?" She fought desperately to keep the smile off her face, but she failed, finally bursting out into a girlish laugh.

"I guess lack of humility isn't the only problem I'm having

today. My foot has been kicking me in the teeth all morning. Forget everything I've said."

We continued in silence. When Cami spoke, she was serious. "Your brother has created a dilemma for me. His outward appearance doesn't meet my expectations for the guy I want to...Well, it's what's inside JB that gives me hope. Some day that will show in his outward appearance."

She smiled. "One of my biggest challenges is explaining JB to my Mia Maids because I don't want them to get the wrong idea. Therefore, JB has become my missionary or my activation assignment."

"I see. So he's really like a special church assignment?"

She nodded and smiled sheepishly. "JB and I joke about that. He'll call me up and say `Hey, do you want to do some more activation work this Friday night?'"

"And you jump at the chance?"

"It has proved to be a very enjoyable church calling."

"So when I come along, I'm just another guy. You prefer the church business end of your relationship with JB."

"When I see you. When I talk to you. When I go to church with you. When I do any of those things, I think of JB. I think that those could all be things he does. I suppose you're right in one way. I do think about you. That kiss..." She hesitated. "That feeling I had when I first walked down the stairs and..." She walked in silence for a moment. "Those were all real. Very real."

"But they were for JB."

"Something happened between JB and me. It happened the first day he stopped to help me. Susan and the rest of the family have never looked past his hair, his beard or his mustache. That's all they see. That night he stopped, I saw all of those things, but I didn't really notice them till later—after I had looked inside him." She turned to me. "Help him, Jacob."

"I've tried."

"Have you given up?"

"No."

"Neither have I."

CHAPTER SEVEN

JB was dressed when I returned to the apartment. He sat on the couch reading *Sports Illustrated*. "How was it?" he asked, not looking up.

"You missed some good meetings," I answered plaintively. "They rolled out the red carpet for me."

"It's a friendly ward."

"Then they found out I wasn't you. They were disappointed. They really like you, JB."

He chuckled sardonically. "You mean they like your haircut and clean-shaven face."

"It's more than that."

"Is it?" He laughed. "Tom Pawlik and his son are my home teachers. He must stop by at least once each week. Maybe more often. Bishop Harrison drops by. He's a good guy. He knows Roger Franco. They both try to work on me. They're determined to make me over into a nice clean-cut missionary boy like you, Jacob. But they're wasting their time."

"Did you have a good sleep?"

JB dropped the magazine next to him on the couch. "No. Thanks to you. I might as well have gone to church. I'd have received less preaching there."

"And you could have sat with your arm around Cami instead of your misshapen pillow," I replied. "By the way, I received a dinner invitation."

JB studied me for a moment. "To the Hardaways?"

I nodded.

"Why is it that I get the strange impression you're cutting in on me?" he asked, maintaining a guarded smile. "Cami does have a sister."

I nodded, pushing my hands into my pockets. "Yeah," I

said, sighing, "but I was told Teresa's too young for me."

"Susan isn't."

"Susan isn't Cami. She's some girl, JB." I breathed deeply and paced the floor, shaking my head. "After spending meetings with her…" I looked at James, who sat on the couch staring at me. It was hard to read him. "I flat out told her I'd like to ask her out. Not in those words."

"You ended up with Sunday dinner instead? What am I supposed to do?"

"We're both invited."

"But one of us has to sit out on the porch?" he asked sarcastically.

I shook my head. "She likes you, JB. I don't mean a little bit. She likes you. You know that perfect guy you talked about, the one you'll saint when you see him?" JB didn't speak or move. He just continued to stare. "You're the guy. And I don't stand a chance. I can settle for Susan or Teresa or Cami's best friend. But I don't have a prayer with Cami Hardaway because you're there.

"This morning I said I was envious. I'm not envious. Shoot! I'm jealous. And I'm ticked off because you can have her, but you won't make the effort to take her. I'd do anything to have her." I shook my head. "And she won't take me. Yeah, she invited me to dinner. But I received the invitation because I'm your brother. Now that's a humility check for you. I've been having them all morning. Because of you."

JB pushed up from the couch and muttered, "It's almost one. Let's get over there. I'll drive."

I didn't officially meet Denton Hardaway until JB and I showed up for dinner that Sunday afternoon. He was a distinguished looking man, about six-three, with thick rapidly graying hair even though he was only forty-seven. From the moment I walked through the door and he took me by the hand, I realized that his most salient characteristic was his cheerful friendliness. I understood why he had done so well in sales. I could imagine walking into his furniture store and wanting to buy an entire living room set just to please him.

"It's good to have you both here," he said after the introductions. Looking at me, he added sincerely, "I've heard lots of good things about you, Jacob. I'm glad I could finally meet you."

I looked past him at Cami, who winked and smiled, giving me an inconspicuous thumbs up. Denton put his arm over my shoulders and pulled me into the living room while Cami took JB's arm and tugged him over to the couch where the two sat down. Denton and I made small talk. He asked about my mission and my plans for work and school. I asked him about his furniture business.

A short while later Cami's two brothers, Justin, seventeen, and Brett, fourteen, came in. They both took after their dad, handsome and friendly. Denton and his two sons started discussing some school things and Cami and JB were laughing and speaking softly. I glanced toward the kitchen where Susan was working to put dinner on. She had changed into a loose-fitting smock and was wearing a bright red apron. I pushed up from the chair where I was sitting and wandered into the kitchen. "I take it that it's your turn to cook," I said, announcing my entrance.

Susan looked at me and smiled tiredly. "Unfortunately it's my turn every Sunday."

I glanced back toward the living room where everyone else was visiting and apparently oblivious to Susan's efforts. "Is that by choice?"

She followed my glance and then turned back to the stove. "Probably family tradition. Or family expectations."

"What did they do while you were in Chile? Wait in there for the good fairy to pop through the door and cook the meal?"

"I have no idea. But as soon as I returned, they seemed perfectly happy to turn the kitchen duties back to me."

"You don't sound too pleased with the arrangement."

"I get frustrated with everybody's helplessness."

"Maybe they just like the arrangement. And you make it easy."

She turned from the stove and studied me. "Are you trying to pick a fight with me?" She tried to veil the question in humor, but there was a shade of seriousness to it.

I shrugged and looked about the kitchen. "I tried that Friday and lost. I was just making an observation. You gave a good lesson this morning."

"Thank you," she replied softly with her back to me. "I

wasn't planning on you being there. But since I'd planned to use my own personal experience from Friday, I was glad you were so I could apologize appropriately. I don't know that I did Friday."

I laughed and added awkwardly, "I'm sorry about Friday too. Do you need some help in here?"

She laughed. "No, I'm doing fine. Go back with the others."

"You're bound and determined to be a martyr, aren't you?" She turned to me, but before she could say anything, I quickly added, "I can whip up some mean potatoes. They were my specialty at home."

"Have you even whipped potatoes before?" she asked, doubting.

"You haven't experienced a real Sunday dinner until you've tried my famous mashed potatoes."

"Would you like to mash the potatoes?"

"I'd love to. We can both be martyrs, you know, commiserate and slave together in here while the others lounge around lazily."

"Can you commiserate and mash potatoes at the same time?"

"Most definitely. I've had a lot of practice. Move over Cinderella and get me a big bowl, a cube of butter, milk, the electric beaters, and…" I stopped when I saw Susan about to tell me how to proceed. I held up my hands and shook my head. "Trust me, Miss Hardaway. I probably won't do potatoes the way you do, but you'll like them."

She started working on the roast and left me to the potatoes; however, I could tell that it was all she could do to not give me a few pointers, but she refrained.

"You know my mom had a hard time getting everybody to help for Sunday dinner. And then one day she came home and just lounged around like the rest of us. Two hours later when our stomachs started growling and the table was still bare she got our attention. Everybody started demanding to know what was going on. She was pretty casual about it. She just said, `Sunday's a day of rest for me too. If nobody wants to work, that's fine. We can fast. If everybody wants to pitch in and help, it won't be hard for any of us.' It worked. Mom was a lousy martyr. But I can mash potatoes now and do a few other things."

"Is that what you're suggesting I do?" she inquired, smiling.

I glanced toward the living room. "They had to do something while you were playing missionary in Chile."

She shook her head. "I don't think your mother's approach would work here. They'd just make a mess, and I'd end up having to clean it."

"Suit yourself, Cinderella."

A few minutes later the family sat around the huge oak table in the dining room piled with food. The place settings, the table decorations and the platters and bowls of meat, vegetables, salad, rolls and mashed potatoes looked like something out of *Good Housekeeping*. Susan Hardaway definitely knew how to fix a meal and make it look wonderful.

"It's good to have JB and Jacob with us this afternoon," Denton commented before he asked Brett to say a blessing on the food. "We hope you'll both feel welcome."

I glanced at JB, who sat across the table between Teresa and Cami. He stared down at his plate without responding, other than nodding his head once in a tacit expression of thanks. "It's great to be here," I said simply. I looked to my right and left where Brett and Justin sat beside me. Susan was at the end of the table facing Denton. "This is almost like eating at home. I like big crowds at Sunday dinner."

"JB has told us a little about your family," Denton said. "Four girls and four boys are a lot around any dinner table."

Dinner was a casual, relaxed affair. No one was rushed. Everybody seemed accommodating and solicitous, making certain that JB and I were well fed and taken care of. And everybody commented about the potatoes.

"They're Jacob's contribution," Susan explained, nodding in my direction. "His own secret recipe."

"Actually Susan didn't think I could do anything in the kitchen, except make a big mess that she'd have to clean up."

"I vote Jacob does the potatoes every week," Brett called out. "Susan leaves too many lumps in hers."

"Do I need to make a public announcement that I was wrong?" Susan teased, raising her eyebrows and cocking her head to one side.

The conversation was spontaneous and natural, covering everything from Sunday meetings to community problems to work issues. Brett began to kid his dad about stopping after church and talking to Carol Boring, a rather young single mother. "I think he might ask her out," Brett snickered. "Of course, like always he'll probably give her a little time to get used to the idea."

"Yeah," Justin joined in, "he'll wait until her kids are all raised. He doesn't want to rush things."

"Before anyone gets another wild romance going," Denton cut in, fighting to remain serious, "she was asking me about a used sofa set."

"Woooo," Cami said, "that definitely has some romantic overtones. They're a bit subtle, but someone with Daddy's romantic inclinations could take that used sofa and..."

"Oh, please," Denton groaned.

Everybody laughed. Cami turned to me and explained, "Daddy is pretty careful when it comes to his romantic activities. I think he's shaken two women's hands in the last eight years."

"Both women were old enough to be his grandmother," Justin chortled.

"Don't believe anything they tell you," Denton said, turning to me.

"Daddy's idea of socializing is going home teaching, attending sacrament meeting and selling furniture," Cami whispered loudly.

"What about Sharon Lewis and Beth Corey and..."

"He took them all to sacrament meeting," Cami grinned across the table at me. "He didn't even bring them home for dinner."

"Jacob," Denton asked, shaking his head, "if you met a nice young lady with whom you wanted to become serious, would you dare bring her here?"

All the kids groaned. I coughed and held up my hands. "Brother Hardaway, I don't think I want to get dragged into this family discussion."

"Chicken," Justin accused. "Dad's just trying to build support with strangers. He likes to think he's the Don Juan of Huntsville, but he only goes out a few times with anybody. If he thinks they're getting serious, he disappears."

"You have no idea how many poor ladies' hearts have been mercilessly smashed by our dad," Cami commented, smiling.

"I will admit that I'm a bit particular about somebody I'm going to date. It's tough dating when you're as old as I am. And can you imagine bringing an innocent woman into this?" he asked, gesturing around the table to his children. "It's bad enough that I have to put up with this abuse."

Everybody laughed and there was a short lull. Teresa was the first to speak. "Do you think you'll ever get married again, Dad?" Her question was serious.

Denton continued chewing a piece of roast. He swallowed, wiped his mouth and stared intently at his glass. Everyone waited for his answer. "There is someone," he said slowly. "And it's *not* Carol Boring."

Everyone looked down the table at Denton, waiting for him to continue. He took another bite of meat as though he had said nothing out of the ordinary. "And?" Susan finally prodded.

He looked up and glanced around the table. *"There's* no and. There's just someone."

"Someone special, someone you're serious about, someone who has proposed to you?" Justin pressed. "What about this someone?"

A huge grin spread across his face. He wagged a finger. "For your information, I'm going to do this on my own. I refuse to take any counsel from my kids. Especially after the abuse that has been heaped upon me over the years. Don't you think that's fair, Jacob?"

"I'm completely neutral," I answered, grinning.

By the time dessert was served and eaten we had been at the table close to an hour and a half. It was a fun meal. There was a jovial closeness in the family that I relished. Of course, Cami had something to do with my feelings. I had been disappointed when I was not seated next to her, but as the meal had progressed, I was grateful that I had been seated across the table from her where I could see her face. It might have been just her friendly manner, but several times during the meal I thought I detected more than the normal glance my way. Twice during the dinner conversation, she nudged me teasingly under the table with her toe and looked away innocently.

"Well, you outdid yourself again, Susan," Denton complimented as he pushed back from the table. "We certainly missed these feasts while you were away."

"Yeah," Teresa called out, "so don't leave again. We starved on Cami and Dad's cooking."

"What do you mean Dad's cooking?" Justin protested. "He made us do the cooking."

"So now show your gratitude and help clean up," Denton ordered, chuckling.

Everybody started clearing the table, hauling everything into the kitchen where Susan started filling the dishwasher and scrubbing the pots and pans in the sink. It wasn't long before everybody just drifted away to their individual quiet Sunday afternoon activities, leaving Susan to do the bulk of the clean up. Cami and JB left the house to take a ride.

Carrying the last platter into the kitchen and setting it on the sideboard, I felt awkward and out of place. "Thanks," Susan remarked tiredly when she glanced over her shoulder and saw I was the only one left.

"What can I do?" I offered, feeling bad that Susan had been left with nearly everything.

She laughed. "Oh, I can get it. We don't make it a habit of putting our guests to work."

I wiped my hands on a paper towel and was about to leave when I reconsidered. "I don't mind. Where can I do the least amount of damage?"

She turned and shook her head. "If the others aren't going to stay and help, I'm certainly not going to have the guests do it."

I laughed. "It's your fault they're not here."

"My fault?" She sounded indignant.

"You probably like getting stuck in here."

"And what's that supposed to mean?" There was a coolness to the question.

"Just an observation." I pushed into the sink and grabbed a scouring pad. "You put the food away since you know where it goes. I'll scrub these."

"Really, I can do it."

"Are you afraid I'm going to break one of these pans? If you want to know the truth, scrubbing greasy pans and mashing potatoes are my specialties. Outside of those two things, though, I'm helpless."

For the next few minutes we worked without speaking while the clinking, clanging sounds of clean up filled the kitchen. "Is your dad as socially backward as everybody makes him out to be?" I asked, attempting a bit of conversation.

"Actually, he's come a long ways the last three or four years. Right after Mom died he had it pretty tough. He and Mom were really close, and her death was so sudden and unexpected. She had a massive aneurysm while she was working in the yard. She died within minutes. Dad was making some deliveries and nobody could get in touch with him until late afternoon." She was quiet a moment. "He almost lost it," she continued softly. "I suspect if it hadn't been for us kids, he would have fallen apart.

"He withdrew a lot. Not so much here at home. He wanted to make sure we were taken care of, but he didn't want anything social. He immersed himself in his work. He was gone a lot so he hired housekeepers and cooks to look after things. If anyone mentioned dating or getting married again during those first two or three years, he shut them off immediately.

"A few months before my mission he became really serious with a lady in Liberty. It was the first time since Mom's death. Although they hadn't announced anything officially, they were planning to get married. Then out of the blue her ex-husband showed up. I guess she'd never stopped loving him, because she took him back. They got married a month or so later."

Susan sighed. "Daddy was devastated. I already had my call to Chile. I didn't know if I should go because I felt Daddy needed a lot of support. I didn't want him retreating into his social shell again." She took a deep breath. "But he insisted that I go. It was good for both of us. He's come a long ways since then.

"He dates now. Fairly regularly." She laughed. "Regularly

for Dad is once every week or so. But he doesn't get serious. Once he told me that every time he went out with a woman, he found himself comparing her to Mom, and none of them measured up. He admitted that he wasn't sure Mom could even measure up to his memories of her."

"So now he has his eye on someone?"

She laughed. "That was news to me. And everybody else in the family. If there is someone, I'd sure like to meet her."

We were quiet again, and then I directed the conversation to Cami, which was where my real interest lie. "What made your sister charge off to ASU and then quit before the year was finished?"

Susan didn't answer immediately. When she did she seemed a little exasperated. "When she graduated from high school, she wanted to get away. She had always planned to go to BYU, but then she and her friend got to looking at all the colleges around the country. ASU just caught their fancy. She begged Dad to let her go. He refused at first, but she kept pestering until he gave in. That's Camille for you, always wanting to go on some crusade or wild adventure."

"What made her come back part way through the second semester?"

"Your brother," she answered simply without looking at me.

"JB?" I shook my head. "But he was down there. Was she trying to get away from him?"

"She didn't think the influences down there were good for him. She convinced herself that if she got him up here in another environment where the Church was strong and she had family and strong friends around, she could bring him around. She lined him up a job and he came." There was a hint of bitterness in her tone.

"But he didn't change according to plan," I guessed.

"Maybe he's changed some. But..." She didn't finish.

"You don't think he'll change?"

"Do you?"

"I don't know," I answered honestly.

"But I think she might change. She might convince herself that if she marries him, then he'll change, just like she thought he'd change if she brought him to Huntsville." She paused a moment and then added, "Cami has a lot on the ball. She's pretty and intelligent. Everybody likes her." She studied me. "No one can resist her radiant friendliness. You like her too," she observed bluntly. She averted her eyes as she began folding a dish towel.

"I'll plead guilty to that." I smiled. "If JB weren't around, I'd probably make a daring move."

"Watching you today, I'd guess that you already have," she retorted dryly. "Cami's also an incorrigible flirt. She doesn't mean to lead anybody on. It's just part of her friendly nature." Susan turned her back to me as she wiped down the sideboard. "But Cami hasn't learned a lot of responsibility yet. I don't say that as a criticism as much as a statement of fact. She's carefree and fun and irresponsible. That's why she could charge off to ASU one month and then pull up stakes a while later and come home without a shade of guilt."

"Maybe that's partly your fault," I remarked.

She turned around. "My fault?"

I considered my comment a moment and then nodded my head. "Does that come as a shock?"

"Are all the problems in this family my fault?" she fired back, not attempting to disguise her irritation. "I'm the one doing the work around here." She pointed to the dining room. "Was I in there lounging around while dinner was being prepared?"

"Maybe you should have been. Maybe you shouldn't be here right now."

"Now I've heard it all," she muttered, turning away and attacking the sideboard with angry energy.

"Sometimes people need to walk on their own. You're not doing them any favors by carrying them. Even if they have to crawl for a while."

She tossed the dish rag into the sink. "Thanks for the help cleaning up," she snipped, pulling off her apron without looking at me. She started from the kitchen.

"Thanks for dinner," I called after her. She ignored my thanks and went up the stairs. "Well, I made some high scores with her," I muttered to myself as I headed for the front door, anxious to get out of the house.

CHAPTER EIGHT

"If you want, I'll go on a walk with you." I turned to discover Teresa lying on the floor on the other side of the sofa. She sat up and gave her head a quick flip, sending her long sandy-colored hair flying off her shoulder.

"How long have you been hiding there?" I stammered.

"Long enough to hear you and Susan fighting."

I shook my head. "We were discussing."

"Sounded like fighting. Susan doesn't like people telling her what to do. She'll get over it, though. What about the walk?" I hesitated. "I doubt anybody else is going to ask you. Especially not Susan." she added pointedly but not unkindly. I was soon to discover that Teresa possessed an unpretentious frankness. If she thought it, she generally said it, not to be cruel, only to be candid.

I grinned self-consciously. "Well, I hadn't planned to ask Susan to go on a walk with me."

"Does that mean you want to go with me?"

"There isn't anybody I'd rather go walking with right now than you, Teresa Hardaway."

She wrinkled her nose, rolled her eyes and smiled, shaking her head knowingly. "That's a bunch of bull, Jacob," she returned, starting for the door. "I know somebody else you'd love to go with."

We walked out the door and strolled slowly down the street. "What makes you think I want to go walking with anybody else?" I questioned, curious to see how perceptive this eleven year old was.

She looked at me askance and then smiled. "Do I look dumb?"

I cleared my throat and looked away, feeling suddenly at ease with this precocious pre-teen. "I'm glad you offered to take me on a walk," I remarked. "I like somebody who's honest. Maybe you can answer some questions."

"I don't tell family secrets," she teased.

I laughed. "Shoot, you're no fun."

We walked in silence for a moment and then she asked, "What do you want to know?"

"You mean I don't even have to pump you for information? You'll just spill everything?"

"Not everything." Her captivating, innocent but sly smile spread across her face.

"Tell me about your family. Not the deep, dark secrets. Just the common stuff."

"Susan told you about Daddy and Cami."

I looked down at her. "How long were you there eavsdropping?"

"Long enough. Nobody told me to leave."

"Nobody knew you were there."

She shrugged. "Do you want to know about my mom?"

"Do you know anything?"

"She was my mom, dumby."

"But you were only two, weren't you?" I pointed out.

"Three, but that doesn't mean I don't know anything about her. I can't really remember her. Just one little clip. She was tucking me in one night."

"And?"

"There's no and. That's all I remember. But I remember seeing her."

"Was she pretty?"

"Not really."

I looked down at her again, shocked and taken back. "I'm not one that fancies everything up. I just tell things straight. I've seen pictures of her. She's not beautiful. Not like Daddy is handsome. I mean, Mom wasn't ugly or anything. She was just kind of plain and ordinary. But Daddy thought she was the most beautiful woman in the world. That's how he tells. They were happy together. Susan's told me that lots of times. She says they always acted a bit crazy around each other because they were so much in love. They were always staying up past midnight, just laughing and talking, like they couldn't get enough of each other. I guess that's why Daddy missed her so much when she was gone."

Teresa thought some more before going on. "She was a teacher. She taught second grade until Susan was born. She liked to paint."

"Some of her paintings are hanging in your house," I commented. "Cami showed me one."

"She was very artistic, not just with her oil paints and watercolors. She had an eye for pretty things."

"She sounds like a wonderful kind of person. I can understand why all of you miss her."

"I didn't really know her," Teresa said frankly, "so I can't really miss her. I know about her from what Dad and Susan have told me. Now they miss her. Really miss her." She looked over at me as we walked. "Do you know what I think?" I turned to her without speaking. "I think Susan's a lot like Mom. She's the one that wants all of us to remember Mom and appreciate her. That's why I think she tries so hard to be like her."

I studied Teresa, wondering for a moment if I was really speaking to an eleven-year-old girl. She was so innocent and straightforward and yet so insightful.

"Do you want to know something else about Mom and Dad?"

"Sure."

"When Daddy first went over to her apartment, everybody thought he'd go out with her roommate. She was a beauty queen from Idaho. Everybody thought Daddy and the beauty queen would make the perfect couple. But Daddy didn't ever pay any attention to her. He said he knew from the very first that Mom was for him. They got engaged after three weeks and were married two months later."

"Somebody ought to write a book about that," I joked.

Teresa shook her head. "Nobody would believe it. It's too corny. And I haven't even told you the really corny stuff."

"But it makes a great story."

Teresa looked over at me through narrowed eyes. "Are you one of those dumb romantic kind of guys?"

"I don't know what kind of guy I am. I haven't thought too much about it. After all, I'm just getting started. I've got a lot of my life ahead of me. I can assure you, though, I'm not going to ask somebody to marry me after two weeks. I'm the kind of guy who has to think things through, bide my time. I'll probably have to date a girl a couple of years before I propose." I grinned.

"You seem like one of those returned missionaries who is married before he's been home two months."

"Now, that's a very unkind thing to say," I muttered, trying to appear offended, but having a hard time keeping a straight face.

"Don't you think you'll get married pretty soon?" Before I had a chance to answer or even act insulted, she rattled on. "If I ever ask you anything you don't want me to know, just say it's none of my business. I can handle that. I'll do the same to you."

I smiled. "You know, Teresa, I'm getting to like you more the longer I'm with you. It's too bad you aren't a little older. I'd ask to marry *you*. That way I could be married before my two months are up."

"And I'd tell you no."

"Dang! You know how to hurt a guy. What's wrong with me?"

"You like my sister."

I gulped. "Which one?"

"Don't play dumb with me. Cami."

"What makes you think I like Cami?" Before she could answer, I quickly asked, "And by the way, is this conversation in strictest confidence or do you go back to the house and broadcast everything?"

"What?"

"Are you going to blab all of this to the whole family?"

She rolled her eyes. "I'm not a blabbermouth."

"All right, what makes you think I like Cami?"

"The way you look at her."

"Cami's JB's girl. And I don't look at Cami any differently than I look at anybody else."

"Be careful," she warned, "your nose is starting to grow big time."

I laughed. "Man, you're cruel."

"I wouldn't mind if you started dating Cami. Or married her."

"I think that's what JB has in mind."

She shook her head. "She can't marry him because he won't take her to the temple. You could. You look like JB. I think you look better than him. And you'd take Cami to the temple."

"So if it were up to you, I'd be walking with Cami right now and you'd be pacifying JB?"

She giggled. "No, I'd still rather be with you, but I'd like you to marry Cami."

"You're sure this discussion is confidential?" I questioned again, feeling just a little nervous.

"Relax. Besides, I'm on your side. Do you know what I thought the first day I saw you?"

"That I was going to be swallowed by your sister."

She giggled and shook her head. "No, after the kiss."

"What did you think?"

"I thought you and Cami made a great couple standing there on the front step kissing. That was pretty good. I did tell the rest of the family about that. Daddy got a little nervous, though. And Susan thought it was dumb. She told Cami to be more careful."

"Cami was the one doing the kissing," I pointed out.

"But you were sure enjoying it."

I laughed. "No comment."

"So now all you've got to do is marry Cami."

"Well, that's quick. All we have to do is kiss and then get married. I appreciate your vote of confidence. Now all we have to do is convince Cami."

"So you do like Cami," she burst out as though that were a new revelation.

"I thought you'd already guessed that."

"That's all it was, a guess. But you do like her."

"You're a devious finagler," I accused, pointing my finger.

"So how are we going to get you lined up with Cami?" Teresa questioned, ignoring my accusation. "You might not believe this, but I'm pretty good at arranging things like this."

I pushed my hands into my pockets as we walked along. I studied the trees and the well-kept yards in the neighborhood. "Unfortunately, I'm afraid that's an exercise in futility. Cami's fallen in love with JB. She told me so herself."

"If she fell in, she can fall out. That's not a big deal."

"But right now she has JB on her mind. Big time."

"I hope not."

"Why?"

She was suddenly worried. "That's what Susan has worried about all along. That Cami would fall in love with JB and then talk herself into marrying him, telling herself that some day he'd get his act together. She doesn't want Cami to be that stupid."

"Susan's pretty protective of your sister, isn't she?"

Teresa nodded. "And Cami probably listens to Susan better than anybody else. Except when it comes to JB."

"Well, I wish I could help you, Teresa, but I don't think I can. I wouldn't mind dating Cami, which would take her away from JB. And I don't know that I can change JB so he's more suitable for her." I heaved a sigh. "Actually, I feel just a little guilty even talking about all this."

"Bummer," Teresa muttered dejectedly.

We continued down the street. "How old are you, Jacob?"

I glanced over at Teresa, but she didn't return my look. "I'll be twenty-two the fourteenth of September."

"Why didn't you go on your mission as soon as you turned nineteen?"

I turned away. "I was waiting for my brother. We had always planned to go together."

"But he didn't go."

I nodded. "So I left without him, seven or eight months late."

"That means that in September you'll be the same age as Susan. At least for a little while. She turns twenty-three in October. You're only ten or eleven months younger than her. That's not too bad, is it?"

"Not too bad for what?"

"Marry Susan."

"You're forgetting one important thing, Teresa. When Susan had a chance to ask me on a walk like you did, she chose to leave me standing in the kitchen."

"That's because you made her mad, all that talk about her being to blame for the way Cami is."

"I'm not sure I rate too high on her priority list."

"I'm not sure you do either, but if worse came to worse, you could always take a long look at Susan."

"I took a long look at Susan. And…" I sighed. "I don't know how precocious you really are, Teresa, but I don't think the chemistry is there between Susan and me."

She gave me a strange look. "Is the chemistry there between you and Cami?"

"Apparently not."

"You think of her. So what does chemistry have to do with anything?"

"I think this conversation is getting out of hand."

"I'm just trying to arrange something for you."

"And you figure that since Cami won't have me, then I should shoot for Susan?" Teresa nodded innocently. "I'm not sure Susan would appreciate that. She might like to find someone who had her as their first choice."

"Jacob, she's almost twenty-three. How fussy can she be?"

"Fussy enough to send me packing."

"I think we can still arrange something."

"Forget it, Teresa." I studied her. "You're a consummate matchmaker."

"I don't know what consummate means." She shrugged. "You probably don't either, but what does any of that have to do with you dating Susan?"

"Why are you so confounded anxious to get me out with one of your sisters?"

She looked up at me and gave me the most beatific grin that I had ever seen on an eleven-year-old girl. "Because I like you, Jacob. I don't even know you very well, but I like you better than any of the guys that Susan and Cami have dated."

I burst out laughing, shaking my head. Reaching out, I put my arm over Teresa's shoulder and pulled her next to me. Then I grabbed her behind the neck and shook her playfully. "You know what's really wrong here?" I mused, still chuckling. "You're going on twelve and I'm going on twenty-two. We're the two that have everything together. We can talk and be honest with each other. We like each other. The whole bummer is that I'm too old for you."

"I'm not looking anyway." She jabbed me suddenly with her elbow and laughed. "Besides, I've got my eye on Tony Barnett. He's not as neat as you, but he's more my age."

"Dang! I'm losing all the way around."

We came in view of the house and the magical candidness between us slipped away. I spotted Susan sitting on a lawn chair under one of the giant poplar trees growing along the south side of the house. Turning to Teresa, I warned, "Now remember, everything we've talked about is…"

"Don't worry," she cut in impatiently. "I'm not going to tell anybody." She got an impish grin on her face. "Shall I leave you and Susan alone?"

"For what?"

"Just in case."

"In case what?"

"In case the chemistry starts working. Some chemistry takes longer to work than others."

"You just stay really close to me, Teresa Hardaway."

Susan looked up as we entered the yard and crossed the grass to where she sat with her scriptures, note pad and teacher's manual spread out on a white, glass-topped lawn table. "How was the walk?" she asked, smiling but cool and distant.

"You should hear all the stuff Jacob told me," Teresa said nonchalantly, pretending to read Susan's manual. There was a sudden uneasy lurch in the pit of my stomach. "I think he must have been a great missionary." She peeked up at me and then turned back to the manual. "I'd like to hear more of his stories." Straightening up, she called out, "Oh, I forgot something. See you two later."

We both watched her race around the corner of the house and out of sight. I began tucking my shirt in around my belt line. "I suspect there's not a lot that escapes that young lady," I commented nervously. "She's quite the girl."

"Did she talk your leg off?"

"Oh," I said slowly, "we both did our share of talking."

"Teresa's a tease. But she knows how to keep a secret."

I laughed. "So I don't have to worry about my innermost feelings being plastered on posters around Huntsville?"

"Not by Teresa."

I fidgeted and pushed my hands into my pockets. "Well, I better get going." I wondered if she would ask me to stay longer, but she didn't. I think she was still irritated by my earlier comments. "Thanks again for dinner," I said, starting to back up. "It certainly beat peanut butter and jelly sandwiches."

"Maybe we can do it again sometime."

"If I promise not to try to straighten out your life?"

She thought a moment and then smiled faintly. I turned and walked back to the apartment.

CHAPTER NINE

Just after the crew had eaten lunch Tuesday afternoon, Roger Franco pulled up in his pickup, leaned out the window and shouted, "I need one of you fellows to pick up a load of materials in Salt Lake."

"Send the gopher," one of the guys called back, nodding in my direction. "He's good at that kind of thing." He grinned at the others.

Without giving me a chance to defend myself, Roger shouted, "Matthews, get down here."

"It'll give you a chance to rest your blisters," JB called to me.

Fifteen minutes later Roger was handing me the keys to a ten-wheel flat-bed truck. "Have you ever driven truck?"

"On the farm. It's been a couple of years, though. I didn't get much chance in Mexico."

"Dang," Roger snorted, "you farm boys start driving truck before you're out of diapers. Once you learn you never forget. This'll be a cinch." He raced through his instructions and directions for the materials pickup. "Beat the afternoon traffic out of Salt Lake and you'll be back by four-thirty or five."

It was six-thirty when I finally returned to Huntsville with the truck. Roger and JB were both waiting impatiently, alternating glares between me and their watches. Roger stomped over to me and burst out, "Good gad, boy, what'd you do, take a shortcut through Cheyenne, Wyoming? It's pushing seven o'clock."

"There was a bit of a mix-up down there. They were loading the truck, and I happened to be in the office. The secretary was showing me some stuff on the computer. I noticed a discrepancy between what you were supposed to be getting and what they were charging you. I saved you four hundred dollars on this load."

Roger looked at me and then at JB. "Four hundred bucks?"

he questioned slowly. I nodded. You picked up on that looking at their computer? What are you, a computer whiz?"

"Well, the secretary was helping."

"Do you know computers?"

"I've played with them a bit. My major's in business."

He thought a moment. "Did you have any trouble with the truck?"

I shook my head and grinned. "I pretended I was driving through the hay fields instead of down Interstate 15. I only forced four people off the road. Of course, I ran over more than that."

Roger walked back and slowly examined the load of materials, pensively rubbing his chin with his thumb. Finally he turned abruptly. "You figure they've messed up on us before?"

I shrugged. "Maybe." I grinned cautiously. "But things could go the other way too."

He tugged on his nose with his thumb and forefinger. "You've just been transferred and given a raise, Matthews. No sense in you wearing blisters on your hands while I'm losing money. You'll do pick up and delivery work. I'm shorthanded in the office too. Do you think you could handle some of the computer work? You know, purchasing and stuff like that?"

"I can probably do that easier than I can hammer nails."

"I can teach a monkey to hammer nails and fetch a saw. I'll try you in the office and on the road for a while."

As I climbed into JB's Firebird and headed to the apartment, he commented without enthusiasm, "Congratulations. You're here a week and a half and you get your first promotion."

"I'm glad you guys sent me on that run," I attempted to thank him. "Of course, I hope Roger doesn't expect me to save him four hundred dollars every time I pick up a load of materials."

"Sounds to me like he wants to make you a junior partner," he returned dryly, putting the Firebird into gear and racing onto the highway.

Nothing more was said as we drove home. After washing up, we both pitched in to stir up some fried potatoes, hamburger patties and green salad. We spoke only when it was absolutely necessary. When we sat down, JB started to eat immediately while I said a quick, silent blessing, which had become our routine. We ate without conversing for the first half of the meal, staring down at our plates and eating while keeping our individual thoughts to ourselves.

Finally I set my fork down, pushed my plate back a couple of inches and leaned my forearms on the edge of the card table. Looking across the table at JB, I asked, "What's happened to us, JB?"

He continued to chew, staring down at his plate. Finally he set his fork down, put his elbows on the table, clasped his hands in front of his chin and sighed, shaking his head. "I don't know, Jacob. I've thought a lot about that. It's just not the same anymore."

"We can't talk to each other anymore without…" I tapped my butter knife on the table. "We just can't talk."

"I've wanted to."

"So why don't you?" I encouraged. "Something's eating you but I don't know what. But I'm listening."

He leaned back in his chair while staring down at his plate. "Jacob, listening is more than hearing. It has something to do with feeling." He wet his lips. "A few years ago," he said softly with a rueful grin, "I would have been happy about your promotion. We'd have gone out and celebrated." He shook his head, picked up his fork and began pushing his food about on his plate. "I've been working for Roger almost three months, but I've been doing this kind of construction for three years. I do good work. I'm not bragging. That's just the truth. Roger let you on because he was doing me a favor. And then you show up and bingo, it's promotion time. Roger could teach a monkey to do what I do."

"He didn't say that."

"While you were in Mexico, I used to think of us working together again. I thought of us fixing up the Bug, hiking, double dating." He shook his head. "There are a hundred things we could be doing with each other."

"So why don't we?" I asked hopefully.

JB dropped his fork again. "There's Cami. I suspect that if I hadn't met her first, she would have fallen for you right away. Her family likes you. The people up here like you. They all want me to be like you." He shook his head forlornly. "And I can't be you, Jacob."

I laughed. "You're describing just how I feel. Everybody I've run into up here has fallen all over themselves to be friendly to me. But it's always been because they thought I was you or that I was an extension of you."

"No, they thought I'd become like you." He shook his head again. "They don't want me like me; they want me like you. They want Jacob Matthews. And if they have to have two of us, they want two Jacob Matthews. They want someone without an earring, somebody sitting in church every Sunday being properly pious."

"You can do all of those things."

He swallowed hard, and I saw a deep foreboding sadness in his eyes. "Just because I went through the motions wouldn't mean..." He pressed his lips together in frustrated hesitation. "It wouldn't change me. I'm still me. And I'm the only one who knows what I am."

"JB, remember in football? You played right linebacker. I was on the left. Nobody could get past us. In wrestling you went 160. I went 152. We were wrestling partners. If you dogged it, I was on your tail. If I dogged it, you climbed all over me. We accepted each other the way we were, but we made each other better."

He was quiet a moment, and then he muttered barely above a whisper, "We'll never go back, not to the way it was. I guess that's what hurts. I dreamed about you coming back and having things the way they were. I can see now that won't ever happen. It's not your fault."

"I don't believe that, JB. That's why I came here. I had a job in Brigham, but I wanted this one, not because Roger gave me a better deal, but because I could be with you. We can make this work."

JB pondered; then with his finger he drew an imaginary line across the table. "There's always a point of no return." Using the imaginary line on the table, he gestured. "If you cross that line, step all the way over, there's no going back. You've made your choice, whether you intended to make it or not. You've still crossed that line, and you're stuck with what you've dished out for yourself."

"And you've crossed this...this line?"

JB shrugged and leaned forward in his chair with his forearms on the table. "If I haven't, I've come so close that it doesn't make much difference. Sometimes you don't know if you've just touched the line, tromped on it or fallen clear across it."

"I don't believe that line is where you think it is. And I don't believe in the `no return' part of your analogy. If there's such a thing, what happens to reformation, change, repentance? I've crossed the line lots of times. But I've crossed back too. That's what the gospel's about. That's what the atonement is for. It's a bridge across that line, so we don't have to stay on the other side.

"None of us makes it back across that line alone. Every single one of us needs help. You're beating yourself because you can't cross back over all on your own. Well, I can't either. But I've learned that someone can help me. That's what the Savior does; he helps us cross back over."

He shook his head. "You haven't crossed the same line I have."

"JB," I pleaded, "tell me what's eating you."

"Spilling my guts all over the table for you to sift through isn't going to change anything."

I wondered what had happened to JB. It wasn't the first time. Although there was a natural curiosity, I wasn't sure I wanted to know everything about JB's life these last three years. I still preferred to believe that it was his selfish pride and unwillingness to act that kept him where he was.

"JB, I don't care what you've done, but you can fix those things."

JB shook his head. "I'd like to be like you, Jacob. Believe me. I'd like to be looking down at someone else instead of up. But some things don't change just because you want them to."

We finished our meal in silence and JB left. I assumed that he had gone over to see Cami. I washed the dishes, swept the floor, wiped down the sideboards and sink. Afterwards I made sure the apartment was in good shape, something I had decided to do several days ago. I was determined to not live in a pigsty, even if I ended up doing all the work to keep things looking nice.

Once the kitchen was clean I didn't have anything to do but sit around the apartment until it was time for bed. I thumbed through some of JB's old magazines, but I couldn't concentrate. I kept thinking of JB with Cami and wishing I was there too. In frustration I shook my head and tossed the magazines aside. "What kind of jerk am I? She's his girl. The last person he should have to worry about is me."

I went to bed early that night. The next evening after JB headed over to Cami's place, I went up and asked Mrs. Pritt if there was something I could do in the yard. She was surprised by my offer and declined, but I persisted. I needed something to do or I was going to start climbing the walls. I mowed her lawn, trimmed her shrubs, and swept her walk and front porch.

The next evening I worked in her garden plot. It hadn't been tilled or planted for a couple of years. I raked up the old leaves, weeds and withered tomato and cucumber vines. I worked until dark. Mrs. Pritt brought me out a glass of cold milk and two thick slices of banana bread. "I've never seen it look so good," she beamed.

I wiped my brow. "If I can borrow a rototiller, we could get a garden in here. The weather's about right."

"I haven't had a garden for a long time."

"You'll have one this year."

The next evening when I came home from work, I found a rototiller sitting on Mrs. Pritt's front lawn. She was waiting on the porch. "Benson Stokes brought his tiller over," she called down to me.

"I'll be right up."

"You sure you're up to this. It's Friday. A young man like you should be out doing some serious courting."

"I haven't had any offers. You're the only girl in Huntsville that's paid any attention to me," I grinned. "I better stick with a sure thing."

JB showered and left the apartment without eating. I was filling the tiller with gas when he pulled away. Mrs. Pritt's garden spot wasn't very big, twenty feet by twenty-five feet. I went over it three times with the tiller before I shut off the motor and dropped down on the lawn to catch my breath.

"There you are, sitting down on the job."

I turned. Cami was standing by the corner of the house smiling. She was dressed in a pair of mid-thigh shorts, a pullover shirt and a pair of sandals. "Sister Pritt said you were back here playing farmer." She surveyed the garden spot. "It looks good. When do you plant?"

I smiled, feeling my cheeks burn slightly. Cami's sudden appearance had taken me by surprise, and I couldn't help feeling a surge of excitement. In fact, although I had tried not to, I had been thinking of her just a few moments earlier. "If Mrs. Pritt can find some seeds, I might put something in tomorrow. I don't have anything else to do."

"Where's your brother?" She looked around.

"I thought he was with you."

"Last night he told me he had to run down to Ogden right after work. I figured he would be back by now, though." She dropped down in front of me and sat cross-legged on the grass. "Is this how you spend your Friday nights?" She smiled. "You know you're breaking some poor girl's heart tonight. You should be out on the town. It's still early."

"It's cheaper working in Mrs. Pritt's garden. And she feeds me."

"You're no fun."

"Besides, the best girl's already turned me down. And she's taken."

She studied me, fighting back a grin. "How did you know Susan had a date tonight? While her sister's left behind to wander around Huntsville all by herself."

I smiled. "Well, I was never one to let a lonely girl pine away at home on a Friday night. Do you want to get something to eat?"

"Maybe I'd accept if I hadn't been your second choice," she teased. She snatched at a tuft of grass and tossed it in my direction.

It was strange how my resolve to keep my distance from Cami Hardaway melted away as I sat and visited. She teased and joked. We talked about home, my mission, our work, living in Huntsville, going to college. She had been accepted to

BYU for fall semester and was leaving the end of August. I was going to be at BYU too. We wondered if we'd run into each other there.

"So this is where you are?" JB's accusing voice broke into our happy conversation.

Cami and I both turned as JB came around the corner of the house and approached us. His face was hard as he glared disapprovingly in my direction.

"Where have you been?" Cami asked lightly.

"Over at your place. Waiting for you."

Cami reached up, took JB's hand and pulled him down beside her. "You said you had to run to Ogden for a quick errand. I slipped over here to wait for you."

"And Jacob here was good enough to keep you company."

"We've had a good visit."

"I'll bet."

I pushed up from the ground. "Well, I better put the tiller away," I mumbled.

JB and Cami left. I put the tiller and other tools away, went into the house and had a sandwich, all the while thinking of Cami. I couldn't have her. All I was doing was aggravating JB and tormenting myself. Once again I determined to concentrate on my work and my relationship with JB. Cami didn't have a role in either.

CHAPTER TEN

Roger called JB and me in to work Saturday. We didn't get off until after seven. By then the only thing I wanted to do was clean up and go to bed.

Sunday morning I showered and shaved and got dressed for Sunday meetings, this time without bothering JB. He was still irritatated that he had found Cami and me together with each other Friday evening although I had explained several times that Cami was the one who had stopped by and all we had done was visit.

As I left for the church, walking instead of driving the Bug, I made up my mind that I was going to stay as far from the Hardaways as possible. I made it a point to go to the church early and find my spot before the Hardaways even showed up

I found a back row spot and waited for the meeting to begin. The prelude music was playing when the Hardaways marched into the chapel and found an empty row toward the front. I made it throught the entire three-hour block without running into any of the Hardaways. Of course, I did attend Susan's gospel doctrine class, but I found a back corner chair and made myself inconspicuous. I also forced myself to not glance in Cami's direction even once.

Feeling pleased with myself for exhibiting such strong self-control, I hurried down the hall at the end of the three-hour block and bumped into Susan Hardaway as she stepped out of the library.

"Dang, I didn't mean to knock you over," I apologized, steadying her and catching one of the books I had knocked out of her arms.

"Hello, Jacob," she greeted cordially. "I didn't realize you had come today."

"I've kept a low profile." I grinned. "Until now."

We started down the hall, both moving in the same direction. "How has work been?"

"I'm feeling better."

"Cami said you've been helping Sister Pritt with her yard and garden," she remarked, sounding pleased.

"It's something to occupy my evenings."

We were quiet for a moment and then Teresa slipped up behind us. "I didn't think I'd see you two together," she called out. "Did she invite you to dinner?"

"Well, not..."

"Are you going to invite him, Susan," Teresa went on before I could answer.

Susan looked from Teresa to me and then back to Teresa. She smiled. "I think you already have."

"Are you coming?" Teresa demanded of me.

"I really don't know if...I should..." I stammered, feeling embarrassed and vulnerable.

Susan laughed. "There's plenty. Come on over. Besides, everybody has missed your famous mashed potatoes. You'll have to promise to make them again."

"This time you can start from scratch," Teresa joined in. "Peel them and everything."

"Teresa has ulterior motives. Peeling potatoes is her job."

I walked home with Teresa and Susan and marched right into the kitchen and started the potatoes with Teresa's help. I was there whipping potatoes with my shirt sleeves rolled up when JB arrived. I could tell that my presence not only surprised him but irritated him as well.

"What's this?" he hissed as he picked up a plate of bread to take out to the dining table. "Are you coming every Sunday?"

"I didn't go around begging for an invitation. They asked me. What was I supposed to do, tell them no because you were going to be here too?" I answered, keeping my eyes on the pot of potatoes but being unable to keep the crispness out of my voice.

Once again I ridiculed myself for allowing my prior resolve to be eroded. I wished I was someplace else, but it was too late now. I took the potatoes out to the table and wandered around the dining room and the living room admiring some of the art work on the walls and shelves. I noticed the initials SH scrawled in the bottom right corner of a portrait of two young girls, whom I surmised to be Cami and Susan when they were younger. "Your mom did this?" I asked Teresa, who was sitting on the sofa.

She smiled and shook her head. "Susan did. She paints too."

"Your sister Susan?" I questioned, taken back.

"The landscape painting is Mom's. The others are Susan's. Some people think she's pretty good."

I smiled. "I'd have to include myself in that group."

"She did all the dry arrangements too. And the two flower sprays on either side of the dining room hutch."

I looked at the dry arrangements and the flower sprays with more interest. My gaze shifted to the kitchen where Susan's back was to me as she put slices of butter on two bowls of steaming beans and corn.

The meal reminded me a lot of my experience the week before. The family talked freely and pleasantly. As they finished the main course and waited for Susan to get the ice cream and hot fudge for nut sundaes, Denton held up his hand and said, "I'd like to make a little announcement."

Everyone stopped talking and turned to Denton, who looked down at his empty plate. He seemed a little reluctant to speak, which was abnormal for him because he was usually so warmly conversant. Everyone became silent and attentive.

"I've been single a long time," he began slowly.

Brett started to grin. "I knew it," he popped off, "after eight years, Dad's finally decided to go on a date."

"Daddy's had lots of dates," Teresa spoke up in her dad's defense, glaring at Brett.

"Yeah, but this is the first time he's ever made an official announcement," Justin snickered, playfully pushing his brother.

Denton held up his hands. He smiled and his cheeks colored. "Actually, this might have progressed past the dating stage."

"Wooo, this is serious," Brett said, leaning forward. "Has Minnie Egan gotten tired of just going to the movies with you without a solid commitment?"

"He's not going to marry Minnie Egan," Cami spoke up. "Are you, Daddy?" she added with a shade of uncertainty.

He smiled and shook his head.

"You're not getting serious with Nan Perkins, are you?" Teresa gasped.

"Why don't we let Daddy tell us what's on his mind?" Susan spoke up, glaring around the table at everyone.

Denton took a quick sip of water from his glass. "During the past four or five months I've visited with a lady at work."

"It's somebody that works for you?" Cami burst out incredulously.

Denton chuckled and shook his head. "No, no, I've just talked to her on the phone. She works for one of our suppliers in Salt Lake. At first it was just business, but after a while we got to talking about family and other things. She's divorced and has three children and..."

"What does she look like?" Justin questioned.

"How old is she?" Brett joined in.

Denton thought a moment and then added, "She's thirty-five. I don't know what she looks like."

"And you're going to marry her?" Justin cried.

"Would everybody just be quiet and let Daddy talk," Susan called out. "He's not going to marry anybody. He's just telling us about this lady he's talked to on the phone."

Denton looked over at Susan and then down at his plate. "Well, actually, we have talked about marriage." He was totally serious.

No one in the room spoke. Everyone just stared with their mouths starting to sag open.

"You're talking about getting married," Susan finally spoke, "and you haven't even seen her. And she hasn't seen you?"

Denton thought a moment and then smiled. "I said we had talked about marriage. Not necessarily getting married ourselves. We've discussed marriage in a general kind of way." He hesitated. "I know this sounds crazy, especially coming from me, but..." He laughed. "I'm going to meet her next Friday evening. I have a feeling things might...develop."

Justin whispered to Brett but loud enough for everyone at the table to hear. "Dad's fallen for a freakin' voice." Then turning to Denton, he added, "What if she's four ten and two hundred pounds? Don't you think you'd better at least ask for a photograph or something before you…"

"He's going on a date," Cami cut him off. "Give Dad some space."

"But he's sounding a little out of touch," Brett fired back. "You're not going to do anything really stupid are you, Dad? I don't know if I could explain something like that to the guys at school."

Dessert was defintely anticlimatic after Denton's announcement. From that point on the entire topic of conversation was Trudy Parsons, Denton's voice companion. The members of the family gradually slipped away from the table, and before long only Susan and I remained.

"It looks like you got stuck again," I commented, surveying the table clutter.

She heaved a sigh. "Doing dishes will be a welcome release after Daddy's bombshell."

"I'll give you a hand," I said, rising and grabbing for the plates on either side of me.

"No," Susan protested, holding up her hands and standing. "Not two weeks in a row."

"You just don't want me telling you how to run your life again," I joked, continuing to clear the table. "I'll keep my comments to myself this time."

"I don't believe that for a minute."

"I can't just leave you with all of this." I motioned to the uncleared table and the kitchen sink. "Besides, I don't mind working for my dinner."

We worked in silence for a while, but I couldn't resist one comment. "You know, you're making welfare cases out of them."

She stopped with both her hands clutching bunches of silverware. "I knew you couldn't keep your mouth shut. Are you going to preach to me again?"

"You need to flat out tell them that they've got to pull their share of the load. You're not going to be around here the rest of their lives. You deserve a life too."

I was expecting a sharp retort, but Susan marched into the kitchen and dropped the silverware into the sink without responding. I assumed she was going to ignore me until she remarked a moment later, "I know this will come as a shock to you, but I did think about what you said last week."

"Hmmm." I smiled and looked about the dining area and the kitchen. "When do they show up?"

"I said I thought about what you said," she sighed. "I didn't say I copied it word for word and posted it to the kitchen door."

"You just don't want to admit that I knew what I was talking about. That's all right," I teased. "Knowing I'm right is satisfaction enough."

"You know, your humility slays me," she muttered, walking past me and giving me a quick, unexpected shove. "It must be hard living with yourself when you're so perfect."

I laughed. "Truce. Let's change the subject. Do you think your dad's serious about this Trudy lady?"

She pondered a moment before responding. "Something tells me he's more serious about this Trudy Parsons than he lets on."

I smiled. "I don't want this to sound rude or…"

"Then you probably better not say it."

I laughed. "I can't help it. I'm in a blunt mood today. Maybe your dad is trying to tell you something."

"And what is that supposed to mean?" she demanded, stiffening.

"Oh, that Denton has things under control and you can go on and have a life of your own. You deserve that much."

"Are you always such an authority on other peoples' lives?"

"I'm merely making an observation. I'm really on your side."

Susan rolled her eyes as she put plastic wrap over the remaining mashed potatoes. "Why is it that doing Sunday dishes by myself wasn't nearly as stressful as when I receive help from you?"

I laughed, shaking my head. "All right, I'll leave it alone. Not because I'm wrong," I quickly added, raising my hand, "but because I want to be pleasant and accommodating."

"Oh, brother," she groaned, "give me a break."

"Teresa showed me some of your art work," I remarked, quickly changing the subject.

Susan didn't comment but she blushed ever so slightly. "I'm impressed. You're good. Have you ever considered selling anything?"

"It's a hobby, nothing more, just something I like to do in my spare time to unwind."

"Your mom was an artist too."

"She's the one who got me started."

"The pupil has surpassed the master."

"Not hardly," she replied, blushing. "Mom had pure talent. She had a natural eye for art. I have to work at it. And I'm pretty traditional. Landscapes and things."

Although she was reluctant to talk about her artistic accomplishments, Susan loosened up and told of watching her mother paint and following her example.

"So if you could do anything you wanted," I observed, grabbing a towel and drying the wet meat platter, "you'd like to find a little cottage in the solitude of some mountain valley and paint your life away?"

She giggled and splashed water in my direction. "The cottage in the mountains doesn't sound bad, but I would really like to write a collection of short stories or maybe even a novella or something. While I was raising my ten kids," she added as an afterthought.

"Only ten?" I questioned, amused.

"Oh, I might feel more ambitious after the first ten, but that's something to shoot for right now."

"Are you a budding author?"

She smiled. "In my world of fantasy."

I found myself relaxed and unpretentious. And Susan wasn't nearly as cold and austere as I had imagined earlier. She had a dry sense of humor and an intriguing way of saying something humorous, but remaining totally serious until smile flickers finally engaged the corners of her mouth and eventually spread into a teasing grin. We managed to finish the dishes in a pleasant fashion.

Just as Susan was turning on the dishwasher and I was wiping down the sideboard, Teresa burst into the kitchen with a brazen announcement: "It looks like Cami and JB are getting pretty serious out there in the backyard. And they're not just talking."

"You'd better mind your business, young lady," Susan warned.

Ignoring Susan, Teresa confronted me. "If you're going to get something going with Cami, you'd better make your move soon."

"What?" Susan almost screeched.

"Jacob likes Cami too," Teresa explained innocently. "What's wrong with that?"

"Now wait a minute," I protested, knowing that my cheeks were scalded purple with embarrassment. "What are you talking about?"

"Well, don't you like her?"

"Yeah, and I like you and I like Susan and…"

"But it's different with us." She grinned tauntingly. She shrugged. "I'm just saying that Cami and JB are getting along pretty good right now. If you have plans, you'd…"

"Teresa," Susan snapped, "what Cami is doing is none of your business. And I'm sure Jacob doesn't have any more interest in what's going on out there than I do." She turned back to the sink.

I glared at Teresa. She responded by grinning broadly, winking and then bounding from the kitchen.

"Well, I'll be on my way," I stammered. "Thanks again for dinner. I promise that I won't make this a weekly event. I'm going to spend Sundays at home in Brigham from now on."

"We like having you, Jacob." She smiled, "I even enjoyed your help this time."

I laughed. "You keep thinking about what I've told you. And do something about it."

"If I do anything about it, you'll be the very last person in this world to know about it."

"That's your pride, Susan Hardaway."

CHAPTER ELEVEN

The next two weeks were busy. I worked long hours each day, even Saturdays. I spent my evenings at the apartment. Sometimes I helped Mrs. Pritt put her garden in, worked in her yard and did simple fix-up work around her house. The rest of the time I read or watched a little TV, always keeping to myself and feeling virtuous for not wasting my money on dates or any other kind of social life. And yet, I had to admit to myself that I was restless and wanted to get out. Even if it did mean "wasting" my money. I was entitled to "waste" some money. Unfortunately, I didn't know who to spend it on. I didn't know anyone in Huntsville, and I was in Brigham only on Sundays. And the fact still remained that my main interest was Cami Hardaway. But she was JB's, and I was determined not to interfere.

I had hoped that things would warm up between JB and me, but even though we lived in the same apartment and worked for Roger Franco, we didn't see much of each other. We lived different lives. After work when JB wasn't with Cami, he was running around with some of the guys at work. He invited me to go with them. I went a couple of times, but their idea of a good time was shooting pool, sipping beers and playing the jukebox at the Ace's Lounge in Ogden. JB didn't drink while I was along, but I suspected he did when I wasn't there.

One Saturday afternoon a couple of weeks after my last dinner engagement with the Hardaways, I was in front of the apartment washing the Bug. Teresa rode up on her roller blades and watched me for a moment.

"Do you think washing it is going to make much difference?" she questioned honestly. "I mean it's pretty wasted. I like JB's Firebird better."

With my hands dripping, I straightened up, looked at Teresa and then back at the Bug. "Just because it's not a

Firebird doesn't mean I shouldn't keep it clean."

She dropped down on Mrs. Pritt's lawn, pulled off her blades and socks and declared, "I'll help you."

As we both scrubbed, Teresa remarked, "I haven't seen you around much. Don't you like us any more?"

I smiled. "I've been busy. And I haven't received any invitations."

She stopped working and stared at me. "Do you still like her?"

"Who?"

"Don't give me that bull. You know who."

I smiled and shook my head. "Cami's spoken for."

"Does that mean we can't be friends?"

"We're friends."

We worked quietly. "Tyson Ethington is getting pretty thick and serious with Susan," Teresa remarked. "But Cory Randall is still trying to make his move too."

"Does Susan date a lot?"

"Since her mission she's gone out as much as Cami. Of course, JB's the only one Cami sees now. Susan dates a lot of guys."

"Who does she like?" I asked, trying to make conversation rather than because I really wanted to know.

"Nobody. She's too serious. But Tyson and Cory like her."

"I suspect she'll want a pretty special guy."

Teresa shook her head. "She'll probably end up marrying some heartbroken widower and be perfectly content in her sadness."

"That's a low thing to say about your sister."

"I like Susan. She's just born a mother and a fuss bug." She studied me seriously. "Are you interested in her?"

I flipped soap suds at her. "You've asked me that before."

She shook her head. "I didn't think so. You're too big of a mess off for Susan."

"I'll have you know that I'm a very serious guy." I picked up the hose and sent a spray of water cascading across Teresa's back.

She squealed and bolted away. "Yeah, you're real serious." She lunged for the bucket of soapy water and we were soon involved in a full-fledged water fight.

It took us a while to settle down and finish the car, but after we did, Teresa turned to me and asked, "Are you going to give me a ride home?"

"Drive you a whole two and a half blocks?"

"I did help you clean your car."

I chuckled. "Hop in."

"You might even run into Cami."

"Wrong. She's with JB."

"Do you want to come to dinner tomorrow?"

"I'm going home to Brigham this evening. I won't be back till Sunday night."

"You're just trying to avoid me."

"I don't want you playing matchmaker."

I spent Saturday night and all day Sunday at home with the family. It was relaxing to be with everyone again, but I found myself missing Huntsville too. At least some of the people there. As I sat down to Mom's huge meal, I had the slight traces of longing for dinner with the Hardaways. I rather wished that I had accepted Teresa's dinner invitation.

I returned to the apartment around nine Sunday evening. JB and Cami were there thumbing through one of JB's high school yearbooks.

"Well, look who wandered in?" Cami greeted as the screen door clattered behind me and I dropped my duffle bag on the kitchen floor. Wearing a white dress with her heels kicked off, she sat next to JB, who wore Levis and a faded denim shirt. Their dress contrasted with each other. As soon as I saw Cami, I was reminded again of how beautiful she was, and the old shade of jealousy stirred inside me.

"I was beginning to wonder if you had moved to another country. I haven't seen you." She looked about the apartment. "But I guess I knew you were still around. The apartment's clean. Of course, one day alone with your brother and it's starting to look a little shabby."

JB tossed the yearbook aside and started tickling her in retaliation for her remark. She twisted away from him and pushed up from the sofa. "Where've you been, Jacob?" she asked, straightening her dress and still giggling.

"Home," I said simply, smiling. "Seeing the family."

Turning on JB, she remarked, "You've never taken me home. Are you ashamed to let your family see me?" JB groaned and slumped down on the sofa. "Will you take me home to see your family?" she asked me unexpectedly, taking my arm and looking up at me.

I laughed. "Sure, how about next Sunday? We'll spend a day."

Cami turned back to JB, still holding my arm, "Jacob's taking me home to see your family next week. Do you want to come?"

JB stared without responding. Although he tried to smile, I knew that Cami's teasing was chapping his good nature. I pulled away from her and picked up my duffle bag. "I'll stop by for you early Sunday morning," I joked, moving toward the bedroom. "But something tells me JB isn't going to let you slip out of town that easily."

"I won't even tell him I'm going."

It was almost ten when JB returned to the apartment after taking Cami home. I was at the card table having a sandwich and a glass of milk. He didn't say anything at first. He got himself a drink and then leaned sullenly against the kitchen counter. I felt I should say something, but I didn't feel like getting into anything with JB right then. I just wanted to go to bed.

"You won't let her go, will you?" JB finally accused, setting his glass down. I kept chewing without answering or even looking at him. "I'll let you use anything else I've got. The apartment's yours. You can take my car whenever you want. Is it too much to ask that you leave my girl alone?"

I finished chewing and swallowed. "What am I supposed to do, JB?" I turned in my chair to look at him. "For the last two weeks I haven't gone near the Hardaway place. I come home tonight. I don't say anything. Cami's the one who spoke to me. She's the one who asked me to take her to Brigham. I didn't give her any encouragement. Maybe if you'd taken her home once, she wouldn't be so curious about going. But that's not my fault."

"You still like her, don't you?"

I chuckled and shook my head. "Talk about a jealous boyfriend," I muttered. "You'll suffocate her at this rate."

"Just answer the question."

I pushed the last corner of sandwich into my mouth, brushed the crumbs off the table into my hand and took my glass to the sink. "There's nothing to answer," I grumbled, rinsing out the glass.

"If I wasn't here, you'd go after her in a minute, wouldn't you?"

I stiffened and flared. "Yeah, I would. And yes, I like her. I'd take her home next week if you weren't around. I'd call her up right now and ask her out if she weren't going out with you. I'd do a lot of things with her if you weren't around. But you are around, and I've left her alone. And if she can't even speak to me or joke with me without you pitching a jealous fit, then that's your problem not mine. Because I'm not going to avoid her like she was the next plague. If that bothers you, then…" I hesitated and finally blurted out, "Then that's tough."

"I just want to know if you're going to leave Cami to me. As long as I'm dating her, you're not going to do anything to cut in on me. Will you promise me that?"

I stared at JB for a long time without speaking. Finally I softened and answered quietly. "I don't know what's going to happen, JB. And neither do you. I'm not making any promises about Cami, the Hardaways or anybody else."

CHAPTER TWELVE

I tried to congratulate myself on living such a Spartan existence, dutifully saving my money and preparing for the time when I'd be able to leave this summer labor and go to school and get on with my life. But patting myself on the back for such virtuous living didn't blunt the boredom of those nights alone in Huntsville.

Early one evening after mowing Mrs. Pritt's lawn, I wandered down to the little store just west of the town park. I was buying some chips and a soda when Susan Hardaway and a guy stepped through the front door.

"Hello, Jacob," Susan greeted me with a smile. "I haven't seen you for a while."

Taking change from the cashier and picking up my plastic grocery bag, I nodded and smiled. "Roger Franco keeps me busy."

"Jacob," she continued, "I want you to meet a friend of mine, Tyson Ethington. Tyson, this is Jacob Matthews, JB's twin."

I shook hands with Tyson and noticed that he then took Susan's hand. I don't know why that bothered me, but it did. I didn't care about Susan, not in any romantic way, but I remember thinking that she could do better than Tyson Ethington. He seemed like a good enough guy, but…As I left the store and headed back to the apartment, I wasn't sure what the but was. I just thought she could do better for herself. I laughed out loud and muttered, "You are lonely. You're getting jealous over Susan Hardaway."

A few days later we were sent home from work a little before four because a drenching summer rain storm dumped all over us. By the time I arrived at the apartment, the rain was slowing down and there was a patch of blue in the northeastern sky presaging sunny skies. Heading up the walk to the apartment door, I realized that I didn't have my key. I went to get the spare from Mrs. Pritt but found her gone. For a few minutes I waited for JB, but when he didn't show, I thought maybe he had stopped by Cami's place. I decided to run over and see if I could find him there. As I pulled up, Cami drove up in her Dad's company Dodge Ram pickup loaded with a sofa set in back. JB's Firebird wasn't in sight.

"You don't know where JB is, do you?" I called to Cami as we both stepped from our vehicles. "I locked myself out of the apartment."

"Smart move," she kidded. "JB told me last night he was going to Salt Lake after work today to look at a four wheeler."

"He's going to buy a four wheeler?"

"Didn't he tell you?"

I shook my head and looked at my watch. "That's great. I could be locked out till midnight."

"Do you have anything planned?"

I laughed. "Not anymore."

She glanced toward the house and then at the load in the back of her dad's truck. "Do you want to play delivery man?" she asked, looking back at me. "Dad promised this sofa set to some friends up the valley. We both thought Justin and Brett were going to be here. It looks like they're gone."

I studied her. She was smiling coquettishly and playing the demure damsel in distress, but she was pretty and convincing. "You're just using me, aren't you?"

"No," she came back, taking my arm and pulling me toward the truck, "I always pay my help. How does a chocolate shake sound?"

"You're a big spender."

"Extra large," she added as she opened the truck door, handed me the keys and pushed me behind the wheel.

"What's JB going to say?" I questioned as Cami climbed into the passenger side.

"This is business," she replied innocently. "You're not planning to get fresh with me or anything like that, are you?"

I looked away and started the truck. "Where we headed,

Boss?"

I don't know what it was about Cami Hardaway, but it didn't matter how long I was with her, even a few seconds, and I started concocting romantic ideas. She made everything so natural. It was as though she stripped away my shyness and inhibitions. We were good friends again. Soon we were both joking and visiting.

"By the way, do you expect me to get this entire sofa set into somebody's house by myself?" I asked.

"I'll help you."

"You?"

"Don't look so shocked. I've been moving furniture for years. It was years before Dad realized that Susan and I were girls. We've just been part of the hired help."

"Did you ever consider waiting for your brothers to show up so they could do all this heavy lifting?"

"Sure," she said, looking out the window, "but then I couldn't have come with you."

I looked over at her. She refused to look at me at first and then glanced my way and burst out laughing. "Just kidding. This is strictly business, Jacob. Turn at the next corner."

It was a struggle for Cami and me to maneuver the sofa into the house, but we finally managed, giggling and kidding each other the whole while. Panting and pushing one another, we raced back to the truck and climbed in. "I'm ready for that chocolate shake," I announced, turning on the engine and starting down the street.

"Let's drive to Ogden and find a Dairy Queen. I'll buy you a blizzard."

"I can handle a blizzard."

The ride down Odgen Canyon with the windows down and the cool canyon air rushing in upon us with the smell of fresh rain was invigorating. More than once I wanted to reach over and take Cami's hand, and I was glad that I hadn't made JB any promises. I couldn't help feeling that my sentiments were not all that different from Cami's. I reflected again on that first kiss several weeks earlier and wondered if it was an accident or a bright omen.

We found a Dairy Queen and climbed out of the truck and then Cami groaned. Her mouth hung open and she looked sheepishly mortified. "Jacob, I don't have any money."

"No money?" I asked, trying to appear shocked and serious. "You hire me to do a job and promise to pay me and you don't even have any money?"

"Do you have any?" she squeaked, cringing and touching the tip of her tongue to her upper lip.

"You mean I get to pay my own wages?"

"I'm sorry. I'll pay you back. Promise." Her cheeks colored and she smiled. "I'm dying for a blizzard."

"Well, if I'm paying for everything," I grumbled, fighting back a smile, "I'm going to get something to eat too. You in the mood for a hamburger and fries?"

"I'll pay you back."

I waved her away and grinned. "Come on." Then I stopped, becoming bold and daring. "I'll buy you dinner on one condition."

"I'm willing to bargain."

"We go to the movie after."

She looked at her watch. "It's only five fifteen."

"There's usually an early feature."

"You're crazy."

"Is it a deal?"

"I could stand to see a movie."

It was after eight when we returned to Huntsville. Susan was on the front lawn watering a dry spot with the garden hose when we pulled up. "Where have you two been?" Susan questioned.

"Making a delivery," Cami answered cheerily.

"It's past eight. Daddy said you took that sofa set a little after three."

"Jacob was helping me and insisted on being paid."

"Paid?"

"Ask Jacob." She jabbed me with her elbow. "Thanks, Jacob." She started toward the house.

"JB has called a couple of times. I told him you were still working."

Cami stopped. "Is he at his place?"

"I think so."

Cami disappeared inside and I started for the Bug. I felt Susan's disapproving gaze on me. I glanced in her direction. "Cami just promised to buy me a blizzard," I explained guiltily.

"I guess that's between you and your brother."

I was going to let the remark slip past and then I reconsidered. "Nothing happened if that's what you're worried about," I said lightly.

"I wonder if JB would see it the same way."

I stopped and looked around and then turned to Susan. "You know, I don't get you. You don't like my brother. You wish Cami would break things off with him, but..."

"But that doesn't mean I think you ought to be pulling things behind his back."

"Pulling things behind his back. I helped Cami with a delivery and then we got something to eat."

"For five hours?"

"We saw a movie too." I sighed. "That was my idea." Susan looked away and continued to spray the lawn. I shoved my hands into my back pockets. "What if I am making a move for your sister?" I joked. I shrugged. "You don't like JB. Maybe you could like me. I'm not so bad." I laughed. "If you overlook a few minor character flaws."

"If you ask me, you're very self-centered. And you're not very loyal to your brother."

I breathed deeply. "You're probably right," I said quietly. "But you don't have to worry." I paused. "I'm not making any moves for your sister."

JB was at the apartment hunched over a four wheeler that was parked on the driveway next to the basement steps. "What do you think of it?" he asked me as I walked up.

"You bought it?"

He nodded proudly. "And the guy delivered it. No charge. Where you been?"

"Riding around. I went down to Ogden."

He nodded, still smiling. "You want to take it for a spin?" he offered suddenly.

I stepped over to it and straddled the four wheeler, bouncing on it to check the shocks. "It's a big one."

"You're telling me." He proceeded to count off all of the four wheeler's attributes, the size of the engine, its maneuverability, its power on a hill. While we were talking, Cami pulled up in her dad's truck.

"Another toy?" Cami called out as she rolled her eyes and strolled up the driveway. "I can promise you that I'm never getting on that."

"You'll like it. Where have you been? I called over to your place several times."

"Making a delivery for Dad."

"Where did you have to go, out of state?"

"I had to find someone to help me unload it." She started circling the four wheeler, taking a closer look. "Hi, Jacob. What's happening?" She winked at me and squelched a smile. "You won't believe this guy I scrounged up to help me unload the sofa set. He wouldn't lift a finger till I promised to buy him a large shake."

"Where'd you scare him up?" JB asked, checking the oil level of the engine.

"Oh, he was just hanging around."

"Anybody you knew?"

"Oh, I've seen him a few times, but he's kind of a strange guy." Surreptitiously Cami poked me so that JB couldn't see. "I should have asked one of you guys to help me out."

"I was picking up my new toy," JB grinned. Nodding at me, he added, "And Jacob here was driving around the country looking for some girl to pick up."

"Really," Cami mused, seeming to pick up interest. "Did you find anybody?"

I stepped off the four wheeler. "Oh, I ran into this girl at Dairy Queen. I offered to buy her a blizzard and she talked me into a full meal and a movie."

"Hey, this sounds interesting," JB spoke up, grinning. "What was she like?"

"Well, you notice that I didn't bring her home to meet the family. I drove by a McDonald's and her mouth started watering, so I dropped her off as soon as I could. Whew! Close call." I jumped suddenly as Cami pinched me on the back.

"Sounds like the girl you picked up," JB joked, "and the guy that helped Cami unload ought to get together. They'd make a wild pair."

"Oh, no," Cami laughed, shaking her head. "If you had seen this guy, you'd know why."

CHAPTER THIRTEEN

"How's it going, Jacob?" Teresa called out one afternoon while I changed the Bug's oil.

"Well," I said, wiping my hands on a paper towel, "I'm still making money, but my social life's suffering." I laughed. "In fact, it's almost dead."

"I heard about your date with Cami last week."

"I did not have a date with Cami," I came back.

"Susan said you did. I heard her talking to Cami."

"What did Cami say?"

"She just laughed. Was it a date?"

"Do you want to hand me that wrench?"

"So there is a chance things might work out between you and Cami?" Teresa ventured, handing me the wrench and looking over my shoulder while I worked.

"Nothing's happening between Cami and me," I answered simply.

"Well, something needs to be happening to you. You're being wasted just sitting around like you are. If I were older you could ask me out."

I laughed. "If you were older, I *would* ask you out."

Teresa giggled. "You'd have to get a better car than this. This is embarrassing."

"Oh, so you're more interested in the social amenities than you are in the guy." I nodded. "I'll keep that in mind."

"I'll bet I could line you up with somebody."

I stopped working and turned to face her. "Let me guess, Cami or Susan?"

"I still think Cami secretly likes you, but you're both too chicken to do anything about it. And Susan..." She considered that possibility for a moment and then went on. "Well, Susan's not interested in you and you're not interested in her so I guess I'm going to have to go out of the family. Tracy Curt."

"Tracy Curt?"

"Yeah, my best friend Jacki Curt has an older sister. She'll be a senior next year."

"She sounds a little young."

"She's cute. And fun. She's a cheerleader."

"Now would this Tracy Curt be ashamed to drive around in this fine machine?" I questioned, patting the rear fender of the Bug.

"Borrow JB's Firebird. That would impress her."

"Get out of here you little matchmaker," I said, closing the rear hood of the Bug.

"Do you want to walk me home?" she asked boldly.

I wiped my hands and started putting the tools and empty oil bottles away. "I'd prefer you waited for me to ask you. I don't like pushy girls. Why are girls so darn pushy these days?"

"Go ahead and ask me then," she giggled, "if it will make you feel more manly."

"Would you like me to walk you home, little girl?"

I caught a fist right in the stomach that doubled me over. "That's what happens when you turn into a smart mouth."

I gasped and tried to laugh. "One thing's for sure," I said after catching my breath. "I don't think anybody's going to take advantage of you." I straightened up. "Young lady, would you like me to walk you home?"

She rolled her eyes. "Come on before you get really corny."

"I'm curious," I said as we walked along. "Since I'm too old for you, who would someone like you be interested in?"

She looked at me. "That's pretty personal."

"But we're good friends. Practically family, assuming one of your sisters will marry me."

Teresa looked away. "There's this one guy. He'll be in seventh grade next year. He's kind of cute."

"Does he have a name?"

"Tony Barnett. I don't hustle him, though."

"You mean you don't ask him to walk you home and stuff like that?" She tried to glower at me but she couldn't extinguish the smile from her eyes. "Do you ever talk to him?"

"He's in our ward. He hangs around sometimes. I've gone roller blading with him before. I think he likes Tanzi Hanks, though."

"Maybe he just needs some encouragement. Do you want me to give him a call and tell him to…"

"No," she burst out, cutting me off. "I don't want you to do anything, and you'd better never mention any of this to anybody."

I laughed and put my arm over Teresa's shoulder. "Do you know what's wrong with this whole crazy situation?" I didn't wait for her response. "As I see it the biggest problem isn't that Cami's going with JB and Susan can't stand either JB or me or that Tony Barnett has a foolish crush on Tanzi Hanks. The biggest problem is still that you're eleven and I'm going on twenty-two. Wouldn't we make a pair? I'm tempted to wait for you, Teresa Hardaway."

Teresa sighed and shook my arm from her shoulders. "I think I'd rather have *you* as a brother-in-law and Tony Barnett as a boyfriend. No offense. Besides, by the time I was old enough, you'd be pushing thirty. That's *too* old." She glanced over at me. "Are you sure you don't want to give Tracy Curt a chance?"

"I don't think so."

"I could bring her by sometime just so you could take a look at her."

"No thanks."

As we reached the Hardaway front yard, I spotted Susan in front on her hands and knees digging in a flower bed. She pulled off her gloves when she saw us and sat down to rest. "I'm returning your lost, wandering sister," I announced to Susan as Teresa and I walked up. I looked down at her work. "You look like a regular little farmer, up to your elbows in dirt." Susan grabbed a dirt clod and tossed it at me. "Do you do all the gardening around here as well as the cooking and housework?"

"Don't start on that again," she said, shaking her head. "I work out here because I like to. It gives me a chance to relax and to think. It's quite rejuvenating. Do you want to try it?"

"I've played farmer for real too much to get very much rejuvenation from it. This looks too much like hoeing corn and thinning beets. I'll just sit here in the shade, watch you work and share some good counsel with you."

"Spare me. Teresa will you go get the hose and turn on the water please?"

Teresa returned with the hose and Susan proceeded to spray the flowers. "Guess who Jacob's going to ask out?" Teresa blurted out. "Tracy Curt."

Before I could protest, Susan turned to me and asked, "Isn't she a little young?"

"I didn't say I was going to ask this Tracy Curt out," I defended myself, giving Teresa a light push.

"He's just trying to play hard to get," Teresa giggled, "but I really think he'd like her if he ever asked her out."

Susan continued to spray the flowers. "I don't think Tracy's Jacob's type."

"She just doesn't want you asking somebody else out," Teresa teased. "She's waiting for you to ask her out."

Without warning Susan turned the hose on Teresa, showering me at the same time. Teresa laughed and darted away beyond the range of the hose; then she turned and raced into the house.

Susan turned the hose back on the flowers, but I could see that her cheeks were red and that she was embarrassed by Teresa's parting remark. I decided to capitalize on her embarrassment. "I've already asked you out once, but you turned me down."

"I didn't mean to spray you a second ago, but the next time I might get you good. On purpose." She smiled faintly. "You give up too easily if you only ask once."

"How about tomorrow?"

She faced me, surprised. "You mean go out with you tomorrow?" I shrugged. "I have something else planned." I detected a trace of regret in her voice and her look.

"Tyson Ethington?"

She hesitated and then nodded.

"I should have known. Now I've been turned down twice. I guess I better check this Tracy Curt out if I'm going to get a date around here."

"Tracy's still in high school."

"But she's available. That's more than I can say for the Huntsville farmer."

She turned the water on me and I raced away. I looked back once. Susan was still watering, but she was watching me. She turned away as soon as I looked back, though.

The next day while I was reading in the shade of Virginia Pritt's front yard, Teresa came by with two girls. One was about Teresa's age and the other one was several years older. "Hi, Jacob, what's happening?" Teresa called out, waving and moving over in my direction.

I set my book down and watched the three girls approach. The older one had short sandy-colored hair and a round face. She was attractive and seemed friendly. "Hey, I want you to meet my friend Jacki and her sister Tracy," Teresa introduced the girls. "This is Jacob Matthews. He's Cami's boyfriend's twin brother."

We exchanged pleasantries and I eyed Teresa suspiciously, but she refused to look me straight in the eye. I couldn't tell how much Teresa had told Tracy Curt, but I sensed that this was definitely not a chance meeting as far as Teresa was concerned, and she did everything she could to get Tracy and me into a conversation while she and Jacki pretended to be engrossed in their own private discussion.

"Jacob, we were going to run down to the reservoir. Billy Evans has his dad's boat and was going to take some of us waterskiing. Want to come?" She asked it like the thought had just barely occurred to her, but I was sure she had been scheming this plot ever since our conversation the day before.

"I'm not sure I'm up to water skiing. Besides, I don't have a suit." I did think Tracy was pretty, but she was also still in high school and I thought the immaturity showed. Perhaps it was more that I just wasn't interested in being forced into a romantic relationship by an eleven-year-old girl.

Teresa eyed me and wrinkled her nose. "Do you mind giving us a ride down to the reservoir?"

I hesitated and then nodded once. "If you don't mind riding in the Bug. You're not so uppity that you won't ride in the Bug, are you?" I asked Teresa. She shook her head.

"Are you going to make me do all the work?" Teresa growled at me as we started for the car.

"I'm not asking Tracy Curt out, Teresa Hardaway," I muttered while Tracy and Jacki walked ahead of us.

"I think she likes you."

"I'm five years older than she is."

"Loosen up, Jacob."

We all squeezed into the Bug, Teresa making certain that she and Jacki took the back seat. As soon as we pulled away from the curb, Teresa called out that she needed to stop at her place to get into her swimming suit, and then we'd go over to the Curts' place so that Tracy and Jacki could change.

As I pulled up to the Hardaways' place, Susan was just walking out to get into the Geo. The three girls piled out of the Bug and started into the house while I stayed by the car, feeling really stupid with Susan for an audience. Susan watched the girls go into the house and then she turned back to me. "I take it that Teresa talked you into the big date." She shook her head. "Tracy doesn't look as young as I thought she was."

I strolled up to where Susan was standing next to the Geo. "Your little sister concocted this whole thing. I am not going out with Tracy Curt."

"You don't have to explain anything to me," Susan said, smiling condescendingly. "Go and have a good time."

"I'm taking them down to the reservoir."

"Tracy will like that." She opened the car door, dropped into the driver's seat and closed the door while I glared at her. "You and Tracy make a good pair." She glanced behind her. "Oh, could you pull your car up just a little so I can squeeze out of here?"

"I want to explain something," I blurted out, feeling horribly flustered and exasperated.

Susan, still smiling, shook her head. "You don't have to explain anything. Your dating is a personal thing. Besides, I'm a little late right now. Maybe another time you can tell me how things went."

Knowing that nothing I could say would change anything, I returned to the Bug and moved it so Susan could get the Geo out of the driveway. As she pulled away, she smiled and waved.

"Why is it that I always feel like such an idiot around her?" I growled.

CHAPTER FOURTEEN

After Teresa's failed attempt to get me interested in Tracy Curt, I drove the girls to the reservoir and then spent the evening at the apartment while JB took Cami out on the four wheeler. Dejected and irritated, I entertained the thought of leaving Huntsville altogether and returning to Brigham to find a job there because things certainly weren't working out in Huntsville as I had once thought they might.

Around eight-thirty, frustration and boredom got to me and I stomped out of the apartment to take a walk. I wandered down to the center part of town, using the excuse that I needed a drink or a snack. It was still fairly light out, although the late evening shadows were moving in and the last traces of sunshine glow were disappearing behind the western hills. I strolled down to the town park. Part way across the lawn, I spotted a girl pushing a bike under the trees. I didn't pay much attention to her until I was a few feet away.

"Why, hello, Jacob."

"Susan?"

"What are you doing out this time of night?" She laughed. "I thought you'd still be baby-sitting Tracy Curt." She feigned a sudden choking spasam. "I mean, on your date with Tracy Curt."

Even though I knew she was deliberately trying to torment me, her remark grated on me, and I felt compelled to explain what had really happened. "Tracy Curt was Teresa's bright idea. I didn't have anything to…"

"You don't have to explain anything to me. That's really a personal matter, and I shouldn't have even brought it up." It was all she could do to keep a straight face.

I resisted the temptation to explain further. "I thought you had a big date with Tyson Ethington tonight. At least that was the excuse you used on me yesterday."

Susan looked down, obviously taken off guard and embarrassed. "He had to go out of town, but I really did..."

"You don't have to explain anything," I said, raising my hands. "I don't want to pry into your personal life. But next time if you don't want to go with me, just say so. I can take a hint." She started to speak, but I cut her off. "And don't bring up Tracy Curt."

"I was just wondering if you'd broken her heart."

"Very funny." I studied her. "You know, I don't think you're nearly as serious and straight-laced as everybody thinks. That's all a facade."

We both laughed. Biting down on her lower lip, Susan looked at the ground. "For your information," she started slowly, "Teresa told me last night what she was planning with you and Tracy. I couldn't resist the chance to tease you since I could see you were going through such well-deserved torture. After all, I thought it was about my turn to find a few chinks in your armor. What are you doing out here anyway, trying to steer clear of my little sister?"

I looked about me. "Oh, I was just looking for someone to bother. Any suggestions?"

She laughed. "We aren't very accepting of your kind in Huntsville, you know, people who go around bothering other people."

I shrugged. "That's why I do most of my work at night when nobody can recognize me."

Susan laughed and shook her head. "I think you're crazy."

"You say that like it was a compliment." She giggled without elaborating. "By the way, isn't it a little late to be out riding your bike? Somebody will run over you on their tractor or wheelbarrow or something. Hasn't your dad taught you better than that?"

"I hate to admit this," she answered as we began walking side by side while she pushed her bike, "but I don't know how many times Daddy has warned and threatened me to not ride my bike at night. I'm also supposed to have my helmet on. I've had every lecture in the book, but I can't help myself. This is when I like to ride. And I'm twenty-two so…"

"Sounds like pure unadulterated rationalization and stubbornness."

"Daddy would agree."

"So you sneaked out of the house."

"Not on my bike."

"So if he saw us together, he'd think I was your accomplice in crime?"

"Most definitely."

I heaved a sigh. "Then why don't we ditch your bike and go for a drink. I was headed to the store for a bottle of juice or something. Do you want to come?"

"I didn't bring any money," she warned me.

"I've heard that excuse before. It must be a family practice. Shoot! That's the only reason I wanted you to come along, so you could buy my drink. Besides, it's your turn to buy."

"My turn. When did you have your turn?"

"Next time. But since you came so ill prepared, I'll cover for you tonight and you pick up the bill the next time."

"And my bike?"

I pointed to a picnic table in the middle of the park fifty feet or so from a light. "Chain it to the table. Nobody'll take your bike unless they want the table too."

We wandered over to the little store and picked up a couple of drinks. "You interested in a walk?" I asked as we stepped from the store.

"Where to?"

"The reservoir looked inviting when I took Teresa and her friends down there this afternoon. I didn't hang around to enjoy it, though."

"Tracy would have loved to show it off to you," Susan giggled, looking away.

"I wasn't in the mood this afternoon."

"You don't want to walk all the way to the reservoir this evening, do you?" she asked, surprised.

"Sure."

"That's not a walk; that's a small journey."

"Maybe we'd better get a couple more drinks then."

"Are you serious?"

"About the drinks or the journey?"

"Both."

Without answering, I returned to the store, bought two more drinks and returned to where Susan stood waiting with an amused look on her face. "You're not like JB, are you?"

"Is that a question or a compliment?"

She shrugged and then grinned as I handed her the second bottle. "No, I'm not like JB. Not any more."

"Do you and your brother compete quite a bit?"

"Not intentionally."

"I guess I don't understand your brother much."

I shook my head. "I guess I don't understand him either," I said plaintively. "Three or four years ago there wasn't anybody I understood better. We used to be really close. Now it's like we're on two different worlds."

"Cami thinks she understands him and can help him." There was no disguising the worry in Susan's tone.

"Maybe she can."

"Can she?"

I considered the question. "I don't know. I thought I could. That's why I came to Huntsville. Now I'm not so sure."

"When Cami first started this relationship, she was on a service crusade. There's nothing wrong with that unless..."

"Unless she falls for him before she saves him."

She sighed deeply. "That's what worries me," she said softly.

I laughed. "JB used to be like that, wanting to help everybody. I was too judgmental. There was this kid in high school, Curtis Reed. He was a little slow but a pretty stout kid. He was in our weights class. Nobody wanted to be his lifting partner. He didn't shower much. He was kind of an outsider. Some of the others made fun of him.

"JB came to me and told me to get another weight lifting partner because he was going to lift with Curtis. You never saw anybody change like Curtis Reed. His senior year Curtis set the bench lifting record for the school. He was showering, dressing nicer, talking with the other guys. JB changed him. That's why he stopped to help Cami out when she had her flat. Most people probably think he stopped because she was a good looking girl. JB would have done the same for the town grump."

We walked in silence, finishing our second drinks. Finally I spoke. "I don't know if we need to restrict our conversation to JB. I'm curious about something. What made you go on a mission?"

"Do I detect a shadow of prejudice against sister missionaries or is it inconceivable that a girl could want to go on a mission?"

"Absolutely not," I said honestly. "I have two sisters who went on missions. The sister missionaries I knew in Mexico were definitely more dedicated and hard working than most of the elders. I'm just curious. You're…" I groped for the right word.

"Yes," she prodded, smiling.

"Well," I blurted out, "you have things together. You're nice looking and…"

"And sister missionaries can't be those things?" she teased.

I laughed. "All right, I've got my foot in my mouth again."

"I had an aunt who went on a mission. My mother's sister. I was ten when she returned. I used to talk to her about it. I made up my mind way back then that I was going to go, no matter what. When Mom died, I didn't know if a mission would ever happen for me. I wasn't sure the family…" She hesitated.

"Could get along without you?" I added, smiling.

"Something like that. But I didn't stop hoping." She sighed. "Daddy knew what I wanted because we had talked about it before. He also knew I didn't think I could just up and leave the family that way. That's when he was getting really serious with a woman. I felt that was an answer to my prayers."

"Nothing or no one tried to dissuade you?"

"Oh, there was a guy at school. He was a returned missionary and wanted to get married."

"And you told him after your mission?" She nodded. "And he wasn't interested?"

"Not in so many words. But he made it clear four months

into my mission when he sent me his marriage announcement."

"Do you have any regrets?"

"Absolutely not," she said with enthusiasm. "I wouldn't trade any of it. I loved my mission."

It really was more of a hike to the reservoir than a mere walk, but the time passed quickly. Becoming comfortable with Susan was a process whereas becoming comfortable with Cami just happened, but by the time we returned to the park, I knew I had misjudged Susan.

It was after ten when we approached the park again where Susan had left her bike. We saw the sprinklers kick on just as we crossed the last street. "Something tells me that your bike is going to get a real washing," I remarked as I saw the huge crystal arches of moving water sweep across the lawns, drenching the picnic table where the bike was locked. "You probably better come back in the morning for it."

"I can't leave it over night. Dad really would be upset if he knew I'd done something like that. I'll have to go get it."

"I was afraid you were going to say that," I muttered.

"I'll be all right," she shrugged, starting toward the bike.

I reached out and grabbed her arm. "And I'm supposed to stand here and let you go in there and get all wet and shout a few encouraging words in the process?"

"Will you go in for me?" she said hopefully at the same time ducking away. "I'm more humble tonight. I don't mind asking."

I put my hands on my hips. "What kind of a gentleman would stand here," I pontificated in jest, "while a lady charged out into the evening mist to face an out-of-control sprinkler?"

"So you *will* go?" She squeezed my arm.

I raised a forefinger. "If I drown out there, I'll be upset."

"If it gets too deep, I'll come in after you."

I shook my head and rolled my eyes. "It's at times like these that I wished I were the damsel in distress."

"Oh, hush up and go get it. Here I thought you were noble and you're just a whiner."

Without saying another word, I charged into the pulsating mist, trying to dodge the half dozen sprays that were firing at me from all directions. I hadn't even reached the bike before I realized there was no way I was going to escape without a little moisture on me, but I wanted to stay as dry as possible.

I staggered to the bike, grabbed it by the handle bars and turned to race back to Susan. I was jerked off my feet when the chain held the bike fast to the table and a pulsating jet spray hit me full in the face, taking my breath away. "It's locked," I screamed, as the cold water plastered me.

"You told me to lock it," Susan called back. I could tell she was having a struggle to keep her laughter in check.

"Where's the key?" I gasped as another watery arch from a different direction cut across me.

"It's a combination. It's 23, 6, 18. I think."

"You think?" I shrieked. I could hear Susan's hysterical laughter. "This is not funny," I shouted, fumbling with the chain and padlock. "I can't even see the stupid lock. How am I ever going to…" My words were cut short as another cold barrage fell across my shoulders as I hunched over the chain.

"What about the street light?" Susan coached, still laughing but trying to suppress it with her hands across her mouth. "Are you drowning yet?"

I shifted my position so the few faint yellow rays from the street light fifty feet away might fall on the face of the combination lock. Slowly, carefully I struggled to find the correct combination. I tried it three times and nothing worked. By then I was drenched and no longer trying to dodge the cascading sprays.

"Try 23, 16, 18."

"You mean you don't know the combination?" I panted.

"I know the 23 and the 18 are right."

"Wonderful. We've only got thirty-six more numbers to go."

After a dozen more attempts, the lock finally popped open. Gasping, shivering and grumbling, I grabbed the bike and charged back to where Susan stood. "There, my good lady. Your bike, clean and polished."

Still trying to bring her laughter under control, she nodded.

"Thanks, Jacob. You're a real jewel." She couldn't hold back the laughter any longer. She turned away, laughing. "I'm sorry," she sputtered between bursts of mirth. "But you looked so..."

"Don't say it," I muttered, trying to maintain my somber composure even though I was about to burst out laughing myself.

Susan finally composed herself and returned to where I was dripping profusely on the sidewalk. She pressed her lips tightly together, attempting to be serious. "Could I ask one question?" she finally managed to say.

"Go ahead."

She took a deep breath. "If I buy the drinks, can we . . ." Her serious composure lasted no longer than that. The remainder of her question was in a gush of giggles, "do this tomorrow too?"

"Only if you go in for the bike and I stand on the sidewalk, hooting and howling while you drown. You know, I think I'm probably going to catch pneumonia or at least come down with some horrible water-related respiratory disease. Then you won't laugh." I shook my head. "On second thought, I think you'd still laugh."

"You're a gentleman," she said, taking a deep breath and wiping some of the water off my face with her hand. "I wish I had a handkerchief or something."

"I wish you had a couple of towels."

She looked over my shoulder. "Oh, look at that," she called out. "The sprinklers are turning off. Isn't that wonderful?" she added in a shaky voice, biting down on her right thumb.

I turned around. Sure enough the sprinklers were turning off on that particular section of the lawn and another line of sprinklers began to sputter and spurt on the far corner of the park. "At this very moment I can't think of anything that makes me happier. What an auspicious turn of events!"

In little girl fashion Susan clasped her hands in front of her and asked, pretending shyness, "Could I ask one more thing of you?"

"Man, lady, you've got a lot of nerve, but go ahead."

"Do you want to walk me home?" She looked around her in a fake worried fashion. "You know it is late, and I did walk to the reservoir with you, and I really do need someone to protect me, and since you're already holding my bike, you could just push it home, and I promise not to say a word unless you want me to."

"You know, you're a puzzle to me, Susan Hardaway. I don't know whatever gave me the impression that there was anything serious or austere about you. You're as dingey as they come."

"You thought I was serious and austere?"

"I thought you were right out of the pages of *Fortune 500*, one of those never-smile, eat-up-the-guys, spit and polish lady executives. That was my impression when I first saw you."

"Whatever gave you a distorted impression like that?" she asked, her laughter beginning again.

"Who knows, but it's gone now. Forever."

"Is that a yes? You'll walk me home? And I'll shut up."

"I'll walk you home. On one condition. We talk. I need to do something to keep warm. Of course, you could always put your arm around me."

"You're soaking wet."

"It would definitely get me warm. After all, I went into the dark, watery deep for your blasted bike."

"We probably should have left the bike chained to the table. Didn't I want to leave the bike chained to the table? Wasn't…"

"On second thought, I'll walk if you shut up."

As we strode across the park, Susan reached over and slipped her hand under and over my arm without getting too close. "Is that holding you enough?"

"Your generosity overwhelms me." I smiled. "But something tells me that I can't be too choosey tonight. I'm already warming up."

CHAPTER FIFTEEN

As Susan and I walked up the driveway, Teresa burst around the corner of the house. "You're making tons of noise. You'll wake up the whole neighborhood."

"Teresa," Susan gasped, "what are you doing out at this time?"

"Sleeping out."

"So why aren't you sleeping? And speaking of waking up the whole neighborhood, that's what you're doing. Keep your voice down. You ought to be in bed."

"How boring! I decided to wait for you two. You missed a great waterskiing party," she said to me. "Tracy looks good in a swimming suit."

"I hope there was someone there to appreciate her," I responded.

"Lots. I think Jody Freeman cut in on you."

"How could he cut in on me? I wasn't there or interested."

"He took her home. You blew your chances, Jacob. That's the last time I'm going to set you up with someone."

Susan laughed. "I didn't realize I was taking you away from the biggest romantic conquest of your life."

"Very funny," I muttered.

Teresa studied Susan and me and then inquired bluntly. "What have you two been doing? Did you have a secret, wild rendezvous?" She gave me a furtive nudge.

"It was a little wild," I conceded, glancing over at Susan, who shrugged and looked away.

"You're wet." Teresa said, reaching out and touching me again. "What happened?"

"Jacob had this really dingey idea to run through the sprinklers at the park," Susan spoke up. "I tried to tell him it was crazy. I even think there's a city ordinance against it. But once

Jacob gets something in his mind, it's hard to get it out."

"Oh, is that what happened?" I asked.

"What's with the midnight conference?" a voice called from the front door. We turned as Cami came down the steps to where the three of us stood on the driveway.

"Is there anybody else we should invite to this gathering?" I asked, turning to Susan. "Do you figure your Dad and brothers want to join us?"

"I was just getting ready to go to bed, and I heard all this racket," Cami said. "I thought maybe there was a special convention out here."

"Looks like JB got you home at a pretty decent hour," I commented to Cami.

"That's because they got in a fight," Teresa piped up.

"We were not in a fight," Cami contradicted, glaring at Teresa.

Teresa looked at me and shrugged. "It sounded like a fight to me. They were arguing in the driveway when Jacki's mom dropped me off here."

"We were discussing JB's four wheeler."

"And you said you thought he needed to have his mind on more serious things instead of running around buying toys. And he said that it..."

"Teresa, what JB and I were talking about is not a public concern."

"I just said it sounded like a fight."

"Teresa," Susan and Cami said in unison.

Teresa turned to me and said flippantly, "I guess it was just a little discussion." Then she added under her breath, "I sure hope they don't ever get into a fight."

Cami took a swipe at Teresa, but she jumped back. Turning back to me, Cami observed, "You look wet. What happened?"

"You'd better ask your sister. Her memory seems to be better than mine. All I know is that I'm freezing to death."

"You need to do something to warm up."

"What do you say we have a quick little game of basketball?" Teresa called out.

I held my wrist up and squinted at my watch in the dim glow from a distant street light. "It's ten forty-five," I remarked.

"We'll be in the backyard. We'll have to be quiet, though."

"What about your dad?"

"His bedroom's on the other side of the house. Besides, he's used to us."

"And the neighbors?"

"You'll have to keep your voice down," Cami spoke up. "Even when you're getting creamed by some girls. You know, no sniveling and bawling and being the usual macho-male poor sport. This is just a friendly game. Something to warm you up."

I glanced over at Susan, who hadn't said anything but seemed amused by her sister's challenge. "Do you guys know how to play?"

"Cami played for Weber High," Susan mentioned casually. "Teresa has played on Little League teams. I shot a few baskets here at home. Nothing very competitive."

"Do I have to stand all three of you?"

Teresa snickered. "He must think he's good."

"I've played a little ball." I tried to sound modest. "In fact, JB and I were pretty good."

"JB isn't here," Cami came back.

"He wasn't the only one who knew how to play. Our ward took the stake championship two years in a row."

"Stake champions," Cami said, whistling sarcastically.

"All right, I've never played with the Chicago Bulls or anything," I said, pretending to be annoyed, "but I can still get the ball in the hoop on a good day."

"Are we going to have to listen to him brag?" Cami asked tiredly, turning to Susan, "or can we just go out and beat him bad and get it over?"

"There's nothing that I dislike more than feminine arrogance," I muttered. "Tell me what the teams are and whether I need to spot you ten or fifteen points."

"Oh, I can hardly wait to get this guy," Cami said. "Teresa, go turn the lights on in back and grab the ball. Susan and I will take on you and Teresa. Unless you think you can take on all three of us."

I shook my head. "But I'll promise to be gentle."

"We'll go to twenty. Do you think you can last that long without a break or should we stop every six points?"

Turning to Susan, who was smiling smugly, I asked, "Is she always like this?"

"Only when she plays ball and knows she's going to win."

"You must think she's good," I remarked as we headed up the driveway and into the backyard.

"She isn't bad. For a girl, of course."

There was a second building in the backyard. It was a wood shop and storage area combined. They called it the shop. In front of the shop was a twenty-five foot square slab of concrete. Mounted on the roof of the shop was a glass backboard. That should have been enough of an indication to me that the Hardaways took their basketball seriously, but I just assumed they were well-to-do and could afford the luxury.

After turning on the lights, Teresa emerged from the shop carrying a basketball. The leather ball should have been my second warning. I took the ball, dribbled around a bit and pushed off a half dozen shots. All but two missed, but the two that hit were swishers, nothing but net.

"How much warm up time do you need, champ," Cami asked me. "This was supposed to be just a short game. We didn't expect you to go through an entire workout first."

I looked at Teresa and Susan, who stood back and smiled. "You know, she's getting on my nerves. Bad. Either she's the first woman NBA rookie of the year or she's got one horrendous attitude." I tossed her the ball. "You can have first outs. Come on Teresa. You guard Susan; I'll take the NBA rookie."

Before I had a chance to get set, Cami took the ball, whipped it across the court to Susan, who slipped under the basket for a quick, easy lay-up.

"Oh, what luck!"

The girls didn't say anything.

Teresa pitched the ball in to me. I dribbled twice and the ball hit the side of my foot. Cami scooped it up and made an easy lay-up."

Grinning sheepishly, I shook my head. "I'm the best player on your team."

"Don't kid yourself," Cami came back. "If we let you on our team, you'd be the worst player. Your outs."

I still wasn't willing to make a good, hard effort. Not against a couple of girls. I let Teresa lob the ball into me again. Immediately Susan and Cami double teamed me and batted the ball away. Cami pushed up an eight-foot jumper that swished through the net.

"I can't believe how lucky you guys are."

"Jacob," Teresa said, "I think you'd better stop worrying about *their* luck and start playing ball before they skunk us."

"Skunk us?" I asked, amused. "That was the last basket I'm going to give to them."

Being down six to zero, I was ready to play ball. But of course, I was too late. Talk about ganging up on a guy; those two didn't let up five seconds. From the moment the ball was in play, Susan and Cami were moving just like a well-oiled machine. Since Cami was the best player, I guarded her, but as soon as I did, she passed the ball off to Susan. At first I thought the only thing Susan could do was make lay-ups, and then she hit two in a row from about fifteen feet out.

I had never pictured Susan as being athletic. Graceful, yes, but not athletic. But as I watched her on the basketball court I could see her talent. In fact, she had more prowess than her sister. Her sister had worked at the game longer, but Susan had an uncanny natural flow to her movements that made her fun to watch.

The game ended twenty to eight. Teresa had made two of our baskets. I was panting and definitely warmed up. I had also had a huge helping of humility.

"Now that you're warmed up," Cami challenged, breathing hard, "do you want to go again. We'll spot you ten and we won't take any lay-ups. We'll just shoot from outside. If you want, we'll play in bare feet or one arm behind our backs."

I looked over at Teresa, who grinned back at me and shook her head. "They creamed us, Teresa," I grumbled.

"I could have told you that."

"You knew they were going to beat us?" She nodded. "You probably didn't even try. You gave it to them."

She laughed. "They beat you fair."

"I've been set up, haven't I? Here I thought you were my friend and you set me up."

"You're not going to accept our challenge?" Cami questioned.

"You mean for another game?"

She nodded.

I held up my hands and shook my head. "I concede defeat. I'll be gracious about it."

"There has never been a guy in the history of the world who has graciously conceded defeat to a girl. They've been patronizing and arrogant in their pretended humility, but gracious? I don't think so. And you haven't started tonight."

"Man, you don't let up, do you?" I grinned.

We all went over to the lawn adjoining the court and dropped into some lawn chairs. "I take it this isn't the first time you've clobbered an unsuspecting guy on this court. I can't have been the first one."

"It's his arrogance showing through," Cami said to Susan. "He doesn't mind getting beat so much if he doesn't have to have the dubious distinction of being the very first."

"Do you think you could beat JB and me?"

"You mean the shooting duo who took the *stake* championship two years running?"

"All right, I'm sorry I brought up the stake championship. Are you willing to take JB and me on?"

"I won't spot you ten points. And I'd want an audience here just so you couldn't deny it when we creamed you both."

I laughed. "I think the stakes are too high. Where'd you learn to play?"

"Practice and hard work," Cami said, simply. "And then Susan pushed me." There was admiration in her tone and look as she handed her sister the credit. "Susan was usually tied up in school and making things work here at home, but she told me if I was going to play, I was going to play better than anybody else, including the boys. We've spent a lot of hours out here playing one on one."

I looked over at Susan. Her cheeks were coloring slightly and she was staring out across the court toward the basket. "You didn't ever want to play yourself?" I asked.

"There was never any time. Playing with Cami was enough. All I needed was a release. And Cami liked the competition more than I did. I didn't mind going after it here in the yard, but," she shook her head, "I wasn't much interested in putting on a demonstration in front of a crowd."

"You ought to see her play softball," Teresa spoke up. "We have a game tomorrow."

"Church?" I questioned.

Cami and Susan nodded and laughed.

"I'd be interested in watching someone besides myself getting creamed by you two. Where do you play?"

"There's a ball field out in Liberty," Cami answered. "Do you want to come?"

"Sure."

"Well," Susan moaned, "I've got to get up in the morning. I better get to bed." She pushed up from the lawn chair and started for the back door of the house. "Good night, Jacob." She smiled and winked. "Thanks for rescuing my bike. I'm sorry about your clothes."

"I'd believe you," I called after her, "if you hadn't laughed so hard while I was doing it."

"It was funny," she returned, starting to giggle again as she slipped into the house.

"Teresa, you head to bed," Cami called to her little sister, who moaned and groaned but pushed out of the chair and moved over to the opposite corner of the yard where a small dome tent was set up under an apple tree. "Turn the lights out before you go," she added.

For a few moments Cami and I sat quietly alone in the dark after Teresa flipped the lights and wandered off in the direction of the tent. "Well, what do you think of Huntsville now that you've been here a few weeks?" Cami questioned, slumping down in her chair and gazing up at the star-studded sky.

"Of all the days I've been here, the first one was the most impressive. It still takes my breath away just thinking of it."

"You're horrible. And you told JB too."

"Well, I figured it would be better that he heard it from me than that he learn it from Teresa or someone else."

"I think he was a little jealous."

"I think he was a lot jealous. So was I."

"You? What did you have to be jealous about?"

"It wasn't for me."

"You are really bad, Jacob Matthews."

We were quiet for a moment and then I couldn't resist asking a question that had been nagging at me all evening. "Was it a fight or a discussion?"

"You're worse than Teresa."

"Just curious."

"Has JB always been so interested in...*things?* I mean, is he ever going to see that there are other things to life?"

Cami pushed up from her chair and I stood with her. We bumped into each other. I don't know if it was just me, but it was like as soon as we touched there was something there. I wanted to reach out and touch her again, take her hand. I had the oddest feeling that she wanted me to do the same, but I didn't want to take the chance. We stood there quite close to each other. I was glad that the lights were off because I could feel a sudden warmth pump to my face.

"I'll drop by tomorrow and pick you both up for the big ball game."

"It starts at six-thirty. Come around six."

We separated, Cami heading for the back door while I strolled around the corner of the house.

"Which one do you like?" a small voice called to me from the shadows at my left.

"Teresa, is that you?" I hissed, a bit startled.

"Who'd you think it was," she said, walking out of the dark so I could see her faint outline.

"I thought you went to bed."

"Are you kidding? While you and Cami were just sitting there in the dark together."

"That's all we did, just sit there."

"I'll walk with you, and you can tell me what happened."

"You're not walking anyplace with me," I laughed. "It's eleven-thirty and you need to get to sleep. Not as much as I do," I added lowly. "And I'm not telling you anything."

"But I'm your secret counselor. You've got to talk to me. If you don't have someone to talk to, you'll get all confused and do something stupid."

"Counselor?" I muttered, shaking my head. "You've just got a horrible case of curiosity."

"Which one do you like?"

"You mean Cami or Tracy?"

"No," she groaned. "You blew it with Tracy. I'm talking about Susan and Cami. Did you and Susan have a good time tonight? She's really not too bad. She'd probably cut her tongue out before she admitted it, but I think she can stand you."

"Just tolerate me?"

"You don't know Susan. She acts differently with you. I mean, she's been really friendly with you. And she really didn't like you to start with. Of course, that was mostly because of JB, but she really didn't have much use for you either."

"How do you know what she thinks? Are you her analyst too?"

"I just know stuff like that. I watch people. There are a lot of things I know about people because I watch them and listen to them. People say and do things that mean a whole bunch if you know what you're looking for."

"I can tell that I need to be very, very careful about what I say and do around you."

"I'll bet right now Susan's thinking of you."

"Good night, Teresa. Go pester somebody else."

"But you have another problem," she called out.

I stopped. "And what problem is that?"

"I think you still like Cami."

"Oh, get out of here."

"And I think she likes you," she added quickly. "Even though she had that `discussion' with your brother tonight, she didn't feel too bad about it because she was thinking there was a chance with you."

"What makes you think so?" I asked the question too quickly and with too much interest. I was certain that perceptive Teresa could pick up those subtle bits of evidence.

"She doesn't want to like you because she's supposed to like your brother, but she can't help it. I wasn't sure at first, but I watched her watch you while you played basketball tonight. She had that look."

"You should have been concentrating more on playing basketball than playing Cupid. We might have won the game."

"And when she came outside in the first place. That wasn't like Cami. Normally she would have just gone to bed. But you were out here so she came out to see you."

"I think your imagination is running away with you."

"So now you've got a problem," she went on, ignoring my comments of denial.

"What's my problem?"

"They both like you. And I think you like both of them."

"For your information, Miss Know-it-all, I like both your sisters. They're both good friends, and you don't have to write any more into it than that. You know what you ought to be? A romance writer. You've got the imagination for it. Good night, Teresa. And stop spying on me. You're making me nervous."

Although I had pretended to discount everything Teresa told me, I couldn't help reflecting on her comments as I wandered back to the apartment. I didn't know how Cami and Susan felt about me. I wasn't sure that Teresa was as perceptive as she claimed to be, but I had to admit to myself that she had read me well. My first attraction was Cami, but Susan had stirred something in me tonight. In fact, she had done something to me even before tonight.

CHAPTER SIXTEEN

"Where were you last night?" JB asked as we sat at the kitchen card table eating cold cereal, toast, milk and orange juice.

"I took a walk."

"It was almost midnight when you dragged in."

"It was a nice night out." I stirred my cereal and asked, "What happened between you and Cami?"

He looked up at me and chewed slowly. "Who said anything happened?"

I shrugged. "Teresa said something."

"Were you over there?" He studied me from across the table.

"I ran into Susan and walked her home." I shrugged and returned to my cereal.

"Did you talk to Cami?"

"She was there."

"That isn't what I asked."

"Sure, I talked to her." I tried to be casual.

"Alone?"

I laughed. "What is this, the Huntsville Inquisition? It was a crazy evening. I was sopping wet because I'd pulled Susan's bike out of the sprinklers for her. When I got to the Hardaways', Susan and Cami challenged Teresa and me to a basketball game." I grinned. "They creamed us twenty to eight."

JB listened, but his expression didn't have even a glimmer of a smile. "So you talked to her alone?"

I didn't say anything for a moment. "Cami and I were there for a few minutes before I headed home."

"You don't waste any time, do you?"

"What are you talking about?" I smiled but I was angry.

"We have a little fight, and you jump in with both feet."

"Oh, brother," I moaned, shaking my head. Come on, JB, are you so jealous that you can't stand to have me say a few words to Cami?" I stared down into my cereal bowl. "JB, are you trying to catch me in some romantic snare? Nothing happened."

We both returned to our cereal in silence. As I scraped my bowl, I remarked, "I know you don't go around begging me for advice, but I'm going to give you some. If you want Cami, you're going to have to make some changes in your life."

"What do you know about my life?"

"Nothing. I wish I did. Maybe I could help you."

"Just leave it alone, Jacob."

"JB, Cami'd probably marry you in a minute, but she's not interested in your Firebird, your four wheeler or anything else like that. She wants you to make some commitments about your life. She wants you to go to church and..."

"And be just like you," he snapped, breaking into my frustrated sermon. "Jacob, just get off my case. I'm not going to go to church and cut my hair and be a mirror image of you. Can you get that through your head?"

I stared at him, feeling my stomach churn angrily. "Yeah," I said huskily, "but I'm not sure Cami does. She's still holding on to the illusion that maybe you'll come around."

JB pushed back from the table, gathered his glass and bowl and took them to the sink. I followed him. "The girls have a softball game tonight. They invited me to go. Do you want to come?"

"I'd probably be in the way," he muttered sarcastically. "Besides, I told Walter Evans I'd help him on his truck."

"Well, if you finish with Walter, run out to Liberty."

That evening I cleaned up and ate a sandwich before heading over to the girls' place. JB came home from work, showered and went to his room. Before leaving the apartment, I knocked on his door. He didn't answer. I knocked again. "Yeah," he called.

Pushing the door open, I stuck my head in the room. He was lying on the bed, staring up at the ceiling with his hands propped behind his head. It reminded me of those evenings he had climbed into bed without praying but being unable to keep himself from thinking about it. "I'm going now." He didn't react. "JB," I said somewhat impatiently and softly hit the door jamb with the heel of my hand. "I like Cami. That's just the way she is. You meet her and you like her. So don't make a federal case out of my talking to her."

"Maybe I ought to let you have her. I'd be doing you both a favor. But I can't wake up one morning and say I don't care about her any more. You don't understand that. You didn't with Leti."

"Leti and Cami aren't even in the same ball park, JB. They're not even in the same county. But you're right, I never did understand you and Leti." I looked away. "This is going nowhere," I moaned, rubbing the back of my neck. "If you want to come to the game, you're invited. If you don't come, don't bother to conduct another inquisition when I get back."

I was still fuming when I pulled up to the Hardaways' place. I climbed out of the Bug and walked up to the front steps. Just then Susan and Cami came out the door. Cami was wearing a pair of mid-calf baseball pants and a T-shirt; Susan was dressed in a T-shirt and a pair of loose-fitting gray sweats. Cami held up a set of keys in her hand. "Hello, Jacob," she greeted me cheerily. "We'll take the Buick."

"The Buick?" I said, smiling. "You'd choose an old Buick over a nice VW Bug? Where's your taste? Besides, I'm the one who said I'd pick you up."

Susan and Cami looked at each other, smiled and shrugged. "Wasn't it one of you that hammered me on my humility the other day? I need to dish you up a bowl. The Bug will do that better than anything. Come on, we can squeeze in."

Just then Teresa pulled open the front door. "Can I come?"

Her two sisters looked at me. "Sure, you can sit up front and shift the gears," I laughed, relieved that I didn't have to choose between the older sisters to sit up front.

Teresa took her role as co-pilot seriously, grabbing the gear shift, shoving it into first and calling out, "Next stop Liberty."

By the time we arrived at the ballpark, I had forgotten about JB and was content to be with the three girls. Cami and Susan walked out on the field to warm up and Teresa and I found a place by ourselves on the low bleachers.

"You're probably wondering why I came," Teresa commented.

I looked over at her and grinned. "You've got a mad crush on me. I can see it in your eyes."

She jabbed me with her elbow and took a long, deep breath. "Believe it or not, I'm the coach."

"You a ball player?"

"I'm your coach." I turned to her. She was staring intently onto the field. Slowly the traces of a smile pushed into her cheeks. "I really don't know if you can do this without me. You've got some tough work ahead of you. And you're pretty green when it comes to girls. All returned missionaries are like that."

"I suppose you know all about bumbling returned missionaries."

"Don't let my age fool you."

I laughed. "Don't worry. I already know you're more cunning and conniving than any eleven year-old kid I know. I definitely need to keep you at arm's length."

She shook her head. "I need to be right there at your elbow, whispering directions. I'm kinda like your romantic radar. You need help, Jacob. Deciding which of my sisters to go after."

"Your sisters would break both your legs if they knew what runs out of your mouth when you and I are alone." I pretended to shiver. "You're eleven going on twenty-five."

"This is all confidential." She gave me another quick, playful jab with her elbow. Winking, she added, "The way I've got this figured, when you make your move you've got to make sure you zero in on the one you really want. Once you start making your moves, you can't change your mind or you'll lose both of them. And then I don't end up with you as a brother-in-law."

I turned away and shook my head. "Do you happen to have the rings and wedding dress picked out yet?" I asked, fighting back my grin. "And where shall we have the reception?"

Her answer was a huge, smug smile. "You're moving too fast for me." She shrugged. "But you've got the right idea."

"Teresa, had I known you were going to be so indiscriminate and bold, I wouldn't have let you come tonight."

"Ah, don't break into a sweat. You worry too much. Now the

big question: If you had to choose right now, who would it be?"

"I don't have to choose now. I don't even have to talk to you. And if you keep this romantic coaching up, I won't even sit by you. And you'll have to find your own ride home."

"I'm just curious. Which one?"

"They're getting ready to play ball."

"Just answer me that one question."

"Teresa," I sighed, "I like both your sisters."

"You can't marry them both."

"But I can be friends with both of them."

Teresa did her famous eye roll and groaned. "Is that all you want, to be friends?"

"I want to watch the game. Cami's up."

"She'll knock it out of the park."

Cami took the second swing and sent the ball sailing out into center field. It would have been a great hit had the center fielder not raced under it. "She should have waited for a better pitch," Teresa grumbled. "Now just because Cami gets out on her first ups doesn't mean she's a bad choice."

"Teresa, this is getting old."

"I won't bug you anymore."

A few minutes later Susan came to bat. "Susan's a pretty good player," Teresa remarked, "but I think she's out of practice. I hope she doesn't get desperate and strike out."

"Your faith is overwhelming."

The first pitch was a strike and Teresa groaned. "She's going to strike out. How embarrassing! I hope she let's them walk her. A walk's as good as a hit."

The next two pitches were balls, but Susan was calm and patient. The fourth pitch was a little low but right over the plate. Susan put all her weight and leverage into the swing. The ball sailed out a half dozen feet over the left fielder's outstretched glove, but before the ball ever landed Susan was racing over the first base bag. I came to my feet as I watched her. Her stride was long and graceful. She crossed home plate a split second before the catcher snagged the ball, which was relayed in from left field. She seemed to know from the moment the ball cracked off the bat that she was going for the home run.

"Wow! Did you see that?" Teresa cheered, pounding me on the shoulder. "She's good, isn't she? Cami says Susan could have been a better athlete than her. I told you she was good."

I laughed. "I thought you were ready to crawl under the bleachers in anticipation of your sister's shameful strike out."

Teresa shook her head and waved me away. "Oh, I got a little nervous, but not bad. Do you kinda like Susan?"

"I'm going to gag you, Teresa."

"I'll shut up."

By the time the game was over, Cami had made a couple of diving catches at short stop. She had two base hits. She went out twice on fly balls to center field. In addition to her opening homer, Susan had a triple and two doubles. She guarded home plate and stopped two runs that would have tied the score. As it was, the girls' team won by two.

"Well, I can tell you right now that I'm not playing softball with you," I joked as I helped the three girls into the Bug.

"You only play against girls if you know you can beat them?" Cami asked.

"Usually."

"He won't play against you two any more," Teresa snickered.

Looking in the rearview mirror at the two older girls, I asked, "Do you know how this little lady runs her mouth?"

"We don't know everything she says," Susan answered, giving her little sister a gentle shove from behind.

"Would you like to know?" Teresa asked innocently, twisting around in her seat. Turning to me, she added quickly, "Should we share our discussion with these two?"

"*Our* discussion? You mean *your* monologue."

Teresa leaned her head out the window and let the wind blow through her hair as she squinted against the cool evening blast. "Where we going to celebrate?" she asked no one in particular.

"Hamburgers are on me," I announced. "Co-pilot, lead me to the best hamburger joint in the valley."

Pulling herself back into the car, Teresa grinned and called out, "You just keep your foot to the floor and hold onto that steering wheel, and I'll show you right where to go."

Teresa navigated us to a little hamburger joint on the fringes of Huntsville. There was something about being together with these three sisters that intrigued me. I kept looking at Susan and Cami and seeing each one's strengths and talents. All the while Teresa sat giving me tacit encouragement. She was a strange, fun-loving, precocious girl. But I liked her. Looking back now, I don't know if I would have made it as far as I did with either of the older girls without Teresa's help. I lacked the boldness that I needed right then to make anything happen, and Teresa definitely didn't possess any inhibitions.

After eating we drove home. As I helped the girls out of the car, Teresa said, "It's still early. We ought to do something."

"We could go in and watch the evening news with Dad," Susan suggested jokingly.

Teresa grimaced and shook her head. "Let's play a game."

"Not basketball," I said, grinning.

"You big chicken," Teresa teased. "We could beat them. I wasn't playing hard last night."

"Gluttons for punishment," Cami kidded. "We weren't playing hard last night either."

I looked at Teresa. "I think they're scared. They caught us off guard last night. Now they don't want a rematch."

"All right, Susan," Cami sighed, heading toward the backyard, "no mercy this time. We tried to let them walk away with a little dignity last night, but their sense of appreciation is lacking."

"You up to another game?" I asked Susan.

She gave me a demure smile. "Well, it probably beats watching the evening news. You'd better be careful around Cami, though. I think she's on the prowl."

"I'm not falling for that. I watch her while you knock the net off the basket. You only pretend to be a struggling player."

This time under the glare of the backyard lights Teresa and I were psyching each other up for the big game. I knew that this was not going to be a casual cake walk. I could see that in Cami's determined glare. She wanted a repeat of the previous night. When it came to ball, there were no concessions on her part.

Coming into the game as the previous night's losers, Teresa and I took the ball out. For the next twenty-five minutes there was no half-steam attempt from either side. We were all panting and perspiring. The score was tied at twenty-eight. Teresa and I had the ball. As I dribbled a moment, waiting to toss it in to Teresa, I couldn't resist the temptation to gloat just a little. "For one aging, out-of-shape guy and a little girl, we haven't played too bad against the women's NBA of Huntsville."

"We didn't want to run away with it this time," Cami chided.

"I thought this was the `no mercy' game."

"The game isn't over. Toss the ball in."

I laughed and winked at Teresa. "These two are sweating like a couple of tuckered-out workhorses, and they have the audacity to brag. Let's finish them off."

As soon as I tossed the ball in to Teresa, both Susan and Cami converged on the ball. For the first time that evening, they double teamed Teresa. Before I could rush to her rescue, Susan had batted the ball away. Cami scooped it up, dropped back to the foul line and went up with a quick, perfect jumper. The ball didn't touch anything but the bottom of the net.

Susan and Cami gave each other high fives as they cheered. "Do you know what your problem is?" Cami said to me as she smiled and tried to catch her breath. "You start running your mouth before the game's over. I'd practically conceded this one to you. Then you started with your championship speech and I said to myself, `There is no way this guy's going to win this game.'"

"We did better than last night," Teresa remarked indifferently.

"You want another one?" Cami challenged.

I looked over at Teresa. She considered a moment. "I think I'm getting my second wind."

The second game was all ours. Teresa and I started playing like a team, and we beat them thirty to twenty-four.

"We can't leave things tied up," Cami said, sprawled in one of the lawn chairs next to the court.

"Cami," Susan protested, smiling and shaking her head. "What are you trying to do, wipe us out?"

"You don't expect us to let them get away with this, do you? First one to twenty."

It was ten-forty when we started the third game, and it was all business from the opening play. Nobody led by more than two points. When the score was tied at 18, Susan stepped out of bounds to toss the ball into Cami. She hesitated a moment and then she hugged the ball in front of her. "I have a suggestion."

"Are you going to let us win?" Teresa taunted.

"There's root beer and ice cream in the house," Susan went on, ignoring Teresa's question. "We've both won one and this one's tied. Let's leave it that way and end with root beer floats."

Cami glanced in my direction. I considered the proposal and sucked in a gulp of air. "I could suffer through a root beer float and accept a peaceful tie."

Susan tossed the ball in my direction. "Come on, Cami. Give me a hand in the house."

Teresa and I dropped into two lawn chairs. For the first minute or so we sat there trying to catch our breath. "Thanks, Jacob," Teresa said softly, seriously.

I looked over at her. "Thanks for what?"

Her eyes were closed. "Thanks for letting me come and hang around with you tonight. Nobody else has ever done that."

I chuckled. "How could I leave my romance coach behind?"

She snickered. "No, I'm serious. You don't seem to mind having a kid around. I mean, I don't feel like I'm in the way. Even though I might be."

I picked a tuft of grass and tossed it at her. As she was smiling and brushing herself off, I asked, "What's my next move, coach?"

"I won't bug you anymore. Besides, I don't know who to bug you about. I think Cami's the one and then Susan."

"Of course, there's no reason whatsoever to consult Susan and Cami," I said in a matter-of-fact manner. "That would just mess things up good and royal."

"Now you're thinking like me. Pretty soon you won't even need to hire a coach."

"I didn't know I'd hired you."

She sat up with a look of pretended horror. "You didn't

think I was doing this for nothing. This is costing you big time."

"So you're nothing more than a conniving mercenary."

"What can I say?" she said, shrugging and dropping back in her chair.

"It appears to me that you say way too much."

"But I keep secrets."

I shook my head and looked away. We were quiet for a moment and then Teresa spoke softly, "There was one other thing I was going to tell you out in Liberty."

"Is this going to be what I think it is?"

"I heard Cami and Susan talking this evening before you came."

"I thought you said you kept secrets."

"This is just information. What *we* talk about is secret. What *they* talk about..."

"Is just information," I finished for her. "You're a corrupting influence," I said wagging a finger at her.

"Susan was glad you moved to Huntsville because she thought Cami might fall for you and that would get her away from JB."

"So Susan's interest in me is for her sister?" I tried to sound casual and disinterested, but there was a tinge of regret in that news from Teresa.

"I believe it *was*. I'm not sure what it is now. She's upset with Cami now because she's acting like she likes you. But I think Susan kinda likes you too. Does that make sense?"

"What are you two conspiring about?" Susan called out suddenly. She was coming out the back door with a tray holding four root beer floats; Cami followed with a handful of napkins.

"I'm advising Jacob," Teresa answered innocently.

"What does she talk to you about?" Susan asked suspiciously. "She's not always this forward and talkative with people."

I looked in Teresa's direction and smiled. "Teresa and I make a pretty good team. And not just on the basketball court. Those root beer floats look like just the thing I need to knock off this terrible thirst."

I left twenty or thirty minutes later. When I arrived home, JB was in the living room, sprawled on the coach waiting. There were no magazines or books around him so he hadn't been reading. The TV wasn't on.

"The game must have gone into extra innings. Lots of extra innings," he remarked as I came into the apartment.

"We messed around a little afterwards." I stepped to the sink to get a drink. "Did you get Walter's truck running?"

"I didn't go."

I studied him. "Why didn't you come to the game?"

"I wasn't exactly invited."

"I invited you."

"That's not the same thing."

I filled a glass and took a long drink. I knew JB wanted to talk. He wanted to know what had happened, but I wasn't in the mood to discuss anything, especially if he was going to challenge everything I did and cast suspicions on everybody's actions.

"You're making quite a hit over there, aren't you?"

I turned on him and as calmly as I could said, "Just so you don't burn up with red hot curiosity, I took Cami, Susan and Teresa to the game. We had hamburgers after. All of us. I took them home. We played a little basketball. Susan and Cami fixed root beer floats while Teresa and I stayed outside and talked. It was just a fun get-together. And you could have been part of it instead of brooding here." I shook my head and rubbed the back of my neck. "Look, JB, I'm entitled to a life too. I'm tired of sneaking around afraid I'm going to ruffle your feathers."

CHAPTER SEVENTEEN

I worked a full day Saturday and decided not to go home for Sunday. JB had patched things up with Cami so I wanted to make sure I didn't interfere. Once again I made it a point to find a secluded spot in the chapel so I wouldn't run into any of the Hardaways. However, Susan's Sunday School lesson was impressive and thought-provoking. I felt impelled to compliment her.

"I couldn't leave without telling you that you did a good job," I said, coming up behind her as she was putting her things up while everyone filed from the room. She turned around and smiled. "I was impressed. I've missed hearing your lessons these last few weeks. The teacher at home isn't nearly as good."

"Why, thank you, Jacob." She blushed and looked away. "I'm never sure how it's going to go until it's over." She cleared her throat. "I was hoping you'd be here."

"I wouldn't have missed it."

I turned to leave. "Are you coming over for dinner?" she asked.

I stopped and smiled. "Is that an invitation or just a question? You probably think that the only time I show up for church is when I want a dinner invitation."

Susan's blush deepened. "It was an invitation."

I laughed and then became serious. "I'll pass today. Thanks, though."

"Maybe you can come over a little later then. You know, to help me with the dishes." She smiled.

I chuckled. "Give me a call and I'll give you a hand."

A while later as I was leaving the church Teresa caught up to me. "Hey, Jacob, I didn't know you were here today."

"I've been keeping a low profile, coach."

"Do you want to hear my latest plans?"

"Get out of here," I grumbled, tugging on her hair.

"I've even got a backup plan in case the first one falls through." I moaned and raised my gaze to the sky. "You're coming to dinner, aren't you?"

"I can't."

"Why?" She sounded surprised and disappointed.

"Susan already asked me and I turned her down. You don't think I can accept your invitation, do you?"

"Why not?"

"I'm going to see if I can spend a Sunday in Huntsville without barging in on the Hardaways' Sunday dinner."

"Hey, I like you barging in."

"The answer's still no."

"I'm going to go to your apartment and drag you over for dinner," she threatened.

"The answer will still be no."

"But coming to dinner is part of my big plan."

"Then the answer is definitely no. I'm going to have ham sandwiches, tortilla chips, root beer and mint chip ice cream."

"We're having something better."

"Teresa, you're not listening to me. No! I am not going over to your place for dinner."

She waved me away. "I'll see you at your place in about thirty minutes."

As I entered the apartment, JB was buttoning his shirt and getting ready to leave for his standing dinner appointment. He watched me enter. "I thought maybe you'd be at the Hardaways'."

I shook my head. "I did receive two invites, though. You'll be proud to know that I turned them both down."

He started for the door and then stopped. "I don't care if you come to dinner, Jacob," he muttered with his back to me.

"It's too late now. Have a good time."

He faced me. For a moment he just stared. Finally he

looked away and sighed plaintively. "Dang it, Jacob, I don't know what's going on. I'm sorry for being a jerk."

"Forget it. Have a good time."

"Come with me?"

I laughed. "Get out of here before I change my mind."

I changed into some slacks but left my white shirt on without the tie. Although I was hungry, I wasn't anxious to go in and fix ham sandwiches. I began to wish I hadn't been so adamant about declining all my dinner invitations.

Thirty minutes after arriving at the apartment, I went into the kitchen and started making my sandwiches. As I was spreading the mustard, there was a light tap on the door. I stopped with the knife in my hand and my back to the screen door. "Teresa," I muttered softly, exasperated. "Teresa," I said more loudly, "the answer is still no. Go away. I love ham sandwiches. And I love to eat by myself."

There was more tapping, this time louder. "Besides, if I go over to your place, I'll just get stuck with the dishes." There was more knocking, but I refused to turn around. I continued to work on building my ham sandwiches. "Look you persistent little matchmaker. I am not going over to your place to dinner." The knocking continued. Chuckling and shaking my head, I set the butter knife down and went to the door and came face to face with Susan Hardaway, who stood demurely with a squelched grin on her face. My mouth dropped open. "I thought it was Teresa," I stammered, pushing the door open.

"After I got home, I realized that my invitation was less than it should have been. I really didn't intend it to come out as a question. I wanted it to be an invitation." I smiled, embarrassed. "Teresa told me that she got turned down because you had already turned me down."

I laughed and shook my head. "Hey, I appreciate your thoughtfulness, but I almost have my lunch on the table."

"Teresa said you might be stubborn."

"Teresa," I sighed, shaking my head and looking at the ceiling, "what would I do without her."

"Come on, break down and have dinner with us."

"I can't."

"Then will you invite me to have lunch with you?" she asked stepping into the apartment and looking around. "This is the first time I've been here. Cami said you kept it clean. She was right. We could use a good housekeeper over at our place. Do you want to come over Saturday mornings?"

"Sure. What's the pay?"

"Sunday dinner."

I laughed.

"You really do have to come with me. Remember my lesson today was King Benjamin's sermon about feeding the poor and the needy and not turning the beggar away. You're just helping me fulfill my Christian duty."

I glanced toward my ham sandwiches sitting on the kitchen counter. "Put them in a plastic bag and eat them for lunch tomorrow," Susan suggested.

"All right. You win."

"Good," she beamed, "now we have somebody to do the potatoes and the dishes." She poked me in the ribs.

"Hey, who's fixing dinner?" I asked as we left.

"I don't want you to get a big head, but I took your advice. Cami and Teresa are putting dinner on today. I haven't done anything. I did offer to get you so you could mash the potatoes, but other than that, they've done the whole thing."

I was a little worried to see JB's reaction when I entered the house with Susan, but he seemed as pleased to have me there as the rest of the family. I whipped the potatoes and felt right at home, glad I wasn't back at the apartment choking on dry ham sandwiches.

At the end of the meal, Susan stood and announced, "Justin and Brett, your turn for dishes."

The two boys started to protest, but Denton cut them off and insisted. As the two boys started clearing the table, the rest of the family drifted from the dining area. I walked out with Susan and we sat in the living room while the other family members went their various ways.

"Hey, I'm impressed," I told Susan as she dropped into an overstuffed chair while I sank onto the sofa across from her.

"You really got these guys whipped into shape." I nodded toward her two brothers in the kitchen. "And Cami and Teresa putting on dinner. Where did you get such a novel idea?"

She glared at me and pretended to be irritated. "Do you enjoy being annoying or does it just come naturally?"

I cocked my head to one side and considered the question. "Does it annoy you that I was right?" I grinned.

She sighed. "You were right. Now does that make you happy?"

"Yeah, because now we're both free and I can help you with your Sunday School lesson. Do you want some pointers?"

"No!" she came back and then laughed and shook her head. "I don't even prepare my lesson this early. I have to think about it first, let things simmer in my brain for awhile. Go for a walk and just think."

"I'll go for a walk with you." She studied me. "Strictly as a Sunday School lesson preparation exercise," I quickly added.

"I'd love to go for a walk. Just to prepare my lesson, though." She giggled. "I'll need to slip into some more comfortable shoes."

"I'll meet you outside."

I spent the entire afternoon with Susan. We walked all over Huntsville and sat in the park. We did talk about Susan's Sunday School lesson, but we talked about so many other things. When I finally walked her back to her place it was nearly seven.

Although we hadn't done anything more than talk and laugh—there was no holding hands or anything like that—when I left Susan, I knew something had happened to me.

The next week I was coming up the canyon after making a trip to Salt Lake for Roger when I spotted the Hardaways' Buick off the side of the road and Susan standing there looking forlorn. I pulled Roger's pickup truck behind her and stopped.

As soon as she realized who I was, she rolled her eyes and turned away. I glanced at the Buick's rear right tire. It was flat. "Hello," I called out as two cars swished by.

Susan turned back to me. "You know what I've been doing?"

I looked at Susan, dressed in a light dress, hose and heels.

"Probably hoping some guy would stop and lend you a hand."

"You're partially right. I've been praying that someone would stop and help me. I've never changed a tire before. But," she added bashfully, "I've been hoping that you wouldn't be the one to find me in this predicament."

I laughed. "Pride is it?"

"Maybe."

"You're not just out here practicing one of the old Hardaway tricks, playing the damsel in distress? This is two times in a couple of months."

"I knew that's what you'd think," she accused, pointing a finger at me. "I was not trying to lure anyone. Especially not you." She smiled and raised her eyebrows. "But since you're here, what do you know about changing a tire?"

I considered the question a moment and then a sly grin pulled at the corners of my mouth. "There's an old Mexican proverb, something about give a man a fish and you feed him a day; teach a man to fish and you feed him for a lifetime."

"Are you going to be annoying again? And it's a Chinese proverb, and I'm not hungry for fish or anything else. I need my tire changed."

"You know this could happen to you on some dark night out in the middle of nowhere."

"But it didn't. It happened right here in broad daylight and you're here dressed in your work clothes, and if you were a gentleman, which might be debatable," she teased, "you would just change my tire so I could be on my way."

"I'll coach you."

"Look how I'm dressed."

"When you get that flat on that lonely dark night, there's no telling how you'll be dressed. I'll walk you through this. It'll be a cinch." She studied me dubiously. "This will be a great learning experience. You might be able to use it as an object lesson in Sunday School sometime."

"I'm going to humor you," she said threateningly, "but if I get my dress dirty…"

She really was a good sport about it. With a little coaching she removed the spare, jacked up the car and was in the process of loosening the lug nuts when a guy pulled up in a jeep. He was about two hundred and twenty pounds with a full beard and long hair with a bright red head band. He looked like a recruiter for the Hells Angels.

"Need some help?" he called out as I stood by the rear of the Buick and Susan struggled with the lug nuts.

"No, I think we've got it," I called out.

Susan stood, panting and brushing her brow with the back of her hand. Her face was flushed.

"I was talkin' to the lady," the guy barked at me. "Does he got a busted back or somethin'?" he growled at Susan, jabbing a finger in my direction.

Suddenly feeling a bit awkward, I answered sheepishly, "I was just teaching her to change a tire."

The guy turned a menacing glare in my direction. "You her old man or something?"

"No, I just happened by and thought I'd teach her how to change a tire so that the next time…"

"Get out of my way," he snarled, pushing past me and taking the wrench from Susan.

"No, wait," I called out in protest, "I was just trying to give her some experience. I can change the tire."

"If you were going to change the tire, you should have done it before I showed. I'm changing it now. And don't get in my way."

While the guy changed the tire, all the while grumbling and hurling insults in my direction, I stood back red-faced and humiliated as Susan fought back a growing urge to burst out laughing.

When the guy finished, he graciously accepted Susan's profusion of gratitude and then he turned on me and growled, "I hope I pass you stranded on the highway one of these days. I'll make it a point to stop and give you a real learning experience."

When Susan and I were finally alone, she couldn't stop laughing. "So much for the Chinese proverb," she hooted. "I thought he was going to pound you with the lug wrench."

"And you thought it was funny."

"No, it was hilarious."

"Every time I stop to help you, the whole experience turns into a disaster."

"I told you I was hoping and praying you wouldn't show up. But I do appreciate your thoughtfulness. I'll make it up to you some day." She started laughing again as I opened her car door and she dropped down inside. "See you later, Jacob."

The following Saturday afternoon I was washing the Bug and Susan drove up on her bike. Wearing her bike helmet, she was red-faced and perspiring. "Where have you been?" I smiled, looking her up and down.

"Riding. I took the mountain road over toward Morgan. It's quite a drive. I thought of inviting you to go with me."

"Too bad you didn't tell me a little earlier."

"I wasn't sure you were in good enough shape. And I didn't want to embarrass you."

"I don't like your condescending attitude."

She laughed. "Do you want to try it sometime?"

"Sounds fun."

"Do you mind giving me a drink from your hose?" she asked, nodding to the hose that was trickling on Mrs. Pritt's lawn. "I'm dying of thirst."

"Sure." I walked over to the hose and dragged it back to where Susan sat astride her bike. As I pretended to hand her the hose, I suddenly capped the end of the hose with my thumb and casually sprayed her, starting with her head and going up and down her body.

Sputtering and squealing, she leaped from her bike and raced into the street. "What was that for?" she gasped.

"It was your turn," I laughed. "I didn't ever get you back for the time in the park."

She pointed at me. "You're still mad about the flat tire."

"That too."

"If I wasn't so hot and that water didn't feel so good, I'd be upset with you."

"Come and get your drink," I said, grinning. "If I can't annoy you, I don't want to even bother."

It was strange how over the next couple of weeks Susan and I bumped into each other. One day I passed her carrying something down the road. I stopped to offer her a ride. She was taking lunch over to the Parkers, an elderly couple who lived a couple of blocks from her place. I gave her a ride and she invited me to go in with her. I learned that Susan had been checking up on the Parkers for several weeks. I tried to imagine Cami doing that.

A couple days later I was getting ready to fix supper when the phone rang. It was Susan. She sounded embarrassed. "I know this sounds crazy. We've got four vehicles and not a single one of them is here. I don't know where everyone has taken off to. And I promised Sister Farnsworth, the Relief Society president, that I'd run a printed program over to a sister in one of the Liberty wards before six this evening." She hesitated. "Could I…" She paused, apparently undecided as to what she wanted to ask.

"Do you want to take the Bug? I'm not using it."

There was a long silence. "I've never driven one," she said slowly.

"I can give you a ride," I offered.

"Do you mind?"

"I was just ready to fix something to eat, but I'm not in any hurry."

"I wasn't going to have anything fancy—melted cheese sandwiches, soup and milk—but I'll share if you'll rescue me this once," she laughed.

"Melted cheese sandwiches and soup sound better than anything I had on the menu. I'll be right over."

We had a tough time finding this lady in Liberty and when we did, we found out that she didn't need the program for another week. Susan was mortified as we climbed back in the car. "I really thought it was this evening," she explained, not able to look at me.

"Sure," I tormented her.

"You don't think…"

"You're just trying to hustle me that's all," I chuckled.

She punched me in the arm. "I do not hustle guys."

Wincing dramatically, I asked, "You're still going to feed me, aren't you? I'm starved."

She feigned anger. "I don't know, especially after your hustling remark." She turned away. "But since I promised, I'll come through."

The ride back to Huntsville from Liberty was too short. As I pulled up in front of Susan's house, I remarked, "I haven't eaten since noon today. I'm starved."

"I'll make lots of cheese sandwiches."

"What do you say we have something a little more substantial?" She looked at me and I quickly added, "On me. I'll take you someplace. Unless you've got other plans this evening."

She looked at me a moment and I was afraid she was going to decline, but she smiled and answered softly, "I'd like that, Jacob."

"Where to then?"

"There's that little place where we ate after the softball game."

I considered the suggestion. "I'm pretty hungry." I chewed on my lower lip and glanced at my watch. "Have you ever been to Maddox?"

"Maddox?" she said, surprised. "You are hungry."

"I'll take you home. Show you my old stomping grounds. Did you know I was a busboy at Maddox for a few months?"

"Are you sure you want to go back? They might put you to work in the kitchen or clearing tables or mashing potatoes."

"Let's chance it."

Our dinner at Maddox evolved into an entire evening. After eating, I took Susan out to the farm. Mom and Dad and the rest of the family were gone so I just showed her around and talked about growing up there. Afterwards we drove back to Brigham and I showed her all of my old stomping grounds—the high school, Peach City, the downtown movie house. We even dragged Main a couple of times just to prove I wasn't out of practice.

It was almost midnight when we headed back to Huntsville, and I kept thinking as we were driving up Ogden

Canyon that the evening had rushed by too quickly. I didn't want it to end.

When I stopped in front of her place and opened the door so she could get out, Susan laughingly remarked, "The next time I ask you to make a quick run to Liberty, you'll turn me down. You'll be afraid I'll take up your entire evening."

"I wouldn't have missed it." I looked down at the ground. "I hope I didn't bore you with my enthusiasm for Brigham and my old turf."

"We'll have to go sometime when I can meet your family."

"We'll do that."

CHAPTER EIGHTEEN

The next afternoon Teresa showed up at my place pushing her bicycle with a flat tire. "Can you fix a flat tire?" she asked when I came to the door.

"I've fixed a few in my time."

"I've got the patches and everything if you've got a pump."

"I've got the pump. Doesn't anybody at your house know how to fix a flat tire?" I joked.

She grinned. "I didn't ask. I wanted an excuse to come over."

I laughed. "Let's have a look."

As we worked on the flat, Teresa lamented, "I think Cami and JB are getting serious again." I worked without answering. "You still like her, don't you?"

"Sure, I like her."

"You're not going to let JB take her, are you? You've got to let her know you're interested. Send her some flowers."

I looked up at Teresa, who hovered over me with her questions. "If you think I'm going to send Cami flowers, you're crazy."

"She likes pink roses."

"I'll tell JB."

"Don't tell him. Jacob, how are you ever going to be my brother-in-law unless you marry my sister?"

I sighed. "I guess I'll have to break down and send flowers to Susan. What kind of flowers does she like?"

"Oh, brother. She probably doesn't even like flowers. She's too practical for flowers. Besides, she's still thick with Tyson Ethington."

"Will he make a pretty good brother-in-law?"

"I think it's between him and Cory Randall. They're a toss up. And JB would be okay, but I'd prefer you."

I laughed and began pumping up the deflated tire. "I guess you're going to have to talk one of your sisters out of one of their boyfriends then. You've got your work cut out for you."

After I'd patched Teresa's tire and she was getting ready to head for home, JB and Cami pulled up. The four of us visited for a while as Cami held onto JB's arm and leaned against him. I could tell their cuddly closeness was bothering Teresa. She kept glancing at me as though she wanted me to do something about it. Furtively I shrugged for her and shook my head.

"Are you doing anything Friday night?" Cami suddenly asked me. "What did you have in mind?"

"JB and I are going to have a little steak fry in our backyard. Real informal. Do you want to come. We invited Susan. She said she'd be there if you were there."

"As a date?" Teresa gasped.

Cami laughed. "No, this is just a little friendly get-together."

"Can I come then?"

"Sure."

"Well, if Teresa's going to be there," I answered, grinning, "I'll be there. After all, we're practically going steady."

She shook her head, punched me and started walking her bike home. "Now don't you stand me up, Teresa," I called after her.

"You're not funny, Jacob," she flung over her shoulder.

Friday after work, JB and I headed to the apartment and cleaned up for the steak fry. We drove over in the Firebird. Before we climbed from the car, Cami skipped down the driveway to greet us. She touched my arm and then squeezed my hand as she said hello, and then going around to JB's side, she grabbed him by the arm and pulled him toward the backyard. "Are you hungry?"

"Depends on if you can cook."

"Susan's cooking, but if you're going to be picky or grumpy or sour-faced, we'll send you back to Sister Pritt's dungeon."

"And where's my escort?" I called after them. "Teresa didn't stand me up, did she?"

Cami turned around and wagged her head. "Tough break, Jacob. At the last minute Jacki called and invited her to a slumber party. If it's any consolation, she debated pretty hard for..." She shrugged. "Well, about thirty seconds." She laughed. "But that just means more food for the rest of us."

JB and Cami moved ahead of me. I followed them around the house to the backyard where Susan was at the grill in a bright red full-length apron over her short sleeve light blue cotton shirt and a pair of denim jeans. Her shoes were kicked off on the lawn. Relaxed and cheerful, she smiled and waved her cooking fork at me.

Although I had tried not to let on, I was excited to see Susan. More than anything I wanted to be right there by the grill talking with her.

"How's the chief cook?" I inquired as JB and Cami dropped into lounge chairs a dozen feet away. My arm brushed hers, and I knew it wasn't accidental. I wanted to feel her close to me.

"I don't think I'll poison anybody."

"We'll let JB and Cami eat first just in case," I commented.

She drew back the cooking fork as though she were going to hit me. I nudged her gently with my elbow. "I want to concentrate my full attention on the chief cook."

"How do you like your steak?"

"Any way you want to cook it for me."

"You're easy to please. Do you want to lend a hand?" She glanced over at JB and Cami. "Something tells me that neither one of them is interested in playing cook. And this whole thing was their idea."

"I'll stick with you. You're close to the food."

"Oh, so you're just thinking of how to stuff your face." She turned one of the steaks. I stepped over to her and intentionally bumped into her. "Actually I wanted to stay close to you," I whispered, quickly looking around. "But only if Teresa isn't spying on us from one of the windows."

"Don't worry about the windows," she whispered. "She's in the bushes with binoculars. On a special assignment from Daddy." She laughed and pushed me with her shoulder.

"Relax. Teresa's over at a friend's place."

I laughed. "Cami already broke the news to me that I'd been stood up by an eleven-year-old girl. That's tough on a guy's ego."

Susan eyed me suspiciously. "What does she talk to you about?" She pointed the fork at me and warned, "And don't give me any of your wild stories."

"She's just trying to line me up with one of her sisters," I remarked off-handedly, suddenly feeling relaxed and bold.

"I wouldn't put it past her, but you're lying."

"Hey, that middle steak is about ready for me. Do you want me to get my plate?" I jabbed her with my elbow.

"I want you to tell me what Teresa tells you all the time."

I laughed. "I already told you. She's in the market for a brother-in-law, and she's smitten by me. What can I say?"

"You've said too much," Susan moaned. She was quiet a moment and then she ask, "So which one is she lining you up with?"

"The best one."

"Oh, you like to play it safe."

I chuckled. "Did your Dad ask you why you were out so late the other night?"

"He didn't know. He was out with Trudy."

"How are things progressing with him?"

"I think pretty well."

"What's she like?"

"We haven't seen her yet."

"What?"

"I think he's afraid, but I'm not sure of what. Either he's afraid we won't like her or he's afraid she won't like us. It's probably the latter."

"Is there anything I can do except stand here and bother the cook?" I asked.

"Oh, maybe if you stand right where you are and keep bothering the cook we'll both be happy."

I casually slipped behind Susan and put my hands on her

hips. As I did, she leaned back against me, her head resting against my shoulder and her hair brushing the side of my face.

"When you say bother the cook," she whispered, "you mean really distract her. We'll be burning the steaks."

A few minutes later we called JB and Cami over and we all sat down to eat. For the entire meal Susan and I didn't say a lot to each other. The conversation involved the entire group, but there was something communicated between us the whole while, whether it was a look, a smile, a foot nudge under the table or a comment with a double meaning that we could smile knowingly about.

Before the meal was over I wanted more than anything for this to be the evening that Susan and I walked to the reservoir. I wanted to be with just her so we could talk and touch and laugh and even be quiet if we chose.

Cami didn't allow for the walk, however. After we had eaten and sat around visiting for fifteen or twenty minutes, she pushed up and challenged Susan and me. "Since we've developed a backyard basketball tradition, we can't end an evening without a game."

"Cami," Susan protested, "we're stuffed."

"Get some shoes," she shouted to Susan over her shoulder as she went to the shop for the ball. "A little activity will let our food settle. JB and I will spot you the two of you a half a dozen points."

Susan wagged her head and looked over at me. "Something tells me Cami isn't going to take no for an answer."

I looked at JB, who was smiling. "You up to getting beat?"

"Only if there's a wager on the outcome," he came back. "Losers buy ice cream for the winners. Nothing cheap either."

Cami was returning with the ball. "JB just volunteered to buy everybody all the Dryers ice cream they want," I called out. "You'll help pick up the tab."

Cami looked at JB. "Don't worry. Losers buy the ice cream."

"Oh, I can handle that." She poked a finger in my direction and asked, "Did you bring your wallet? No rain checks tonight."

I pulled Susan up. "First one to ten," I said to Cami and JB.

"Ten?" Cami protested.

I held my stomach. "I'm too full to go past ten."

"We'll put you away before your stomach even knows you've fallen out of your chair."

Susan returned wearing an oversize T-shirt, her denim jeans and a pair of white Nikes. "Oh, she's serious about this," JB teased. "Do I need to go home and get my Jazz jersey?" He laughed. "She's going to be bent out of shape when we beat them."

"Let's throw something else into the wager," I called out as I took the ball from Cami and started dribbling across the court. "Losers clean up. The other team can take a long, leisurely walk."

JB smiled at Cami. "I never did like doing dishes. And it's been a while since Cami and I had a long, leisurely walk."

Susan crossed the court with a knowing look. She bumped into me. Before snatching the ball, she purred so only I could hear, "I expect to win this. You've made the stakes pretty high."

Turning my back on JB and Cami, I muttered, "I didn't know you were such a Dryers ice cream fan."

She pushed off a quick jumper. "I can take or leave the ice cream." She snagged the rebound from her own shot and tossed the ball to me. "We'll take first outs," she called to Cami and JB. "We'd like to wrap up this little scrimmage in about five minutes."

The game went longer than five minutes, but Susan and I pulled it off together. It was like we were in perfect sync. When we hit ten points JB and Cami were only six. They insisted that we go to twenty because they were just getting warmed up. We still beat them, twenty to fourteen. They insisted that it was just our very, very lucky day.

"All right," JB called out when they finally conceded defeat, "what flavor will it be?"

"Rocky Road," Susan spoke up.

"I'm a chocolate chip mint man myself," I said. "Why don't you just get one of each so we don't have to choose."

"I hate to break this to you," Cami grumbled in fun, "but you've got to settle on one flavor."

"Come on," JB joined in, "if they're going to be such whiners we'll get them each their favorite flavor. I'm going to have to listen to Jacob brag all night about being the backyard champion of the world; the last thing I want to do is listen to him complain about not getting his very own flavor of ice cream."

"I think they're both a couple of sore losers," I called out. "If you're going to grumble about paying up your bet, then forget the whole thing."

JB pointed at Susan and me and grinned. "If I were you two, I'd practice while we're gone because when we get back we're going to want a rematch."

"Practice?" I questioned, feigning surprise. "If we practiced any more, we'd really cream you."

The bantering continued until JB and Cami went around the house to get into the Firebird. I dropped down on the grass and stretched out with a soft groan. "I didn't know you were such a jock," I commented to Susan as she slumped into a lawn chair a few feet away.

"I'm not crazy about that terminology." She kicked me gently. "Especially if it's applied to me. It sounds so…gross."

I propped myself up on one elbow. "Do you ever wish that you'd had a chance to play like your sister?"

She smiled ruefully, leaning her head against the back of the chair. "Oh, there were times that I felt a little cheated, that I wished that I didn't have to grow up so fast." She shrugged. "I knew it had to be that way. But I wanted Cami to be the best she could be. There was satisfaction in helping her."

She laughed and shook her head. "There were times when Cami didn't want anybody for a mother, especially not her older sister. We had our run-ins, but for the most part we got along. We both learned where our limits were."

"But you didn't have a chance to shine."

"I had other things that interested me. My art and my crafts. When everyone else was in bed, I liked to stay up and paint or work on a dry arrangement or something else. Sometimes I'd write."

"I'd like to read some of your stuff."

"That's all it is, stuff. And nobody reads it."

"Nobody?"

Smiling, she stood up and grabbed the ball from the lawn. "Do you want to play a little one-on-one?"

"You let people see your artwork."

"I'm a better painter than a writer."

"So you wouldn't consider sharing anything with me?"

She chuckled. "I might consider it. Some time." She threw me the ball.

I laughed and pushed myself to my feet. "I don't know if I'm up to your intensity, but I'll play a slow game."

The game was all fun, no rules, no one keeping score. We were careless about fouls, bumping and jostling each other, tugging the ball from one another, pushing, tripping, laughing, complaining, one shouting "no fair!" while doing something underhanded.

Susan went for a lay-up, dribbling about once and running the rest of the way. "Traveling!" I shouted. She ignored me, giggling so hard that she couldn't push off the shot so she started running away. I chased after her, grabbed her arm and started fighting for the ball. It was a free-for-all. Then the ball was knocked loose. We both went for it but pulled on each other to stop the other one from getting it. I finally grabbed her, pulling her away from the ball but pulling her into me. Suddenly we were facing each other. My arms were around her waist, pulling her toward me. She was pressing against my chest with her hands. We were both laughing and then we looked at each other. She gradually relaxed. I held her. Slowly I pulled her closer. Our eyes closed and our lips touched. It was short. Our lips separated momentarily and then we kissed again, this time longer with much more feeling.

It was strange, but as I kissed Susan the second time, I couldn't help thinking of Cami's kiss weeks earlier. There was no comparison between the two. I knew right then that I cared for Susan, more than I had ever cared for anyone ever before. And it wasn't the kiss. The kiss was merely the culmination of the feelings and connections that had developed so between us.

"I think too much intimacy during the game is against the rules," Susan said huskily as our lips parted. She blushed, but

I still held her.

"We weren't playing by the rules."

We heard JB and Cami coming up the driveway. We hadn't even heard the car pull up or the doors slam. Surprised, we separated immediately and I snatched up the basketball. We were standing four or five feet apart when JB and Cami came around the corner.

"So you *have* been practicing," Cami chortled. "They're worried. Are you in panic mode?" she asked Susan.

Susan looked at me, smiled and winked. She shook her head. "I don't think you'd call it panic mode. We were just working out a little strategy."

"We practiced some moves that will really surprise you," I said, walking past Susan and bumping against her.

"Do JB and I need to get worried and have a few warmup sessions ourselves?" Cami questioned.

"I don't think any warmups you do will change anything."

"Oh, these guys are *very* confident," JB taunted as he began to dig out the first scoop of ice cream. "Maybe we shouldn't have left them alone."

"We did just fine alone," Susan answered.

Susan and I didn't sit by each other as the four of us ate our ice cream. She sat across from me, next to Cami.

"Let's have that rematch," JB said, standing up and setting his ice cream bowl down.

"I think you two have clean-up duty," I said, turning to Cami and JB. "Susan and I get to go on the walk. Remember?"

"Don't you want to play first?"

Susan pushed out of her chair and stretched a little. "I think we better walk off some of this ice cream."

"Do you want some company?" Cami asked

"I think you'd better get on those dishes. I don't want to get stuck with them."

We walked around the corner of the house a couple of feet apart, but as we disappeared from sight, I reached out and took Susan's hand. She pressed up against me, and I put my arm around her waist and started down the street.

"Do you remember the first time I saw you?" Susan asked after we'd walked a ways.

"Remember? I only recently recovered from the frostbite." I flinched as she poked me in the ribs. "You did shock me."

"I thought it was revulsion, not shock."

She jabbed me again. "Something clicked in my brain that day. It was like a little voice whispered to me, `You're going to get to know this guy!' I almost fell over. Especially since I still thought you were JB. But I was seeing a different person. I had built up quite a defense and even dislike for your brother because I was trying to protect Cami. To finally find myself even thinking something positive was more than I could handle. I assure you I tried to drive those thoughts out of my mind. Completely."

"That's why you were so..." I groped for the right word. "So aggravatingly antagonistic that Friday you ran out of gas."

She laughed. "That was a wild Friday. I think I would have been cranky with anyone, but you really threw me. I was actually excited to see you at first. But then I told myself that I was being a stupid schoolgirl and I needed to get a grip. I guess in a way I was angry with you because I was finding that I liked you and I blamed you for doing that to me."

"Man, I was really in a lose-lose situation."

"When you asked me to go out to dinner, I was sorry I had to turn you down." She took a deep breath. "I kept telling myself I was being stupid. I was sure you liked Cami."

"I did at first," I admitted, smiling. "But things change." I coughed. "Since this is confession time," I joked, "I was a little afraid of you to start with. Then when you gave your Sunday School lesson, that was the first time I ever really had a chance to study you and see you in a different light."

We walked and talked till past midnight, unaware of the time passing, wanting to be together. When I finally walked her home, the Hardaway house was dark and JB's car was gone.

CHAPTER NINETEEN

I worked Saturday, all the while wishing I had asked Susan to do something with me in the evening, but I hadn't. I decided to wander over to her place as soon as I got off work.

Teresa was out front with her friend Jacki when I dropped in. I visited with them. Before long we were joking and playing around. I was about to ask Teresa if Susan was around when a white Grand Am pulled up.

Tyson exchanged pleasantries with Teresa and me. To him I was just another neighbor hanging around. After speaking with us, he sauntered to the front door where Brett invited him inside.

"Susan's got a big date?" I remarked to Teresa, trying not to reveal the disappointment I felt.

She looked at the closed front door through which Tyson had disappeared. "Yeah, I think she's getting pretty serious. I figure she'll be engaged before the summer's over. Tyson'd be engaged right now if Susan weren't so slow." She thought a moment and then added, "Did you know that Tyson's already graduated from college and works for a computer company in Salt Lake? He makes good money. He's thinking of buying a house."

"Sounds like Susan's got a good deal going there," I commented, thinking of my own situation—a year of college behind me, working construction to pay for tuition, driving an old VW Bug.

A moment later Susan and Tyson emerged from the house. Susan spotted me as she came down the walk. She smiled. "Hello, Jacob, how are you this evening?" I hoped to see disappointment or panic in her face, anything that would indicate that she wished she were with me instead of Tyson Ethington. I didn't detect anything like that. She was cheerful and friendly as she greeted me and walked with Tyson to his car. The only thing that gave me any comfort at all—and it was very little—is that she wasn't holding onto his arm or taking his hand as they came down the walk.

"Are you going to be out late?" I called out suddenly, trying to sound as though I were kidding. "Remember curfew."

Susan turned and laughed. "What time do I need to be back, *Daddy?*" She emphasized the daddy in a playful manner.

I swallowed, deciding to push my luck. "Well, ten o'clock would be nice."

"Ten?" Tyson cut in laughing. "It's Saturday night."

I shrugged. "Maybe ten-thirty then."

Tyson laughed and opened the door for Susan. She was about to slip into the car, but paused and called out without looking at me. "What happens if I come back after ten-thirty?"

"The whole evening will be ruined."

She dropped down into the car. "I'll remember that."

"They won't be back until way after midnight," Teresa remarked as Tyson and Susan pulled away.

A few minutes later I drove back to the apartment, feeling more lonely and discouraged than I had ever felt since coming to Huntsville. More than anything I wanted to be with Susan Hardaway right then. I reflected back on my bantering about curfew. I had meant to relay a secret invitation to Susan. If she had only picked up on my message. She had said she'd keep it in mind. Was that her answer to me? I wanted to believe it was.

All evening I rattled around the apartment, restless and despondent. I considered packing up and driving to Brigham for the weekend so I could get completely out of the situation, but I knew that wherever I was that weekend, I was going to think of Susan.

A little before ten I got cleaned up. I showered and dressed up in clean Levis and a fresh button shirt. At ten-fifteen I walked over to the Hardaways' and hung around in the shadows, feeling stupid but desperate.

"This is really dumb," I muttered to myself as I paced with my hands stuffed in my pockets while I peered around me for fear someone would see me. "You'll get picked up for loitering or being a nuisance in the neighborhood," I growled. But

I didn't leave.

The minutes ticked past ten-thirty and then ticked toward ten forty-five. "Give it up. She probably hasn't given you a second thought all evening." And yet, I couldn't quite believe that. That's why I stayed.

Suddenly a white car cruised around the corner, and for a moment I was captured in the glare of the headlights. The car stopped at the Hardaways'. I turned away, hoping they hadn't recognized me. And then I hoped they did. I wanted Susan to know I was out here. I waited, holding my breath and feeling my heart hammer in my chest, feeling horribly stupid but holding on to the faintest hope that my fantasy was reality.

Tyson opened the door and Susan stepped out. They spoke for a few moments by the car and then Tyson walked around to the driver's side, climbed in and drove off. Susan turned and started very slowly up the walk toward the house.

I wanted to break into a wild sprint, but I walked instead. Susan was still a dozen steps from the front door when I called out, "You're late." I had a hard time keeping the excitement from my voice. "I was wondering if you were going to stand me up."

Susan turned around. In the shadows I couldn't see her face so I wasn't sure what her reaction was until I heard her giggle. "So it was you out there."

Slowly walking toward her, I said, "We did say ten-thirty."

She laughed and moved in my direction. "You know, Jacob Matthews, you are totally bonkers. Saturday night curfew?"

"It was a wild shot." I was almost close enough now that I could reach out and touch her, but I still couldn't see her face, just her silhouette against the glare from the porch light. I looked away, feeling awkward and vulnerable. "Actually, I felt kind of crazy hanging around in the shadows like that, but I kept wondering..." I laughed. "It's probably a miracle that one of the neighbors didn't call the police and report a distraught prowler terrorizing the neighborhood. I'm sorry that..."

Before I could finish, Susan reached out and took my hand. "I'd have died if you hadn't been here," she said softly.

I squeezed her hand and laughed, my whole body sighing with relief. "Then I wasn't totally crazy?"

"I didn't say that," she came back quickly, pushing up against me and laughing. "We're probably both crazy. Dangerously so."

"Shoot, I don't mind being crazy as long as I have company."

"So what now?" she asked, looking at me. "Here it is eleven o'clock, when most people are finishing their..."

"Have you eaten?" I cut in.

She laughed and we began walking toward the street. "I'm embarrassed to think about this whole evening. Tyson and I drove to Salt Lake to a wedding reception for one of his old college friends. He asked me if I wanted to go for something to eat, but I was too nervous."

"Why?"

"It was your fault. All evening I'd been thinking of your strange 10:30 curfew and I just knew I had to get home. Finally I told Tyson that I wanted to go home. I kept telling myself I was being stupid that you had just been joking, but..."

"I'm glad we both agreed to be stupid tonight," I said huskily. "I was serious when I said the evening would be ruined if you didn't come back. Ruined for me."

We were quiet a moment and then Susan said reluctantly, "I'm starving." She squeezed my hand. "Shall we sneak inside and whip something up really quick?"

"Come to think of it," I confided, "I haven't eaten anything either. I was too worried about you getting home on time."

"I can make a really mean tuna fish sandwich."

"Any tuna fish sandwich would be really mean to me. I gave up tuna fish when Mom stopped sending me to school with a sack lunch. But I know where there's this eating place..."

"Jacob, it's eleven o'clock. What about curfew?"

"Curfew? Who said anything about curfew? This place is open twenty-four hours a day. It's a trucker's paradise."

"This is crazy," she giggled, glancing back at the house. "You want to go to a truck stop?"

"You don't have to drive a truck to go there. My stomach's growling. I feel faint. We've got to do something quick." I started pulling her toward the street.

We walked to my apartment, giggling, joking and basking in the exhilaration of this magical summer evening. I'd never sneaked off with anybody until that night. We drove around the south end of Pine View Reservoir and saw the reflection of the night skies in the black, placid waters. I loved driving down the winding canyon with Susan next to me, talking peacefully about anything that came to our minds. I had never felt so at ease with anyone. It seemed as though each time we were together I relaxed more and more.

When we found the Flying J Truck Stop just off I-15 west of Ogden, we slipped inside and found a corner booth in the back of the place and stuffed ourselves on garden salad, chicken fried steak, baked potato and hot cherry pie a la mode.

"Something tells me we should have settled for tuna sandwiches," Susan moaned as I helped her into the Bug. "I'm so full I can't move."

When we returned to Huntsville, we took the old route over the mountain that drops down into Liberty. When we reached the summit, we pulled off the road, climbed out of the car and gazed down on the twinkling lights of the entire Huntsville Valley.

"I've never been up here at one o'clock in the morning," Susan whispered as she folded her arms and leaned against me with my arm over her shoulder, pulling her close. "It's gorgeous. If I'd known how breathtaking it was, I'd have come up here before."

"You have to realize," I retorted playfully, "a lot of the effect has to do with who you're with."

She laughed softly and bit my thumb. "You might be right."

Susan's house was completely dark when we finally pulled up. Quietly we walked to the front door. On the front steps Susan turned and stiffly and formally shook my hand and declared, "It was a very fine evening, Brother Matthews, even if we did break curfew." Then she started to snicker, covering her mouth with her hand to stifle the noise.

I pulled her close and kissed her gently. We were both quiet for a moment. Reaching up, she brushed the side of my face with her hand. "You are coming to dinner tomorrow, aren't you? No, I guess it's today," she corrected herself. "And," she added, "it's not a question. "Jacob, you are coming to dinner," she said firmly but happily.

"Well, you know me, always looking for a free meal."

"Oh, I almost forgot. Daddy's bringing Trudy to dinner."

"The famous Trudy, the one with the romantic voice?"

Susan laughed. "The very one."

"Maybe she doesn't want an audience. Are you sure I should be here for such an auspicious occasion?"

"Somebody has to do the potatoes and the dishes."

"I knew there was a catch."

"But this time you won't have to eat on the back porch. We'll let you sit up to the table with the family."

"As long as I keep my place and don't say anything."

She laughed again. "Goodnight, you crazy man." She turned, opened the door and disappeared.

CHAPTER TWENTY

I was late getting up for meetings Sunday morning. I had to rush to make it to the church on time. Once again I met Teresa, Cami and Susan as they were scurrying across the parking lot.

"Late as usual," Teresa called out to me.

"We've still got three and a half minutes," Cami corrected her. "And nobody better be sitting on our bench."

"Daddy's bringing Trudy to dinner today," Teresa announced excitedly. "He's going to her meetings in Salt Lake and then bringing her up here. I hope she's not fat and ugly."

"Teresa," Susan scolded.

"Well," Teresa came back innocently, "you don't want her to be fat and ugly, do you?"

"Remember what Daddy said. Looks don't mean anything."

"That's easy for him to say. She won't be his stepmother. I don't know if I want a stepmother."

"She's coming to dinner, not moving in with us," Cami said, as I held the door open and the girls slipped in ahead of me.

"Sit with us, Jacob," Teresa called out, stopping inside the door and taking my arm. She smiled up at me. "You can be with me today." She became suddenly serious and formal. "Everybody will think you're my date. And they'll be soooo jealous." Unable to maintain her formal air any longer, she snickered and then composed herself as we marched into the chapel area. I ended up sitting between Teresa and Cami.

As soon as the benediction was said in sacrament meeting, Teresa announced in a loud whisper, "Jacob's coming to dinner today."

"I am?" I questioned, feigning surprise.

"You are. I just invited you."

"Maybe you'd better get your sisters' consent first," I cautioned loud enough for both Cami and Susan to hear.

"I can invite someone to dinner if I want." She scrunched up her nose and winked at me. "After all, you're my big date today. That allows you certain privileges."

"I still think you'd better ask your sisters."

Reluctantly Teresa turned to Cami and Susan. Cami smiled over at me and winked. "I think it will be all right if you bring your date to dinner. As long as he doesn't slurp his soup and otherwise make a total nuisance of himself," she added, nudging Teresa.

Teresa looked over at Susan, who appeared to be tiredly disinterested in the whole arrangement. "Does Jacob have to *always* come to Sunday dinner?" She sighed heavily.

"Don't mind her," Teresa said, turning back to me. "She's just got Tyson Ethington on the brain right now."

Susan, attempting to remain serious, responded in a deadpan, monotone fashion. "Actually, Jacob, I'd love to have you come to dinner today."

"See," Teresa said gleefully, "it's all settled."

"But he does have to do the dishes afterward," Susan added as she turned and moved toward her Sunday School class.

"Don't pay any attention to her," Teresa exclaimed, rolling her eyes. "Now you can walk me to class. But don't get fresh when you drop me at the door. I can't stand guys that get fresh. I feel like punching their light out."

"I'm not the first who's ever walked you to class?" I asked, pretending to be shocked and hurt.

Teresa's eyes twinkled. "You're the first today." And then she giggled. "Actually, you're the first in my whole life."

"Like I've told you before," I teased, "the only thing wrong with us is that I'm eleven years too old for you."

At the end of the meeting block, Teresa caught me and walked with me outside. "Don't you think we better wait for your sisters?" I asked when she wanted to start for home right then.

"They'll come in the car. I want to walk." Looking away, she added as we stood on the church lawn, "Cami's getting serious."

"I thought everybody knew that."

"No, it's different now. I heard her talking to Susan yesterday. She wants JB to make some commitments."

"Commitments?"

"You know, about going to church, going to the temple, stuff like that." She looked up at me and said sadly, "That means she's getting really serious."

"And how does JB feel?"

She shrugged. "I didn't hear that part."

"Were you eavesdropping?"

"Me?" She smiled slyly. "Never. They just weren't very careful about what they were saying and who was listening."

"Well, I hope Cami can get JB to make some commitments."

"You do? Why?"

"Because he's my brother and I love him. Cami could be good for him."

"But where does that leave you if Cami gets serious with JB?"

I pondered a moment. "What are my chances with Susan?"

"Lousy! She's in love with Tyson Ethington."

"Tyson?"

Turning to me and in a low, serious voice, she confided, "Tyson didn't drop Susan off until almost two last night."

"How do you know?"

"I got up for a bathroom trip. She'd just barely come in. She was humming and singing and dancing around. Have you ever danced with your sister at two o'clock in the morning? She was totally dingey. That's not like Susan at all." She sighed and added with a sorrowful resignation, "She's in love. Big time!"

A moment later Susan exited the church and spotted Teresa and me. As she walked over to us, I asked, "Do you want to walk home with Teresa and me?"

"I think maybe I better," she said primly. "You both need a chaperon." Turning to Teresa, she commented, "I'm going to have to report you to Daddy. I don't think he knows you've started dating. He won't approve. He's definitely opposed to girls going out with older men."

"Really!" she countered dubiously. "He's nine years older than Trudy. I'd say he's a little old for her."

The three of us walked along with Teresa between us jabbering most of the while. When there was a brief pause, I quipped to Susan, "Teresa tells me you had a big night last night with Brother Ethington."

Susan glanced in my direction, smiled and then looked down at Teresa, who kept her eyes straight ahead. "She did, did she?"

"She said you stayed out pretty late too. Didn't you remember your curfew?"

"Oh, I remembered," she said, looking away, smiling faintly, "but I got involved and..."

"Let's not ruin things by talking about Tyson," Teresa cut in.

Everybody at the Hardaway house was scurrying madly about, trying to get things ready for Denton and Trudy's arrival. Susan and Cami fired off commands, and the boys, Teresa, JB and I responded as well as we could. Justin was the first to spot the Buick pull into the driveway. "They're here!" he blared.

Brett and Teresa raced to the window to get their first peek. "Get away from that window!" Cami threatened, herding them back into the dining room.

"Can't we just see what's she's like?" Teresa whined.

"You'll see soon enough," Susan reassured her pleasantly.

We all listened as Denton and Trudy walked up the walk. They stood outside the door for a moment visiting while the rest of us waited anxiously for the grand entry. When the front door opened, everyone inside held their collective breath.

I have to admit that I was expecting someone squat, homely but cheerful, and comfortably amiable. Trudy Parson was definitely cheerful and amiable and her effervescent aura was contagious, putting everyone at ease. But she was more than that. She had short blond hair, blue eyes and a fair complexion. She was rather small and petite, especially next to Denton Hardaway's six-foot-two frame. She wore a peach-colored dress with light tan heels and captured everyone with her friendly engaging smile. Once Denton introduced her to us, she remembered us. She had a keen mind and a quick wit. To say that all of us were impressed would have been a gross understatement. After meeting Trudy, I was sure I knew why Denton had emphasized to the family that he didn't want anyone to get caught up in personal appearance. He wanted all to know that he had fallen for Trudy long before he knew what she looked like.

Dinner was a wonderful and relaxing experience. Trudy told about herself. She had two children—Lisa, seven, and Rhett, eleven, both of whom were spending Sunday with their grandparents in Salt Lake. She had been divorced five years earlier. The only time she was reticent at all was when she mentioned her divorce. She simply explained that it was a trying time in her life, one that took her several years to recover from, but it was in the past and she was moving forward.

At one point Brett ventured an intriguing question: "Since you only knew Dad by voice, did you get a little nervous when he wanted to see you? I mean, he could have turned out to be..." He hesitated and then blurted out, "Well, a real jerky-looking guy."

"We both went by faith," Denton spoke up, laughing.

Trudy looked around the family circle, cringed and smiled, reaching over and taking Denton's hand. "I have a confession to make. I cheated. A couple of the delivery men at my place had dropped things off at your dad's store."

"So you asked them?" Brett grinned.

"I just asked them what he was like." She glanced over at Denton. "They were both very impressed."

"I didn't know your faith was so shaky," Denton responded.

"I still didn't know what you looked like. Not exactly."

Although the Hardaway children were a bit reluctant at first to have Denton dating anyone too seriously, I suspect that if a vote had been taken that Sunday afternoon, the vote would have been unanimous to extend official family status to Trudy Parsons.

As soon as dessert was out of the way and we had done some more visiting, Trudy took a huge breath and exclaimed, "This was wonderful!" She began gathering silverware. "I speak to do the dishes." Looking at Denton, she asked, "Do you want to help me. Or don't you do dishes?" She laughed.

"To be honest," I spoke up, "the only reason I was invited today was to do the dishes, so, Sister Parsons, you'll have to do dishes another time." I stood and started clearing the table.

"I think Justin and Teresa are forgetting whose turn it is," Cami called out.

"Hey, if Jacob wants to do dishes," Justin came back, "I don't want to spoil his fun."

"You're a good man, Justin," I said knowingly. "I knew you wouldn't want to disappoint me."

"Jacob isn't doing the dishes," Cami insisted, glaring first at Justin and then at Teresa.

"I'll rescue Jacob," Susan said, standing. "We'll do them together. The rest of you can take the afternoon off. But," she added in warning, "if anyone is within earshot of the kitchen at the end of thirty seconds, I'm recruiting you for a dishes detail."

There were no further arguments. Within a few minutes Susan and I were alone. "That was a nice touch," I said, bumping against her as we both hauled plates to the kitchen sink. "We're alone."

"We better be or whoever is close by is taking our places."

"I think we can safely say that we'll have the kitchen area to ourselves then," I mused.

I never enjoyed doing dishes as much as I did that afternoon. Susan and I visited, scuffled with and bumped into each other, flipped water at one another. What should have taken us thirty minutes took us close to an hour.

As we were wiping down the kitchen counters, I bumped into her. I discarded the damp cloth and reached my arm around her waist. "Are you getting fresh with me?" she asked huskily, looking about to see if we were still alone. "Nobody's ever gotten fresh with me in the kitchen."

"Now you know why I volunteered to do the dishes."

Susan pressed up against me and whispered, "And that's why I volunteered to help you." I pulled her closer and kissed her on the lips. As we parted, she smiled and said, "I'm inviting you to dinner next week too."

"Do I get to do the dishes again?"

"I insist."

"Will you help?"

"I wouldn't miss it."

We heard footsteps approach. We moved away from each other, both of us taking up our damp cloths and attacking the counters again, which were already clean. A moment later Cami stepped into the kitchen. "I have a huge favor to ask," she announced seriously.

Susan and I looked at Cami, then at each other, and finally back at Cami. "I want you both to go with JB and me to that regional young single adult fireside at the Ogden Tabernacle tonight."

"I don't know anything about it," I said.

"One of the General Authorities is speaking. I don't remember which one. I want JB there." She added, "I think he would feel more comfortable if you went, Jacob. And," she went on, turning to Susan, "I think he would go along with it better if Jacob wasn't just a tag-along. You know, if you came too, like it was kind of a family thing."

"You mean all four of us drive down to the fireside?" Susan questioned, seeming to be reluctant about the arrangement.

"What about Tyson?" I broke in.

"Jacob," Cami chided, "we're just driving down to the fireside together. It will be as harmless as the steak fry Friday, just a little family get-together."

"Has JB said he'd go?" I wondered.

"I haven't asked. I wanted to make sure you two would help out. JB needs this, Jacob."

I shrugged. "Hey, if it will help JB." I turned to Susan who managed to keep a straight face. "Will you give it a shot?"

She took a deep breath and considered the proposal a moment. "I suppose I can do that. This one time."

"Should you call Tyson?" I asked, sounding concerned.

She thought a moment. Smiling, she shook her head.

Cami grinned. "You're both wonderful. I owe you both something. I don't know what it is, but when I think of it, I'll pay up. I promise." She disappeared out of the door.

Susan and I looked at each other, smiled and then burst out laughing. "Are you ashamed to tell your family about me?"

Susan stepped over to me, took my hands and kissed me. "I didn't want to embarrass you."

"So you want me to be very discreet this evening?"

"Should we bring Teresa along to sit between us?"

"No," I fired back. We both laughed.

That evening as we climbed into the cramped back seat of the Firebird, Susan and I entered from different sides of the car. For the first little while, we were both quiet but secretly holding hands and poking one another like a couple of goofy junior high kids. We got to laughing and Cami finally turned around in the middle of her conversation with JB and demanded quizzically, "What's wrong with you two tonight?"

I held up my hands in innocent fashion and confessed with a straight face, "Your sister keeps making passes at me."

"You two are crazy tonight!"

The fireside and the ride down and back were wonderful. JB and Cami were so caught up with themselves that they didn't pick up on Susan and me. However, when we returned to Huntsville and Susan and I emerged from different sides of the car, Cami remarked casually, "As much fun as you two seemed to have tonight, you ought to do this again."

"I don't think Tyson would go for it," I chortled.

"I think you'd better leave Tyson out of this," Susan warned. "Good night, Jacob," she called over her shoulder as she started for the house with Cami and JB coming behind her.

"I was kind of hoping you'd wait for me down by the corner in about five minutes," I called after her.

Cami and JB laughed at my silliness. "You'd better take him up on it, Susan," Cami encouraged.

"I'm going in the house. It's late." She paused at the front door and added, "But if I change my mind, which corner?"

"The one between here and my apartment."

"Don't hold your breath," she laughed, disappearing inside.

I strolled down to the corner and waited under the streetlight. Five minutes later Susan appeared. "I want you to know that I sneaked out of the house, using the back door," she confessed, taking my hand.

"You're still ashamed to admit you have anything to do with me," I kidded.

"It's too much fun this way."

It was almost midnight when I walked Susan back to her home. "I didn't know being crazy could be so much fun," she said. "However, sometime we're going to have to come out in the open."

"I think I prefer being discreet."

CHAPTER TWENTY-ONE

"What did you think of the fireside?" I asked JB the next morning as he dragged in late for breakfast. I had gotten up and fixed toast, scrambled eggs and juice for both of us.

He pulled the corners of his mouth down, pretended to frown and then smiled. "It felt all right. I haven't done anything like it for awhile." He shook his head. "Maybe I'm just kidding myself, though."

"Why do you have to be kidding yourself? You used to do that kind of thing all the time, and you didn't trick yourself into liking it. Give the Church a chance, JB."

"The Church isn't the one with the problem." He turned to me and quickly changed the subject. "You and Susan seemed to hit it off all right. I've never seen her like that."

"Oh, I guess we were both in a crazy mood. How are things going with you and Cami?"

He considered the question. "We had a good talk last night. In fact, we've had some pretty serious talks the last few nights." He set his fork down and brushed at some bread crumbs about his plate. "I know what I want," JB answered slowly. "The question is whether I can have it."

"You can have whatever you work for."

JB shot a quick, defensive look in my direction. "It doesn't have anything to do with what I work for. It's just where I am."

After work I wandered over to the Hardaways'. I had a chance to visit with Susan, but there was always someone else there, Teresa, one of her brothers or Cami. In fact, I stopped by the Hardaways' Tuesday and Wednesday also and the same kind of thing happened. It wasn't that I didn't like my association with Susan's family. I liked them. But I wanted to be with Susan. Alone!

Wednesday evening Susan and I were sitting on her front

lawn when Teresa came bounding out of the house with a football. Without warning she tossed me the ball. "Help me practice my receiving," she stated. "I'm going to play football when I get to junior high. I can play way better than most of the guys. There's no reason they should get all the playing time."

While Susan watched, I played quarterback and Teresa zigzagged about the front lawn trying different passing patterns and catching most of the balls I threw. That's how we were when Tyson Ethington pulled up. As he stepped from his car, I waved and lobbed a pass to Teresa. Susan pushed up from the lawn and strolled down to meet him. The two of them visited by the car a moment and then they wandered down the street.

Teresa was completely indifferent to Tyson until he and Susan were out of earshot, then she bounced over to where I stood poised to throw another pass. "I told you that I thought Tyson and Susan were getting serious. I wonder if he's going to give her a ring."

"Isn't that just a little premature?"

"You mean immature?" She shrugged. "Maybe but they're probably dumb enough to do it anyway." She studied me a moment and then added, "You know, Jacob, I think if you had showed up here sooner, before Susan got all sick over Tyson Ethington, she might have gone for you. She's nicer to you now. You're a lot younger than her, but when a girl gets as old as Susan, she can't be too picky."

"And choosing me would certainly mean that she wasn't picky at all, that she didn't have a bit of discriminating taste."

"Huh?"

I laughed. "Nothing. Run out for a pass and get your mind back on the game."

Fifteen minutes later Susan and Tyson returned. Tyson said good-bye to Susan and then waved to Teresa and me. Climbing into his car, he pulled away. Susan returned to where she had been sitting, which was a few feet from where I was tossing touchdown passes to Teresa. She was quietly reflective for a moment and then she commented so only I could hear. "I told him I needed some time and space."

"How did he take it?"

"I didn't tell him about you."

"That's what I figured because he waved to me when he left. Like I was just an old family friend."

Not being able to get the private time with Susan that I wanted, I decided to try something new. Thursday afternoon I had to pick up some materials in Salt Lake. On my way back I stopped at a small floral shop and picked up three roses in a small crystal vase. Susan had told me where she worked so I found her insurance office on Washington Boulevard and personally delivered them.

She wasn't expecting me and was working at her computer when I came into the office. I came up behind her and set the flowers on the corner of her desk. "Jacob," she gasped when she saw the flowers and then me, "what are you doing here?" She smiled, looking around.

"The ladies up front said I could stay as long as I talked insurance." I pulled up a chair and sat down.

"Talking insurance might get a little expensive for you."

I shook my head. "Not if I just talk and don't buy." She reached out and took my hand. "What do you say we set up an appointment later on. Let's do dinner tonight and catch a movie. Something informal. Have you ever had jumbo shrimp at the Utah Noodle?"

"No, but it sounds good."

"How long will it take you to be ready to go?"

"Six-thirty?" I nodded. "You don't think we're making anyone suspicious, do you?"

I grinned and shook my head. "You're way too old for me."

Susan bit down on her lower lip to hold back the laugh. "I'll see you at six-thirty." She thought for a moment. "Do you think we need to sneak off so we don't arouse suspicions? After all, we don't want people thinking you're getting serious with an older woman. And I don't want people thinking I'm going out with a young boy."

"Maybe we'd better meet at the park," I suggested huskily. "But," I added, "whatever you do, don't bring that lousy bike of yours. And let's leave Teresa home. I don't think we need a chaperone."

"Six-thirty at the park then," she whispered and winked.

I squeezed her hand, stood and spoke loud enough so the two ladies up front could hear me. "Well, Miss Hardaway, that helps me understand that insurance policy a lot better. Thanks so much for your time."

"Sir," one of the ladies spoke as I started for the door. I stopped and turned. "The flowers aren't necessary when you're talking business," she said very seriously. Then she smiled warmly. "Come back again when you can stay longer. And you won't even have to talk insurance."

I grinned and nodded. "I'll do that."

That evening at six-thirty I was sitting on a park bench in the Huntsville park watching two pigeons clean up a popcorn spill left by some earlier picnickers. I was excited to the point of nervousness, not nervous to be with Susan but nervous that she wouldn't appear soon enough.

I spotted her approaching the park about the same time she saw me. I didn't take my eyes off her. She strolled casually toward me. When she reached the park bench, she sat down on the opposite end without saying anything. For a moment we both sat there, trying hard not to laugh.

"Should I have brought my dark glasses, trench coat and hat?" I asked, without looking in her direction.

"I don't speak to strangers who wait for unsuspecting young women."

Standing slowly, I looked about me without glancing in Susan's direction. Casually I sauntered to the end of the bench where she sat with her legs crossed and her arms folded. Dropping down next to her, I put my arm around her shoulders and pulled her close to me. "Actually, I'd just as soon stay here all evening with you as long as you won't scream and make a nuisance of yourself."

She began to giggle. "I think I prefer a little more privacy."

"Let's go then," I said, standing and pulling her up with me. "You look beautiful," I commented. "I couldn't take my eyes off of you as you came across the park."

"I was rather taken by the stranger on the park bench. I want you to know that I usually don't run off with strange men I meet in the park." She laughed. "I'm not sure if Huntsville could handle a rumor like that."

I chuckled. "JB offered to let me take his Firebird. I should have brought it. That would get the tongues of Huntsville wagging. They'd think he was stepping out with Cami's older sister."

"The more we talk about this, the more I think we better get out of town as soon as possible. I didn't even tell Daddy where I was going. Not exactly. I know they don't suspect I'm with you."

Susan and I went to dinner at the Utah Noodle, but when it was time to go to the movie, we decided against it. Neither one of us was interested in sitting through a movie. We chose to take a ride instead, visiting about our growing up years. We came to understand how much we were alike, how our feelings, beliefs and goals were intertwined.

It was late when we returned to Huntsville. "I don't think I'll drop you off at the park," I teased as we pulled into town. "Even knowing there's a chance someone will recognize me sneaking around your place tonight, I want to make sure you get home safe and sound."

"I think I can sneak in without anyone seeing me."

I took her hand as we pulled up in front of her house. "The night goes by too fast. We're going to have to do it again."

"You won't have to twist my arm."

"Some of my old missionary companions are getting together for a picnic tomorrow in Orem. Will you come with me?"

"Will they razz you about running around with one of those old sister missionaries?"

I smiled. "Not when they see you. They might drool a little bit." I shook my head.

Saturday morning I left with Susan for Orem before JB crawled out of bed. Susan's family wasn't up either. As I joined my missionary companions and their dates at the park in Orem, I introduced everybody to Susan. She was gracious, friendly and confident. Rusty Thomas, one of the companions I had had shortly after entering Mexico, smiled at me after the introductions were made and commented in Spanish, "She wasn't the girl you were waiting for, was she?" he said, trying to embarrass me.

"I wasn't waiting for a girl," I returned in Spanish. "I was hoping to find one like this one."

"You're lucky. You did really well. She's good looking. Does she have a sister?"

I grinned. "She is, isn't she?" I responded again in Spanish. "She does have a sister, but don't you have someone?" I nodded to his date.

"I'd like to see what your girl's sister is like."

"You'll have to ask Susan."

Turning to Susan, who had been sitting very quietly, amused by Rusty's comments, I said, still speaking Spanish, "Do you think your sister Cami would consider going out with a guy like Rusty?"

Susan smiled and in impressive Spanish replied, "I think she's pretty serious with your brother, isn't she?"

Rusty's eyes widened and his face turned a deep red. "Maybe we'd better stick to English," he stammered, abandoning his Spanish.

Susan fit in perfectly with the group. She joked freely with my old companions, both in English and Spanish. She made the experience a fun one for all of us. It was as though she had been part of this group from our old missionary days in Mexico.

After leaving the park, Susan and I drove up Provo Canyon and took the cut off to Sundance and drove over the Alpine Loop. We stopped at the summit and took a short hike through the trees and the summer grass and wildflowers.

We found a fallen log and stopped to rest. "It's so beautiful and peaceful up here. It reminds me so much of the hills around Huntsville," Susan commented softly, leaning against me as I put my arm around her. "I'd love to have a little cabin up here."

"It wouldn't be much good in the winter."

"Oh, I'd especially love it in the winter," she sighed. "We

could build a blazing fire and curl up in a quilt and read a book or just sit and talk. No interruptions."

"You mean you're inviting *me*?"

She leaned up and kissed me on the cheek. "Maybe. If you're nice."

Susan and I had dinner in Salt Lake at a little Mexican restaurant on State Street. We walked around Temple Square and then walked up to the State Capitol Building on the hill. It was growing dark by then and we seemed to have the place to ourselves. I didn't want the day to end. It was as though we were catching up on a long absence and being apart was just too frustrating.

I finally took her home a little before midnight. The porch light was on, but the rest of the house was dark. I kissed her gently on the lips. Quickly she pushed away and held up her hand. "Just one moment." She opened the front door a couple of inches, reached in and turned off the porch light. "Now we won't be putting on a demonstration for the whole neighborhood and sending rumors rushing about the streets of Huntsville."

After kissing her, I opened the front door and she disappeared inside. I stepped off the front steps and headed across the lawn to the Bug.

CHAPTER TWENTY-TWO

The next morning I shaved, showered and got ready for church. Before leaving the apartment, JB came into the kitchen dressed in a shirt and tie and Docker slacks! I almost choked.

"You going to church?" I asked, trying to cover my surprise.

"I thought I would."

"You picking Cami up?"

"She doesn't know." He felt nervous and awkward. "I've never gone to church with her," he explained, wetting his lips. "I've gone to church socials and things. The fireside last Sunday was the first...well, meeting that I've been to."

I cleared my throat. "How long's it been since you been to church?"

He turned away. "I've gone a few times, in places where they don't know me." He shook his head. "It's always been..." He shrugged and took a deep breath and turned back to me. "It's always been uncomfortable."

"That's because you haven't gone enough," I suggested.

He shrugged. "I decided last night, after I dropped Cami off, that I was going today." He pulled his car keys from his pocket. "I'll drive."

"I'm glad you're going."

"I wish I were," he muttered. Then he smiled plaintively. "Do you mind if I make a suggestion?"

"Go ahead."

"Leave the earring here."

He considered the suggestion and then chuckled. Reaching up with both hands, he removed the stud earring and set it on top of the fridge. "That probably won't change anything," he commented lightly.

"It might make some other people more comfortable, though."

The prelude music was still playing when JB and I stepped into the chapel. I spotted the Hardaways in the middle section about six rows back. Susan and Cami were on the end of the row closest to us. There was a six-foot empty section on the end of the bench.

Cami looked up and spotted JB. At first I was afraid she was going to fall off the bench, and then I wondered if she was going to re-enact the passionate embrace that she had tried on me at our first meeting. JB sat next to her, and I sat on the end of the bench. Cami took his hand and arm and squeezed. She was smiling and tears were on her cheeks as she looked toward the pulpit.

After sacrament meeting, Susan hurried to set up her gospel doctrine class. I walked down the hall with Cami and JB. Between the chapel and the Relief Society room JB was stopped a dozen times by different people telling him how happy they were that he was there. I could tell he was moved but still uncomfortable. He experienced the same reception when he went to priesthood meeting.

Cami invited both JB and me to dinner. Denton was visiting Trudy and her family in Salt Lake so dinner ended up being a rather casual affair with the kids, JB and me. JB and I spent the better part of Sunday with the Hardaways, but there wasn't anything romantic. It was all very relaxed and casual, more like a family gathering, and JB and I were old family friends. JB seemed to relax, which reminded me of his old self when we were younger.

The rest of the week ended up about like that comfortable Sunday. It was as thought JB and I were informally adopted into the family. We had home evening there Monday. Teresa made a special request to be in charge of the lesson. It was on marriage. There was nothing subtle about her.

Tuesday evening JB and I went over to the Hardaways' and helped Justin and Brett change the oil and filters on all four vehicles. The whole family eventually got into a service mood and joined in washing and vacuuming the cars, which ended up in a wild water fight as darkness settled.

Wednesday evening the three girls surprised JB and me by bringing us dinner, which we ate in our basement apartment. It was their way of saying thanks to us for working on the cars the night before. After we ate and cleaned up, Teresa talked us all into playing UNO and proceeded to beat all of us soundly.

Friday evening Denton invited Trudy and her two kids to drive with us above Huntsville and have a cookout. We feasted on burnt hot dogs and blackened marshmallows and endured Teresa's horrible ghost stories, which she insisted on sharing with the family, hoping to send us all into blood-chilling shock. Eventually, sitting around the dying campfire, Justin and Brett brought up the Hogle Zoo, reminiscing about visits there when they were younger, and Teresa cried "deprived child," declaring that she had never been to the zoo. Not only did she finally get Denton to commit to take her some day, she talked him into taking her the next day as well as the entire family, Trudy, her kids, JB and me.

Saturday morning all ten of us squeezed into the Suburban and journeyed to the zoo to appease Teresa. Although it was a hectic day, and I got stuck in the backseat between Teresa and Justin while Susan sat in the seat in front of me, I had a wildly entertaining time. Susan and I did snatch some time together wandering around the zoo and eating at Liberty Park. We finished the day by going to Temple Square, which was Cami's suggestion. She said that she wanted JB to feel the wonderful spirit there. She wasn't much more subtle than Teresa.

JB and I finally returned to the apartment around ten o'clock, and we were exhausted. We both showered and then crashed for a few minutes on the sofa and overstuffed chair in our cramped living room space. We chuckled about the activities of the day, and then JB became serious.

"Could I ask you a couple of questions?" he ventured cautiously. "Church questions," he clarified.

Not since our high school days had JB and I ever really had a gospel discussion. Back then we both talked, but now he was speaking as though I were the authority. I felt strange in that role.

He sat forward on the edge of the sofa and stared at the floor. "You've been on a mission and stuff," he began, "and I haven't paid much attention to those kinds of things. Not during the last two or three years." He reflected a moment. "What is there to repentance? I mean, what does it cover?"

The question took me completely by surprise. Repentance seemed like such a basic, simple principle, and yet here my own brother, who had grown up in the same home as I, didn't understand it. I knew this was a delicate time because the wrong word, the wrong tone, the wrong explanation could turn JB away, turn him away at a time when he was finally reaching out.

I cleared my throat. "Well, repentance covers about everything. That's why we have it. If you do something wrong, then you can repent and through the atonement you're forgiven."

"I know what it can do," he said somewhat impatiently. "I want to know what it covers. I know it doesn't cover everything."

"It covers everything in your life, JB."

JB looked up and studied me a moment. "You don't know that, Jacob."

He was right. I'd judged him. Trying to recover from my blunder, I smiled and said, "Well, you haven't killed anybody, have you?"

JB continued to look across the room at me. "This isn't a confession," he answered. "I just want to know what's covered."

"Murder isn't," I said simply. "And denying the Holy Ghost. Besides those two, everything's covered." We were both silent a moment, and I added, "Now just because something's covered doesn't mean it's not difficult to repent. It all depends on the transgression. It's not just a matter of saying, `I want to repent.'"

"How do you know?"

I considered that a moment. I touched my chest. "Most of the time you know right here. If you're honest with yourself, you just know that one thing is more serious than another." I coughed. "If you figure it's serious, you go to the bishop. You tell him. He's the judge."

JB smiled faintly. "I haven't talked to a bishop, not like that, for a good long..." He shook his head. "Forever, it seems."

"Maybe you should."

"I don't know whether I could. Especially if it didn't make any difference," he added quietly, standing up.

"Cami loves you, JB. There isn't anything she wouldn't do for you."

"Sure there is, Jacob. You told me so yourself. She won't marry me the way I am." Without waiting for my reply, he went to his room, closed the door and went to bed.

For a long time I remained on the sofa staring at the place where JB had sat a few minutes earlier. I didn't know if I'd helped him. I shook my head. I didn't even know where he needed help. However, I knew intuitively that I couldn't force him. If he ever decided to open up, it would be his decision. I just needed to make certain I was ready.

Sunday morning JB was waiting for me to go to church. "I'll give you a ride," he said as I came down the hall cinching up my tie. "I told Cami I'd pick her up this morning too."

"She knows you're going?" He nodded. I smiled. "I'll walk. The two of you need to be together."

I didn't think JB could have chosen a better Sunday to attend church with Cami. The bishop spoke in sacrament meeting about the Savior's love for all of us, about his mercy and how the atonement embodied all of that.

Susan's lesson was on Alma the Younger's sincere, honest repentance. It was a beautiful lesson. Frank Norman spoke up and attempted to derail her line of instruction by pointing out that the Church was full of people who went through the motions but were living a lie because they hadn't repented and that some of them might be beyond repentance. Susan didn't lose her composure, though, and very adeptly she addressed Frank's objections and still imbued her lesson with the beautiful truths of the atonement.

It was as though everyone there that day understood what JB needed and delivered it to him in a most loving, sincere and insightful manner. I felt confident that after this day JB would look at things in a different manner. I was correct, but I wasn't prepared for what that way would be.

JB and I went to the Hardaways' for dinner after services. JB was quiet throughout the meal. The happy, comfortably relaxed JB whom I had observed over the past two weeks was absent. He seemed distracted, even hurt. His behavior confirmed to me that the meetings that day had a moving impact on him.

After dinner Cami and JB went into the backyard and talked. They were there a long time. I remained inside and visited with the rest of the family. Around four JB left and Cami came into the house. I didn't get a good look at her as she went up the stairs, but she seemed upset. I thought I detected tears, but I couldn't be sure. Tears could mean a lot of things.

In the late afternoon Teresa persuaded Justin, Susan and me to retire to the backyard and play a quiet game of crochet. At least it was supposed to be quiet and subdued, which I found was impossible when you played with Teresa, who turned everything into a wild, exhilarating competition. We had to play several rounds until she won, which Justin graciously and furtively allowed her to do so that we could finally quit and have popcorn and sodas before Susan left for an evening meeting. I volunteered to walk with her over to the church.

"My family is having a mini-reunion this Saturday in the park. Daddy's two brothers and his sister and their families will be here. I think Daddy is planning to make an announcement."

"About Trudy and him?"

She smiled and nodded, strolling along beside me. "I just picked up on something he said yesterday in Salt Lake. I know he's getting serious."

I laughed. "I think he's been serious a long time. Even before he met her. I suspect he would have done something earlier, but he didn't want to appear as though he were rushing things."

"Maybe," she sighed, "but I think everything will be out of the bag Saturday." She turned to me. "You have to be there."

"Can I pick you up?"

"Of course."

"I mean, really pick you up, in broad daylight for everyone to see."

"Well, I don't know about everybody, but whoever is at the

park can surely see." She nudged me with her elbow. "You don't like this secret romance?" she asked, laughing.

"Well," I started slowly, pushing my hands into my pockets and looking about me as we walked, "most of the time it's not too bad, but whenever we do something with your family, I always get stuck on the opposite side of the room or the car from you."

"I think they're afraid we'll get into a fight or something if we get too close to each other."

"We need to disabuse them of that notion," I said stiffly and then grinned. "We don't fight like we used to." I shook my head, chuckling. "And I still get the impression that Teresa is bound and determined to line me up with Cami."

"Teresa," Susan said kindly, wagging her head, "she's the one who's going to be most disappointed. She has been so sure things were going to work out differently."

"Oh, somehow I think Teresa will adjust really well. I think I know Teresa better than some of the rest of you."

Susan looked at me. "What *do* you two talk about?"

"I'm sworn to secrecy."

CHAPTER TWENTY-THREE

I didn't return to the apartment immediately after walking Susan over to the church. I wandered around town for a while, feeling calm and peaceful as I considered how the summer had progressed.

I returned to the apartment as the sun was disappearing behind the western hills. JB's Firebird was parked in front, but the lights were off in the apartment. I assumed that JB had decided to go to bed early. Slipping inside, I was careful not to let the screen door clatter shut, although there wasn't much I could do about the annoying whine from the hinges and the metal spring.

I flipped the light on, just long enough to get my bearings and make certain there was nothing in the middle of the floor before I navigated across the room to the hall. I started across the room and reached back and turned off the light, but as I did, something caught my attention out of the corner of my eye. I stopped in the blackness, sensing something amiss. It was then that I caught the distinct, troubling stench of alcohol.

Slowly I groped for the light switch. I turned it on and glanced into the living room. JB sat slumped on the couch, his face stony and bitter, his eyes staring at me angrily. In front of him on the coffee table was an open bottle of partially consumed Jack Daniels.

For a long moment we stared at each other. JB glared at me from the couch, his eyes and posture challenging a comment from me, daring me to object. Soon a smoldering ember of anger prodded my tongue. "Straight to the Jack Daniels," I remarked bitingly. "You don't even build up to it with a couple of cold beers."

"Let me worry about what I drink and don't drink." I thought there was just the slightest slur to his words, and I knew that anything he said would be tainted by the whiskey.

I moved toward him, glaring down at the whiskey bottle. "I suppose if you want to drink, that's up to you. This probably isn't your first time."

"It's not."

"But," I added, my gaze shifting from the bottle to JB, "why don't you drink it someplace else?"

"Someplace else?" he snapped angrily, his eyes flashing sharply. "This is my place, or have you forgotten?"

"I live here too."

"Because I invited you. So if you don't like what I drink, then find the door. I'm not begging you to stay."

I couldn't understand what was happening. After all, JB had started going to church. Cami's hopes were up. This was like slapping her in the face. I could feel my heart pound in my chest, and my breathing became deep and heavy. "This became my apartment the day I started paying half the rent. It doesn't make a bit of difference who was here first. And I don't appreciate having some smelly drunk fouling up the place."

JB's lips curled into a grin that looked more like a snarl. He reached for the bottle, held it up to me and then took a long, hard drink for my benefit. I wanted to slap the bottle from his hand. I decided instead to shame him. "This is a nice conclusion to a Sabbath day, after you've taken Cami to church and made her believe you're doing something with your life. She'd be really impressed if she could see you now."

He set the bottle down, leaning back and closing his eyes.

"I thought things had changed," I muttered, cuttingly. "I thought you'd decided to crawl out of the gutter, not find a deeper hole to wallow in."

"Nobody asked what you thought," he retorted hoarsely without opening his eyes. "I've always been something out of the gutter to you. Ever since Leti Trujillo. That's why you never figured I was good enough for Cami."

"You don't care what Cami thinks?" I scoffed, disgusted with him.

"It doesn't make much difference what anybody thinks."

"I get sick just looking at you."

His eyes opened. "You like it from up there, don't you?" he accused. "Looking down that holier-than-thou nose of yours. You're so high and mighty. You've never tried the view from this end, have you? You get a different perspective from here."

"I don't have to wallow in your filth to appreciate where I am."

"Where you are?" he taunted. "And where are you? Up on your self-made pedestal, looking down on the rest of us scum. You're plenty proud of where you are. And you're glad that nobody else can climb to where you are because you don't want it to get crowded up there. You like your exclusive status."

"If I'm up there," I argued, "you could be there just as easily as I can. But you won't get there sucking on that whiskey bottle or lying in bed Sunday mornings."

He laughed sardonically. "For your information, Mr. Righteousness, this bottle isn't keeping me down." He shrugged. "It just gives me a little comfort while you pass judgment. You like being the proud judge, don't you?"

"You're drunk," I muttered, turning away. "It's bad enough smelling you without having to listen to you too."

"I'm not finished," JB snarled, pushing himself up from the couch. I stopped and turned while he approached. He was steady on his feet. He reached into his shirt pocket and pulled out a small roll of bills. He thrust them into my face. "There's your half of the rent money for this month. All of it. Take it and get out. This is my place."

For a moment I looked at the money, then at JB. "This is my place too. I'm not crazy about the booze." I shrugged. "But I'm staying. I like the work. I like the people here in Huntsville."

"You mean you're waiting for Cami," he flared. "You're waiting for her to dump me so you can have your turn. Ever since you showed up, you've had your greedy eyes on her. That's why you'd like to call her over. You'd like her to stick her nose up at me like you do. Then you could march off with her, all smug in your piety."

"You don't know what you're talking about. And it's not just because you're drunk."

JB tossed the money in my face. "Take it and get out!" he shouted.

"I'm staying," I said steadily, struggling to remain calm. "I could throw you out. And it wouldn't even be a struggle." I started to turn. As I did, JB reached out and grabbed my arm just above the elbow. Jerking me around, he stood in my face. "I don't want to get rough with you, but I want you out of here."

"You're drunk," I responded barely above a whisper.

Out of nowhere his hand flashed and smashed across my face. The burn and shock of the blow staggered me, and I stumbled backward. There was an immediate surge of anger. My first impulse was to charge at him with my fists flying, but I fought down my anger and struggled for calm control. Slowly I reached up and touched my cheek. "I'm not going to fight you, JB. But I'm going to stay." I turned and went down the hall to my room.

For a while I sat on the bed and stared at the wall. I heard muffled voices, and I wondered who was here; then I realized that JB was talking on the phone. I heard him return the receiver. A moment later he was dialing again and talking. I wondered if he was talking to Cami.

Pushing up from the bed, I went into the bathroom to brush my teeth. I looked in the mirror. The red lines of JB's fingers were still clearly evident on my cheek. My anger had cooled and finally dissipated, replaced with baffling confusion.

When I returned to my room, the bills JB had thrown at me were scattered across my pillow. I slowly retrieved them to return them to him. As I turned, I found JB leaning in the doorway. We stared at each other a moment without speaking. Some of the hardness had melted from his face. "The money's yours. You'll need it. I'm leaving first thing in the morning. You can stay. The rent's paid up through the end of August. That's my gift to you."

"I don't need you to do me any favors," I said, holding the money out, my anger returning.

"Maybe I want to do you a favor," he muttered submissively. "Don't be so proud to accept a little help. I was going to help you some on your mission." He shook his head without taking his eyes from me. "I didn't. This is my contribution to your mission." He sighed and looked away. "I'm sorry I hit you," he said hoarsely. "You didn't deserve that. You didn't deserve the things I said." His voice broke ever so slightly at the end. "That slap was really for me. I'm the one who deserves it. I'll be out of here soon."

"Where you going to find another place up here?" I challenged.

"I won't be staying up here," he responded, turning and shuffling back to his room. "I'm going back to Arizona. I've already called Roger. And I called my old boss in Arizona. He says there's a spot for me there on one of his crews. You can have this whole valley to yourself, including Cami. She's liked you all along. And you deserve her."

I watched him enter his room and close the door. I had a hard, hurting knot inside me. I forgot the Jack Daniels. I forgot his cutting words and his sharp, unexpected slap across the face. I remembered instead a time when we had gone to visit our Uncle Wesley. He was well to do. He told us that we could both have our own room during our week's stay with him. We declined. Instead we took turns sleeping on the floor during that entire week because we wanted to be in the same room together. Now we couldn't stand to be in the same house with each other. Not even in the same town.

I looked down at the money in my hand. I didn't want the money, but I sensed that JB wanted me to have it. Needed me to have it. Without any strings attached. I dropped the bills on my dresser and glanced through my open door to JB's closed one. Taking a tenuous breath, I walked across the hall and knocked.

There was a pause. "It's not locked."

I turned the knob and pushed the door open. JB was lying on his bed staring up at the ceiling. "Thanks for the money," I said gently. "I'm sorry about anything I said out there. I make a lousy judge. I don't know what your life's like."

"Everything you said was true."

"JB," I ventured uneasily, "maybe I have looked down my nose at you. But I've wanted you to be..." I groped for the right word.

"Like you," JB filled in. He turned and looked at me. There wasn't anger in his eyes, only a deep-down sorrow. "I can't be like you, Jacob. I wish I could. I can't."

"Nobody wants you to be me."

He smiled ruefully. "Oh, yes they do. They want me to be a clean-cut, returned missionary, go-to-church-every-Sunday Jacob Matthews." He shook his head. "It works for you."

"You can do that too."

JB heaved a heavy sigh, looked up at the ceiling and closed his eyes momentarily. "That's where you're wrong," he said, opening his eyes again. "I made myself believe they'd work for me too. That's why I went to church today and last week. I went through the motions. All week I did. I almost went down and cut my hair and shaved off my mustache. But nothing else changed. Except I saw how far I was from where everybody wants me to be."

"Cami believes in you."

He nodded. "And that's the pain of it all, Jacob. I was a hypocrite today. I could keep being a hypocrite. I could even convince Cami I was like you." He touched his chest with his clenched fist. "But in here I'd know it was a lie. I can't do that to Cami. I love her too much to do that to her."

"You can change. It won't be easy. It isn't easy for anyone. But you have to be willing to try."

He laughed, a sad, poignant laugh, one that later haunted me. "Oh, Jacob, you don't know how willing I am. Not long ago I told you about crossing that line of no return. Well, Jacob, I've crossed that line. Oh, how I wish I never had. I've thought a thousand times how I might go back and change just a few things, things that would have kept me from that dark line. But you don't retrace those steps."

"I don't know what you've done, JB, but you haven't crossed that line. JB, I haven't led a perfect life. No one has. That's what repentance is for. That's what I spent two years of my life doing, showing people in Mexico how they could cross back over that line and be clean. I know it can be done. *You* can do it."

He was quiet a moment and then he asked, "How well do you know the story of King David?"

I thought a moment and then shrugged. "I know it, I suppose."

"I don't know the scriptures very well. I haven't gone to

them much. But I know David's story. He had everything. Then there was Bathsheba."

"Bathsheba wasn't his downfall," I pointed out.

"I know. Even after he committed adultery, he could've turned back, but then he crossed the line, when he sent Uriah to his death. And did David feel bad? He suffered. He mourned. He wished a thousand times that he hadn't crossed that line, but his tears and sorrow couldn't change things. I wish I didn't know David's story so well."

"I don't understand."

"I've crossed the line," he said plainly.

"I can't believe that. That's just an excuse. Does Cami know you're giving up?"

He nodded slowly. "I told her this afternoon. I had to. I couldn't keep living a lie. There are a lot of things I'm not, but I don't have to be a hypocrite. I can spare myself that one sin."

"Does she know you're leaving?"

"I said it was a possibility."

We were both silent for a moment. JB was the first to speak. "I'd like to ask a favor of you."

"Sure," I responded willingly.

He hesitated. It was difficult for him to speak. "You've liked Cami. From the very first day you met her. She's that way. Everybody likes Cami. Once you told me that if I wouldn't take Cami the way she deserved to be taken, then I needed to step aside so someone else could." He paused. "I can't do for Cami what she deserves. You can."

I thought for a moment before responding. "Do you suppose there's any reason to maybe run something like this past Cami?" I smiled, shaking my head.

"Don't worry, she likes you."

"There's one other small detail."

"What's that?"

"I'm not interested anymore."

"What?" He said it like I had made the most preposterous statement. "Nice try."

"I'm not saying that I don't think Cami's a great girl. She is. She's a wonderful friend." I shook my head. "But I don't have any romantic interests there. Not anymore."

"Maybe once I'm out of the picture you'll revive some of those romantic interests."

"She'll always be a good friend. Nothing more. Don't leave Cami for me." Turning, I left him lying on the bed.

CHAPTER TWENTY-FOUR

JB was still in bed the next morning when I was ready to leave for work. Nervously I tapped on his bedroom door. There was a long silence. I was about to knock again when he mumbled, "What do you need?"

Pushing open the door, I stuck my head into the room. "You're serious about not going to work today?" I was hoping that he had just slept in and would come firing out of his bed in a panic.

"Roger knows I'm not coming. I'll be packing today. I'll be out of here at noon or a little after."

I hesitated. "Are you sure about this, JB? I mean, yesterday was a lousy day."

"It wasn't just yesterday."

"You can work things out. Take some time to think things over."

"I've been thinking things over for a long time, even before I came to Huntsville. This isn't something that just popped into my head last night."

"So I won't see you after work?"

"I'll be on the road by then."

I stood there for a while, fidgeting. "So this is good-bye for a while?"

He breathed deeply and then exhaled slowly. "I guess so. You know," he added before I could speak, "we've had some rocky times, but..." He forced a grin. "Well, I'm glad we had it. And the last two weeks were better." He shook his head and looked away. "Except for me popping you last night," he said contritely. "Is your face all right?"

"A little cut in my mouth. I'm all right. I probably needed it."

"No you didn't. You haven't needed any of the garbage

I've dumped on you." Kicking off his sheet, he sat on the edge of the bed. We stared at each other. "You better get out of here or you're not going to have a job. And I don't think I can get you on in Phoenix." He smiled wryly, stood and held out his hand. "See you around, Jacob."

I ignored his outstretched hand, stepped over and hugged him. We stood there for a moment, squeezing each other in the first brotherly embrace that we'd shared since our football and wrestling days; then we relaxed the hug and I stepped back. "Good luck," I said softly, backed out of the room and left.

The rest of the day I thought of JB, worried and fretted over him, but I was at a loss as to what I could do. I don't know how many silent prayers I offered that day, hoping for some inspiration.

In the afternoon I went to a lumber yard in Ogden to pick up some doors. I was unfamiliar with the place and stepped into the front office for directions. "James? James Matthews?"

I found myself face to face with the receptionist. For a fleeting moment I thought I was looking at Leti Trujillo, an older, changed Leti, but the features were so strikingly similar. My mouth dropped open.

"Is that you, James?" she asked again, smiling and coming toward me. I sensed an impulse on her part to hug me, but seeing my surprise and uncertainty, she hesitated. "You don't remember me, do you?" She laughed. "Just the other evening I was thinking of you."

"Leti?" My voice was an incredulous whisper as though someone had played a wild, inconceivable joke on me.

She laughed again, and as she did, I could see it wasn't Leti Trujillo. "You remember me. Victoria, Leti's sister. You better remember me," she warned with a grin. "As many times as you and Leti stopped by my place."

"I'm Jacob, not JB...I mean, James," I stammered, still stunned and perplexed, remembering that Leti had always called JB by his first name. She had thought James sounded distinguished.

The smile on Victoria's face dimmed in obvious disappointment. "Oh, I thought you were James."

"No, I dropped by to pick up some things for Franco Construction."

"Oh." She stepped back. "What do you need?" she asked helpfully, retreating from her friendly stance to a more professional one.

"I came to pick up some doors," I said, groping in my shirt pocket for a purchase requisition while still studying Victoria. She had short, black curly hair and dark eyes. Her face was narrow, smooth and pretty.

"Oh, you're the one picking up the doors and frames." I nodded. "I'll see if they're ready." She picked up the phone and spoke to someone in the yard. "It'll be ten minutes," she explained, hanging up. "You can have a chair if you'd like." She nodded to three padded but simple black chairs along the outside wall in front of the office counter. I didn't move, remaining just inside the door, while Victoria returned to her desk. "How is your brother?" she inquired, losing the professional tone, becoming more friendly again. "It's been years since I've seen him."

"He's okay," I stammered, my mind still jumbled.

"I always liked James," she said, smiling at me. She became a little more serious as she added, "You were always a little more..." She hesitated, then smiled to break the bite of her remark. "Well, a little more stuck on yourself. I knew you before I knew James."

"We knew each other?"

"We had trig together as juniors." She shrugged. "Only first semester. I dropped out."

"Oh, I think I remember. You were..." I stopped as the hazy recollection returned.

"Yes, I was pregnant. I got married."

The memories became more clear. I remembered a painted, defiant but pretty girl in my trig class. It was no wonder that I had not associated the Victoria before me with that girl. They were such opposites. I didn't know what to say. She sensed my awkwardness and tried to help. "But that's behind me. I had my second little girl eight months ago." She took a small golden-framed picture from her desk, stood and handed it to me. It was a picture of Victoria, her two young daughters and a blond handsome guy who seemed very much in love with these three beautiful girls. The picture was taken in front of the Ogden Temple.

"Is this your husband?" Nothing made any sense. I didn't know who she had married her junior year, but I was certain this guy wasn't the one.

"My first husband didn't stick around," she explained simply. "He wasn't even there when Jessica was born."

"I'm sorry."

"No need to be. I don't have any regrets. I met Troy a couple of months after my divorce. He had just returned from his mission in Guatemala." She smiled. "I had never liked Mormons. Except James," she quickly added. "There was something about James that intrigued me. He had a certain goodness. It wasn't put on. It was just there.

"I didn't have very high regard for him after Leti died. The last time I saw him, he was walking out of her funeral mass, and I remember wondering why he wouldn't stay till the end. After all, he had promised to marry Leti.

"But I couldn't ever forget him and the influence he had had on Leti. I guess on me too. She had decided to join the Church. And all the while I thought James had just messed up her mind. But I couldn't completely believe that either. So when I met Troy, I thought of James.

"When I gave the Church a chance, everything fell into place. Troy baptized me. Even though I was divorced with a little girl, he treated me like..." She bit down on her lip and stared out the window. "I think he treated me the way Leti imagined James would have treated her. We were sealed a year later."

I was too dumbfounded to say anything. She laughed happily. "This will probably shock you, but I'm a counselor in my ward Primary presidency. When we were in trig together, you didn't think that would happen. Ever."

"What do you mean James was going to marry Leti?" I blurted out.

Victoria hesitated, reaching for the picture I still held in my hand. She took it. "You didn't know?"

I shook my head, my legs feeling weak and rubbery. Victoria turned away and replaced the picture on the corner of her desk. "It's just as well. She was killed shortly after that."

Dazed, I turned and walked to the window, staring out at the company truck. "I hope I didn't say anything I shouldn't have," Victoria offered worriedly. "You and James were always so close. I just assumed you knew."

I felt a sick heaviness in my stomach as though someone had thrown open a forbidden door, and I was gazing in upon a very personal secret. Now everything leaped into focus.

The phone rang. When Victoria hung up, she said, "They're ready to load the doors. Here's your yard slip and receipt. Just give the yellow copy to Chance. He'll be the big guy in bib overalls on the forklift." She stepped to the counter. "I'm sorry if I said too much."

"No, I'm glad I had a chance to talk, Victoria. I'll tell JB I saw you."

"And tell him thanks for being such a good friend. To both of us." She smiled sincerely. "If he has a chance, have him stop by and see me."

My drive back to Huntsville was something out of a perplexing dream. It was as though Victoria had introduced me to a stranger who turned out to be my brother.

When I arrived at the apartment, JB was still there, putting the last of his things on the front seat. Hurriedly I parked and leaped from the VW. "I was hoping that you'd still be here," I burst out.

He slammed the car door and nodded. "It took me a little longer than I'd figured." He turned and smiled ruefully. "I did a little cleaning too. I didn't realize how dirty I'd let things get." He glanced back toward the house. "It probably isn't cleaned up to your standards," he explained kindly, "but it's better than I've cleaned since I got here." He sucked in a breath of air, brushed at his pants and shirt. "Well, I guess this is it." He held out his hand.

"You're not going to have something to eat first?" I shrugged. "You might as well stay the night and get an early start in the morning."

He shook his head. "I've been snacking all day. I'm fresh. If I get too tired, I'll pull off the road and sleep." He looked away. "I've got a million things racing through my brain. It'll be good to drive and think."

We were quiet for a moment and then I commented casually, "I ran into Victoria Trujillo today. I guess she's not Trujillo any more."

JB turned, his face a mask of shock. "Victoria? Leti's sister?"

I shook my head. "I thought I was looking at Leti. After a minute I could see the difference, but right at first…"

"Victoria was never as pretty as Leti," he cut me off.

"She was pretty today," I came back lightly. "Real pretty."

"No one was as pretty as Leti."

"Well, I didn't know either one very well. I went to pick up those doors and frames. She works in the front office. She thought I was you." I grinned. "She was disappointed when she found out I was just your brother."

"I've been a little afraid to run into Victoria," he remarked.

"She's been baptized."

JB's head jerked around at me. "Victoria?"

"She married a returned missionary. They've been sealed in the temple." I chuckled. "She's in the Primary presidency in her ward. She looks like a sharp girl."

"Victoria Trujillo?"

I nodded.

"Did she say anything about Leti?"

Swallowing, I gnawed lightly on my thumbnail. "She told me a couple of things," I admitted gently. "I'm sorry, JB. I didn't know you were in trouble."

He turned away, stared into the street over the roof of the Firebird. I stepped over to him. "It's all behind you, JB. You don't have to beat yourself with it."

"Beat myself?" he asked, turning to face me. For a long while JB was quiet, staring off into space, but I detected the turmoil that churned within him. "Victoria didn't tell you everything. Maybe she doesn't even know."

"I know you promised to marry Leti." I couldn't look at him when I added, "And I suppose there were some complications there."

JB leaned against the Firebird with his elbows on the roof while he pressed the heels of his palms against his eyes. "Oh, Leti," he said softly. "I always believed she was going to come around. I was the one who showed her something better. You don't know how much she wanted a better life. She really did. Then," he added softly, "I let her down."

"That doesn't mean everything's lost."

He pulled his hands away from his face. A tear broke away and started down his cheek. He quickly wiped it away and tried to blink back the others that threatened. "I meant to tell you. I almost did a few times. I needed somebody to talk to, someone to listen. I didn't need anybody to tell me how wrong I had been. I knew that. I just needed to talk."

"I didn't ever make that very easy, I guess."

He smiled wanly. "Remember when we had the fight in the barn when I almost broke my leg trying to break your head?"

I nodded, thinking back, suddenly ashamed.

"I tried to tell you then."

"But I had too much to say."

"Telling you wouldn't have changed anything."

"I could have understood. Instead of judging. It's not too late, JB."

"Not if it had ended there. It didn't." He breathed in slowly and exhaled in a sudden blast. "Leti had been kind of thick with this other guy when I first met her."

"Marcus Roper," I remarked.

JB nodded. "He was no good, but she kept seeing him. She tried to break things off with him, but he kept pestering her, promising her the moon. And who was I? A dumb high school kid. Then Victoria told me that Leti was expecting." His voice quavered.

"And you told Leti you'd marry her?"

"Sort of. When Victoria first talked to me, more than anything I wanted Marcus to be responsible. That was his style, not mine. I didn't want to get married. Not at seventeen. It wasn't fair. We'd just slipped. All my plans went up in smoke. No mission. No college. No temple marriage.

"I thought of all the things that might happen that would change the circumstances. Marcus could be the father. Leti could miscarry. I could walk away and deny that anything had ever happened. Leti could just disappear."

"Did Leti know how you felt?"

"She was having a hard enough time. But the day before she died, I opened up to her." He shook his head. "I didn't blame her. It wasn't her fault any more than it was mine. In fact, it was more my fault because I knew better. I should have been the one to keep us from falling into that hole. She knew I couldn't go on a mission. Even if she refused to marry me, a mission was out because there was a baby.

"There was only one thing that would correct the problem. And that was if everything disappeared. Leti, the baby, everything. I had even hoped for that," he said, his voice full of emotion, the tears now running down his cheeks. He was no longer trying to force them back. We were having that talk we should have had four years earlier had I been willing to listen.

"I remember thinking that if something happened to Leti, then everything would be all right. I tried to push that thought away, but it kept coming back and seemed like the only escape. I didn't tell her that. I don't remember exactly what I did tell her. She must have suspected, though, sensing what I was pointing to in my own selfish way. So when she took that last ride, she did it at my encouragement. Not from what I said, but what I felt. I guess it was everything I didn't say to Leti that told her I wanted her gone. Any way she possibly could."

"What are you saying?"

"She climbed in her car that night and disappeared. For me. So I could walk away free."

"You don't know that." But even as I denied what JB was telling me, I understood the magnitude of what he was saying.

"She was doing what she thought I wanted, what she thought would help me because I was too cowardly to accept the responsibility for my own actions." JB stared at me, the devastating despair in his eyes. "I didn't drive her into that embankment. But…" He covered his eyes with his hand for a moment and fought back the emotion.

"It's over, JB," I said lamely, knowing even as I said the words that they were empty solace.

"Yes," he responded, his voice cracking, "Leti's proof of that. And I can't take a Cami Hardaway and hope she'll cover up for my foulness. All I do is pull her down and deny her what she deserves."

I didn't respond, but my silence was confirmation enough. He heaved a sigh and pushed himself away from the car. "Since Leti's death I've made my share of mistakes, figuring it didn't matter anymore." He turned back to me, shaking his head. He tried to smile but he couldn't hide the sorrow. "I think of home and what I was taught there. I can't deny those things. They're true even if I've locked myself away from them. I've never repeated what happened with Leti. I've come close with some girls, but there was something inside me that wouldn't let me recross that line."

"That's a good sign, JB. It shows you want to do what's right. Leti said there was a goodness in you. Victoria said the same today."

He laughed sadly, shaking his head. "The only goodness is what I hope for. I dream about being good, but when everything is said and done, it's not there. It's gone. I lost it four years ago."

"I don't believe that, JB."

"I can take satisfaction in something," he said, ignoring my denial. "I've never done anything to Cami that I have to be ashamed of. I haven't gone to church. I haven't done the things that you do. But I haven't done anything to her that I'm ashamed of. She's as clean now as when I first met her. I've never even come close to the line. I've loved her. And now the best thing I can do for her is the hardest thing for me, and that's to walk away. Not just break things off, but walk away completely so she can have her life, so she can reach up instead of crawl down. That's why I'm leaving."

"But, JB, there's a way back for you."

"You don't know how many times I've wished that. I wish I would have married Leti. We'd have made it. Things weren't lost. I know she would've joined the Church. Things would've been hard, but...."

"You don't have any idea how envious I was of you when you went to Mexico." The tears welled in his eyes. "I'd have given anything for that. I still would." He choked back a sudden unexpected sob. "I'd give up the earring, the hair, the beard, the car, the job, everything if it would just make a difference and mean that I could go on. Like you. I suppose that's why it's been so hard to have you back because every time I see you, every time Cami sees you, I'm reminded of what I might have had. I'm reminded of what Leti might have had."

"Have you ever talked to the bishop?"

He smiled wanly. "For what? For confirmation of what I already know? Maybe that's the one sliver of hope I cling to. Maybe there is a chance. But if I went and my worst fears were confirmed, then even that tiny sliver is gone. Maybe that tiny sliver is all that keeps me living. I feel like a guy dying of cancer, and I'm hanging on, hoping someone will come up with the cure. Now you understand why I know David so well. I've read his Psalms and they're not merely words of poetry. They're a picture of my own soul. And not a pleasant picture."

"JB, the gospel and the atonement aren't for just a select few. If the atonement extends to just a few, then it's a horrible illusion. It's for you too, JB, but you have to have faith, faith that you can be healed. You said you feel like the man with cancer waiting for someone to discover the cure. The cure's here. But you have to accept it. You can't run away from it. Believe me, JB."

I couldn't convince him. He was determined to leave. "When will I see you?" I asked.

He shrugged.

"Where're you staying?"

"I'll go to Brad Holliday's place. He's an old buddy of mine. I'll be working on his crew. I left his phone number on the fridge in case something comes up." JB extended his hand to me. I shook it. "I'm glad we talked," he said. "I feel better."

It was strange that for the first time in four years we had finally broken down the wall between us, and now we were separating indefinitely. "JB, I know there's a way for you. God hasn't turned away from you. He doesn't do that. I know it."

"I guess I'm too ashamed to ask him." He looked around longingly. He pulled out a letter. "I'd appreciate it if you'd give this to Cami."

"You ought to talk to her yourself."

"I explained a lot of things to her. I couldn't bring myself to tell her everything. I've tried to write those things in the letter." I took the letter. "Take care, Jacob."

We hugged each other; then JB climbed into the Firebird, started the engine and closed the door. "If you see Victoria again," he said, "tell her hello for me."

"I wish you had a chance to talk to her yourself."

"Maybe I will. I'd like to tell her I was sorry for everything," he smiled. "Some day I might have that chance." He waved and pulled away.

CHAPTER TWENTY-FIVE

I didn't go to work Tuesday. I told Roger I needed some time to myself. I stayed in the apartment. I had attempted to clean the place when I first arrived in May, but I had resented doing it because I felt I was cleaning up JB's filth and clutter, which wasn't my responsibility. This day was different, though. I wanted the place clean, not for me, but for JB. It was a strange notion. Here I was cleaning everything for him after he had already left, but it was the only thing I could think to do for him.

As I cleaned, I discovered myself—not a pleasant discovery. I had always assumed that JB had been the one to fail spiritually. I had gone to church, been a missionary, done all the things that good members are supposed to do, but I had ignored the weightier matters, the genuine demonstration of charity for JB, for Victoria, for Leti and a host of others. In all my efforts to do the right things, I had neglected the sincere loving service and concern for others that were such integral aspects of the gospel.

When I finished the apartment, it was clean. But empty! And all the cleanliness would never compensate for the solitary loneliness there.

I took a ride up into the hill country around Huntsville, tormented by my inability to help JB. Desperately I hoped someone else would reach out to him. Cami had the influence and the inclination. The irony was that I had been the one who had wanted to pull Cami away from JB. Now more than anything I hoped that Cami wouldn't give up on him.

I thought of Leti Trujillo. I was smitten by a horrible guilt as I realized that four years earlier Leti had been reaching out to JB. Perhaps at that time in her life, he was the only one who could have helped her. And I had resented that. JB had seen Leti's potential as a human being; I had seen her merely as a lost cause to be discarded before she contaminated JB. I had wanted Leti Trujillo to disappear; her fatal accident had accommodated my wishes.

JB, on the other hand, had reached out to Leti and to Victoria and others. That goodness that Victoria and Cami had seen in JB was the very thing I was so deficient in. JB had neglected the little acts of righteousness that I had been so proud of in my own life, but he had not neglected charity.

In my mind I had always accused JB of erecting the wall between us. I saw now that I had been the smug mason of that wall, etching my name in every brick. JB had even attempted to pull the wall down. He had tried to open up the secret door to his soul and invite the one person in who should have understood him. I refused the invitation.

I hurt for JB, more than I had ever hurt for anyone else in my life. For the first time his pain became my pain. That afternoon as I drove through the hills around Huntsville, I thought of the challenge to bear one another's burdens and to mourn with those that mourned. I had failed miserably. I found myself blinking back tears of sorrow and disappointment, sorrow for JB and disappointment in my unwillingness to help him.

I was reluctant to go to the Hardaways' that evening. I wanted to see Susan. I needed to talk to her. But the thought of delivering JB's letter to Cami frightened me. Susan answered the door when I arrived. "Is Cami here?" I looked down at the letter in my hand. "I have something for her."

Susan called Cami and she came in. "JB wanted me to give you this," I said quietly.

She took the letter and held it without looking at it. "Did he go?" she asked quietly.

I nodded. "Yesterday evening." I looked away. "I'm sorry." Swallowing hard, I added, choosing my words carefully, not knowing how explicit JB had been with Cami, "I haven't been much help to JB. I didn't realize until just yesterday that…well, that JB's had some challenges in his life. I think I might have helped him at one time." I shook my head. "I don't know any more. I think maybe I waited too long to try."

I didn't stay at the Hardaways' that night. I needed to be by myself; and yet, I was miserable alone, haunted by all the things I might and should have done to make a difference in JB's life.

Around nine o'clock there was a soft knock at the apartment door. Susan was there with a soda and a small plate of sandwiches, carrot sticks, chips. "I didn't know if you'd eaten," she explained as I pushed open the screen door. "Are you hungry?"

I smiled faintly. "You know, come to think of it I am a little hungry. I just haven't felt like fixing anything."

As I ate Susan's simple supper, we talked. "These last four years I haven't understood JB. Now it seems too late for me to do any good."

"What happened? Can you talk about it?"

I told her about JB and Leti. I didn't go into all the details, but I think Susan understood. I explained my own critical manner. I told her of the last two days, of my own self-discovery.

"JB believes that because of what happened, no amount of good can save him. He feels totally helpless." I shook my head. "He told me yesterday that he has come to understand King David. Since I've talked to JB, I can't keep one short passage in the New Testament out of my mind."

"What's that?"

"When the Pharisee and Publican go to the temple to pray. The Publican is humble and feels reluctant to even raise his eyes. He merely pleads for forgiveness. The Pharisee, on the other hand, is proud of his righteousness and can't seem to even tolerate to be close to the less holy Publican." I breathed deeply and exhaled slowly. "It's strange how you hear a passage like that and the characters are faceless individuals. Today they became real people with real faces. And the Pharisee had my face."

Susan reached across the card table and took my hand. "I haven't been very accepting of JB. Cami would tell me that there was goodness there." She shook her head. "I didn't want to hear that. I preferred to point out all his flaws. I'm sorry, Jacob."

Wednesday I got off work a little early. I showered and put on new clothes when the phone rang. It was Teresa. "Can you come over for a few minutes, Jacob?"

I hesitated. "Right now?"

"Yeah. And hurry."

When I arrived at the Hardaways', Teresa opened the door and invited me in, escorting me into the living room, where she directed me to sit on the sofa and left the room without further explanation. Soft music was playing. Other than that the house was quiet. I sat on the sofa several minutes and then Cami came down the stairs barefoot, dressed in knee-length shorts and a cotton blouse.

"Hello, Jacob," she greeted me. She came in and was about to sit in one of the overstuffed chairs across from me when Teresa darted into the room and plopped down in the chair ahead of her.

"Why don't you sit over there on the sofa with Jacob?" she asked.

Surprised, Cami looked down at Teresa and then over at me. Smiling, she shrugged and remarked, "Well, Jacob, I think I'll sit on the sofa with you." She dropped down on the opposite end of the sofa from me and pulled her legs up under her.

"Do you guys want something to drink?" Teresa blurted out. Before we could answer, she charged from the chair to the kitchen. She reappeared with a small tray containing ice-filled glasses of SevenUp and a dozen Oreo cookies on a saucer. She set the tray on the coffee table, handed us each a drink and offered us a cookie. Cami and I studied Teresa, then looked at each other, smiled and shrugged.

"There are more drinks and cookies in the kitchen if you want them."

"Aren't you the dutiful little servant girl today," Cami commented to Teresa, grinning and winking at me.

"I thought you might like some drinks and things while you talked."

"While we talked?" Cami questioned.

Teresa sighed and looked around as though she were hearing the music for the first time. "Don't you just love this song. It makes me feel so romantic." She turned and started from the room.

"Romantic?" Cami asked so only I could hear. "Did she say romantic?"

"I think that's what she said." We both laughed and sipped

our drinks.

After a quiet moment, Cami asked, "What did you need?"

I turned to her. "What did I need?"

Cami nodded, picking up a cookie. "Teresa said you wanted to talk."

I looked at the plate of cookies, my drink and then over at Cami. "I didn't say anything about talking to you," I said, shaking my head. "Teresa called a few minutes ago and said to come over. That's all I know."

"She called you?"

I nodded and then it was like a light coming on. We were alone, the soft "romantic" music, the drinks, sitting on the sofa together. I started to smile, shaking my head in disbelief.

"Do you need anything else?" Teresa called out, sticking her head in from the kitchen.

"Teresa," Cami asked bluntly, "what's going on?"

Teresa stared at us a moment and then in exasperation she blurted out, "Talk. Talk to each other. Do I have to do everything? You're alone. Do something. JB's gone and isn't coming back. This is your chance."

I about choked on my SevenUp. I could feel my cheeks warm, and I didn't feel that I could glance in Cami's direction because she was probably feeling suddenly uncomfortable too.

"Jacob loves you, Cami," Teresa burst out. "He's always loved you. And you've loved him too. There's nobody to stop you now. I can't coach you every step of the way." Turning, she sped from the kitchen and up the stairs, leaving Cami and me with our mouths open, looking at the place where Teresa had disappeared.

Cami and I were awkwardly silent for a moment. I decided to attempt a touch of levity. Clearing my throat, I remarked, "When love dies, Teresa doesn't even let Cupid's corpse get cold before she's hatching another love scheme." I shook my head and nervously rubbed the back of my neck. "There's something that I've wanted to tell you, Cami."

"Maybe I better speak first," Cami cut me off. "I think this is partly my fault." She took a deep breath and made the verbal plunge. "I have liked you, Jacob. A lot. I've even told Teresa how I've felt. I know she thinks you're wonderful. And you are a great guy and everything. It's just that I couldn't..." She stopped. "I love your brother, Jacob. I don't know what's going to happen between JB and me. I have no idea. But just because he's moved away..." she stammered uneasily. "What I'm trying to say, Jacob, is that even though I think you're a wonderful person, I can't change how I feel about your brother, and..."

"This cuts me to the heart, Cami," I interjected lightly.

"Jacob," she pushed on, "if I've led you on in any way, I'm sorry. I didn't mean to. I've enjoyed being around you and everything. You've been a wonderful friend. But that's what you've been and I..."

"Can I say something?" I called out, holding up my hands. She stopped. I studied her a moment and smiled. "The thing that I wanted to tell you is that Susan and I have been dating for a while and..."

"Susan?"

"We haven't been terribly open about our feelings toward each other, but..." I smiled. "Actually we've grown quite close."

"You and Susan? She hasn't said anything to me."

Just then we heard a car pull in the driveway. Cami looked at me. "That's probably Susan," she announced.

A moment later Susan came into the house, greeted both of us and sat on the overstuffed chair across the room from the sofa. I cleared my throat and explained, "Teresa's been playing Cupid this afternoon."

"With you two?" Susan questioned slowly.

I nodded and smiled. Clearing my throat and leaning forward, I went on, "I've been trying to explain to Cami about us. I've told her everything."

"Everything?"

I laughed. "Well, not the intimate stuff."

"So she knows?" I nodded. Suddenly standing up, Susan said, "So what am I doing sitting clear over here like I was a sister missionary and you were my interviewing zone leader?" She walked over and dropped down next to me, taking my hand.

Cami stared. "Are you in on this?" she asked Susan. Susan nodded. "I mean are you faking this whole thing?"

"What do I have to do, sit on his lap and kiss him?"

"That might be a start."

Susan leaned over and kissed me on the lips, which was almost as much of a surprise to me as it was to Cami.

Cami shook her head incredulously. "This is not the Susan I know."

I proceeded to tell Susan how Teresa had tried to set up Cami and me. We were all laughing when Teresa came down the stairs. Halfway down the stairs she stopped and studied the scene before her—Cami and I on different ends of the sofa and Susan in the middle. "Well, what happened?" she demanded indignantly.

"Things just didn't work out between Cami and me," I explained with an indifferent shrug of my shoulders.

"Jacob says he's going to try Susan for a while," Cami added.

"You are both so dumb," she suddenly flared. "This isn't even funny. You love each other and you're going to be so sorry you didn't do something about it. And it's your own fault. I hope you're both miserable." She turned and charged back up the stairs.

We all sat there with our mouths open and then we began to snicker and finally burst out laughing. "Do you think you should have tried the kiss in front of her?" Cami asked.

"I'm not sure she was in the mood for anything quite that graphic just now," I answered, wagging my head.

CHAPTER TWENTY-SIX

Thursday afternoon Roger sent me to Ogden to deliver some loan papers to the bank. I was ready to head back up the canyon to Huntsville when I passed within a few blocks of where Victoria Trujillo worked. I had been thinking of her and her sister. Suddenly I felt a compelling need to talk to her, to apologize for how I'd thought and felt about her and Leti.

I glanced at my watch—a few minutes after five. I knew she might have already left, but I still drove over. There was a closed sign on the office door, but I could see Victoria inside. I waited for her. She closed the door, checked to make certain it was locked and then turned and started for her car, a white two-door Neon. Then she spotted me. "James?" she asked again, a hopeful tone in her voice.

I smiled plaintively and shook my head. "Wrong again."

She laughed. "I thought maybe you had talked to your brother and he stopped by to see me. Did you come to pick something up? We're closed."

I shook my head. "I want to talk to you." She looked down at her watch and then at me. "If you've got a few minutes." I looked around, feeling self-conscious standing there in the parking lot. "There's a little park a couple of blocks from here. We could drive over there."

She debated a moment and then nodded.

We reached the park and walked across the grass to a picnic table under a huge willow tree. We sat on opposite sides of the table. She touched her wedding band and twisted it on her finger. Looking up, she smiled and commented, "I usually don't go to the park and talk to guys."

I blushed. "I thought of that as we were driving here. I'll make it quick. I had to talk to you once more. Then I won't bother you anymore."

"You haven't bothered me." I gazed out across the park. There were a half dozen kids screaming and playing on a swing set fifty yards away. "After I talked to you on Monday, I..." I hesitated.

"I felt sorry for saying as much as I did," Victoria apologized. "I assumed that you knew everything. You and JB were so close."

"Not close enough. Maybe if we had been that close things would have been different." I cleared my throat nervously. "I'm sorry I wasn't more tolerant when we were in school together. You were right about my looking down my nose. It hasn't been until recently that I realized what a bad habit I've developed. I'm sorry that I didn't see you as JB did. I hope you don't have bad feelings toward him. He really cared about you and Leti."

"I don't have bad feelings toward James. I liked him." She laughed. "And Leti was so in love with him. With the other boys she knew she had always felt like she was the strong one, the one in total control. She was beautiful and talented and knew how to use both. Then James came along, so innocent, so caring, so totally different from any guy Leti had ever known.

"At first she didn't know how to deal with him, but then after they'd been seeing each other for a couple of weeks she came to my place in Logan. That was where I was living then. She said, `Vicki, I love this guy.'

"Well, you can imagine what my reaction was." She smiled and shook her head. "I had a good laugh." She was serious. "But this was different from anything that Leti had experienced. I could see that. She saw something in James that she had never seen in anyone before."

"And you saw it too?"

"Not then. Leti and James came to my place several times. I didn't warm up to him at first. I think that's because I was envious. My marriage certainly wasn't all that great, and here Leti seemed so happy and excited even though they were both really young. She was changing. And I couldn't understand that. James wasn't domineering and demanding, but Leti melted under his quiet, innocent influence."

"When did you find out that Leti was...expecting?"

"Who told you she was expecting?" She asked the question with a touch of incredulity.

"JB told me."

"Recently?"

"A couple of days ago when I told him you and I had talked."

"Leti wasn't expecting."

"What?"

Victoria studied me for a moment, seeming to be undecided about what she should say next. "Leti only thought she was expecting. I guess I always assumed James knew that."

"I'm lost."

"Everything turned out negative," Victoria explained uneasily. "The test, I mean. Even if she had been, it happened before James and her."

Suddenly this puzzle, which had seemed to fall into place a few days earlier, was cracking up before my eyes. "But I thought that was the reason she and JB were getting married."

"It was."

"You're confusing me." I shook my head, unable to focus on anything because everything kept changing just when I thought I understood it.

"I've probably done my share of confusing." She tapped her long nails on the tabletop.

"If Leti wasn't expecting," I stammered, "why did she…" I swallowed, uncertain how to phrase the question. "Why did she kill herself?"

"Those were just rumors," Victoria responded quickly, warmly. "They spring up every time someone like Leti dies unexpectedly. Leti would never have done anything like that. I know that for sure."

"JB believes she did," I said hoarsely. "And he feels responsible."

Victoria looked across the table at me, genuine shock and puzzlement in her look. "Why?"

"He thinks she did it to…free him. If that isn't true, what is? And how do you know?"

Victoria looked away from me, staring back at our cars parked along the street. For a long time she was quiet. Finally she turned to me. "He probably hates me."

"JB?"

She nodded.

"No. In fact, he wonders if you hate him."

"For what?"

"For what he did to Leti."

Victoria placed her elbows on the table and pressed the palms of her hands together. The tips of her fingers touched her chin. Slowly she closed her eyes. "This is all my fault then," she whispered.

Opening her eyes, she began to talk. "I was already married when Leti came to me thinking there might be a chance she was expecting. She had been trying to break things off with this Marcus Roper guy. He was a lot like the guy I first married. A real charmer as a boyfriend, but a genuine jerk as a husband. Then James comes along at the tail end of that relationship. I didn't want Leti to end up like me. I knew James and Leti had...well, slipped up. So I figured Leti could have married James as easily as she could marry Marcus Roper, and he would have been so much better for her.

"I was the one who told James that Leti was expecting. He asked her and she confirmed it, but James didn't ever realize that he was not the one. Leti was upset with me because she said I'd lied to James, and she hadn't had the courage to tell him what had really happened. She was ashamed too. I tried to tell her that it didn't matter. I said that she should marry James and things would work out because he was the one she really loved."

Victoria shook her head. "I couldn't convince her, though. She decided that she was going to explain everything to James. She was still torn because he had promised to marry her, and she loved him. I argued with her. But she thought too much of James to do that to him. She had made up her mind she was going to talk to him, even if it meant losing him for good."

"So why doesn't James know this?"

"It took Leti a while to build up her nerve to tell him. By then the doctor had told her she wasn't expecting." Victoria paused and stared blankly out across the park. "I was the first one she came to. We stayed up late. I argued with her. She refused."

Victoria turned to me and smiled ruefully. "It was almost two in the morning when Leti left my place. I knew she was tired. I should have insisted she stay with me, but I was angry with her and felt she was throwing away a perfect opportunity. But Leti was happy and at peace with herself." She shook her head. "She didn't take her own life. She simply fell asleep at the wheel. And if anyone's to blame, it's me because I didn't invite her to stay the night with me."

As I listened to Victoria, it was as though a huge, horrendous weight was lifted from my shoulders. What she had said didn't change the original immorality, but it certainly changed the tragedy of Leti's death.

"I'm sorry if James has thought something else all this time. That's my fault because I was the one to tell the first lie."

"Would you do me a favor? And JB a favor?"

"What?"

I pulled out my wallet and handed her a scrap of paper with a phone number written on it. "James is going to be staying at this number. Give him a call. I don't even know if he would believe you if you talked to him, but it might change some things in his mind."

Victoria took the scrap of paper and studied it before folding it and holding it in her hand. "I'll try to call him." She smiled and looked around. "And I think maybe we had better be on our way before someone gets suspicious about us."

Driving up the canyon after speaking to Victoria, I thought of JB and his burden, a burden that wasn't as great as he had imagined. I had to talk to him, reach out to him, ask his forgiveness as well as help him see that there was an escape from the guilt weighing him down.

As I drove, a terrible thought crept into my mind. Would JB resort to the same out that he had presumed Leti had taken? Chilled by the possibility, I knew I had to reach him, intervene before he erroneously convinced himself that his sliver of hope was a mere illusion.

As soon as I reached the apartment, I called Brad Holliday's place in Phoenix. JB hadn't arrived, and Brad hadn't had any contact with him. JB had left three days earlier, more than enough time for him to make the trip.

"I'm going to Phoenix," I announced to Susan that evening.

"When?"

"As soon as I know he's there."

"What about your work?"

"It'll have to wait. I can't let this one chance slip away from me. It could be my last."

"I can go with you. We could take one of our cars." She held up her hand and smiled, anticipating my objection. "The Bug might not make it. And right now it's important that *you* make it there. A relief driver might come in handy."

I smiled, comforted by her support. "I wouldn't mind the company either. I'll let you know as soon as I hear something."

I called Brad Holliday's place the next morning. Brad was gone, but his wife answered. JB hadn't arrived during the night. As soon as I returned home from work Friday afternoon, I called again.

"He showed up a little past noon," Brad's wife explained. "We have an extra bedroom and I told him to move his things in. Then I had to go to the store and do some shopping. I wasn't gone more than two hours. When I returned, he was gone. He just left a note saying thanks."

"Did he say where he was going?"

"No."

"Was he upset when he arrived?"

"He wasn't very talkative. He'd been on the road a long time, just kind of wandering around the country. He seemed to want to be alone."

"Is there anyplace he might have gone?"

"You could call later and talk to Brad. He might know something."

A dark foreboding wormed its way into my brain. I dreaded and yet braced myself for the worst, praying with all my heart that he wouldn't take that irrevocable step across the definitive line of no return.

I called Brad Holliday later that evening, but he couldn't help me. JB hadn't talked to anyone there. I was more than nervous; I was frantic.

Saturday morning I called Brad again, hoping that perhaps JB had returned, but he hadn't. Roger had asked me to work Saturday, and all day I agonized over JB's disappearance.

Saturday evening was the Hardaways' family reunion at the Huntsville park. I didn't feel at all like going, but earlier in the week I'd promised Susan that I'd pick up some things in Ogden for the picnic. I felt obligated to attend even though my mind and emotions were a churning torrent of fears and apprehension.

After work I decided to stop by the apartment to call Brad Holliday before going to pick things up for the picnic. It was a little before four o'clock when I turned down the block for home. My stomach lurched excitedly. The Firebird was parked in front.

Leaping from the Bug as soon as I turned off the engine, I bounded for the basement steps. "JB," I shouted as soon as I pulled the screen door open. "JB, where are you?"

There was no answer. I looked in his bedroom. Part of his things were piled on the bed. Then I heard the shower. I hammered on the door with my fist. "JB, is that you?"

"You just *thought* you got rid of me," he called out above the echoing splash of the shower. "I hope you don't mind my dropping in again."

"Mind! What are you talking about? This is *your* place."

"It's so clean I thought I was in the wrong apartment. I hardly dared touch anything. I'll try not to mess it up."

"What do you mean, mess it up? It was messed up because you weren't here."

"It feels good to be back."

"Where have you been? I've called Brad Holliday a dozen times."

"I just took my time going down, doing some serious thinking."

"I've got to talk to you. But I've got to run down the mountain to pick up some things for the Hardaways' family picnic. I'll be right back."

"I've got an appointment."

I assumed he meant Cami. "I'll be back in less than an hour, depending on the traffic in the canyon. We'll go to the picnic together." I was jabbering more than making sense.

He laughed. "I don't have an invitation."

"Then I'll stay home from the picnic." I turned to leave and then stopped. "JB," I shouted through the door, "I'm glad you're back. I kept thinking of you, wishing you were here."

The shower continued to run, but JB didn't answer. I stood there, thinking of something I hadn't told JB in years. Over the last few days more than anything I had wanted to tell him. I had told myself that if I ever had another chance, I wouldn't hesitate. I hammered on the door with my fist. "JB," I called out, my voice quavering slightly.

"Yeah," he called back just loud enough for me to hear.

"JB, I love you." I choked, blinking back a mist. "It's been so long since I've…" I swallowed. "I just wanted you to know that, JB." I turned and charged from the apartment, feeling a rush of relief.

It took me almost two hours to drive to Ogden, pick up the napkins, paper plates, cups, plastic utensils and chips before heading back up the canyon. When I reached the apartment, JB was gone. His things were still piled on the bed so I knew he'd be back. I had passed the Hardaways' home on my way back from Ogden, but his car hadn't been there.

It was approaching six-thirty and I had to be over to the Hardaways' by seven. Hurriedly I climbed into the shower, hoping JB would return before I had to leave again. While I was getting dressed, Susan called and asked if I'd pick up two bags of ice.

"Something good happened," I told her. I laughed. "I'll tell you when I see you, but I'm not going to Phoenix."

I got dressed, hopped in the Bug and drove over to the convenience store and bought the ice. It took longer than I had expected so it was after seven when I swung back to the apartment. The Firebird was there.

I was late, but I had to see JB, even if for a few minutes. Bursting through the screen door, I headed for the hall, but before I could take two steps, I stumbled to a halt. JB sat at the table with a glass of ice and a half-empty bottle of soda in front of him. My mouth dropped open. His mustache was gone. His hair was clipped short. The stud earring was missing. He was dressed in a pair of white slacks and a light blue short-sleeve dress shirt. I hadn't seen JB looking like this since high school.

"Hello, Jacob," he greeted me quietly, smiling and lifting his glass of ice and tipping it in my direction. "I stole one of your sodas. I was dying of thirst. That's what talking too much does."

I realized that my mouth was hanging open. I closed it, swallowed and then ran my tongue over my lips. "You..." I gestured in his direction and then shrugged, completely taken back. "You look...different. But great," I quickly added with a grin. "Awesome!"

His face colored and he set his glass down, pouring the rest of the soda in. He watched the drink fizz and foam for a moment and then he turned back to me. "You don't know how strange I feel. Weird. I almost scared myself looking in the mirror. I thought I was looking at you."

"That's enough to scare anyone," I joked.

"No," he said, shaking his head. "It felt good. To look like you." He set his glass down, pushed his chair back and stood. Smiling while his cheeks colored with self-conscious embarrassment, he held his arms out and looked down at himself. "I keep wondering if this is really me."

Slowly I walked over to him. I know he wasn't expecting me to do anything wildly out of the ordinary, but I was so relieved and happy to see him, I couldn't help myself. Without warning, I threw my arms around him and pulled him close to me in a bear hug. "You don't know how glad I am to have you back, JB." My voice cracked with emotion. "I've missed you. I love you, JB. I wish I'd told you that a long time ago."

All of a sudden JB and I were both crying. Not saying anything, just battling our emotions. We both sat down at the table.

"I called Brad's place," I stammered, "hoping I'd catch you. You finally showed up and then took off again. Brad's wife didn't have a clue where you'd gone. Then I really got worried." I was babbling again. "I didn't know if I should call the police or something, but I didn't know where to tell them to even look for you, and..." I caught my breath and stared across the table at him. "Dang, it's good to see you."

"I've done a lot of thinking the last few days." He rolled his moisture-covered glass in his hands as the ice tinkled softly. "I kept thinking of all the things you had told me, you know, about the atonement and repentance and forgiveness. I hadn't ever allowed myself to think of those things. It was always too painful because I was sure they didn't apply to me. You made it sound like there might be a chance, even for me."

"There is. I know it, JB."

He swallowed. "Before I reached Brad's place, I made up my mind that I needed to find out for sure what my chances were." He looked down at the table. "I had thought a number of times that I had been at the very bottom. But I really hit bottom this time.

"I was in the mountains of Arizona outside Flagstaff when I finally came to the conclusion I couldn't go on like this." He paused. "I knew I had to get on a different train or I had to get off the train permanently." He looked up at me. I could see the fear in his eyes. "I was ready to bag it all. I hadn't prayed for months." He shrugged. "Years, I guess. But I pulled off the road and prayed. I was willing to do anything."

He seemed to relax as he spoke. "Something happened to me up there in the trees with no one else around. For the longest time as I prayed I couldn't shake the old agony. I felt so unworthy to even pray, but I didn't stop. I couldn't. Something in my heart told me if I stopped I'd be letting go of my very last lifeline.

"It was then that I started to feel peace. It was just a shadow at first, but I felt loved and understood. Soon I was consumed with the feeling." He shook his head. "I didn't want to leave that place. That grove of trees was the only place I had ever found peace in the last four years. I still wasn't sure what was going to happen, but I sensed that a door would open somewhere, sometime."

"I talked to Victoria again," I offered, hoping to help him.

JB nodded, smiling weakly. "She called me."

"Victoria?"

"She said you'd given her the phone number. That's why I left Brad's place. It was like, as soon as Brad's wife went out the door, the phone rang. Victoria and I talked for a while and then I told her I wanted to sit down with her face to face. We had lunch today."

"So you know about Leti?"

He nodded. "It doesn't make anything right. I made mistakes four years ago. But I was relieved that Leti didn't take her own life, that she had made some decisions before the accident." He shook his head. "I still wish I could have helped her." He wet his lips. "I loved Leti. I've loved her ever since. If there's been anything that's kept me from blowing everything since her death, it's been my memory of her. I have felt responsible for her. I still do. But I sense she's all right now."

He took a slow sip of soda and set the glass down. "It wasn't until I met Cami that I found someone that I could love in that same way. I guess it was knowing Cami and then having you come back that made me see how far I was away from where I wanted to be. I called Bishop Harrison this afternoon. He agreed to meet with me."

"That's where you were?" I asked, surprised.

He nodded. "As soon as I set up the appointment, I found a barber. I wanted to walk away from my old life. I know that changing my outside isn't the most important thing, but it's a start, and I wanted to get started.

"I had a talk with Bishop Harrison, a talk I should have had a long time ago." He shook his head. "I'm not sure I was ready then. I told him everything. I don't know where things will end, but I'm willing to do whatever's required." He looked at me. "I still want to go on a mission." He smiled sadly. "It won't be like we planned. You know, the two of us together, but I don't care how long I have to wait or what I have to do."

"Did Bishop Harrison think there was a chance?"

"He needs to talk to the stake president. It might be six months, a year. But it doesn't matter. When I used to think of going on my mission, I knew I couldn't, that it was impossible for someone like me, but I told myself that if I ever found a way, I'd go, regardless of the cost."

"What about Cami?"

He thought for a long time. "I don't know how she feels. She knows about my past. Knowing that, she might not be interested." He shrugged. "But I couldn't ask her to wait anyway. I don't know how long the wait will be. I've reconciled myself to the wait. The wait doesn't worry me. I won't expect her to wait. She deserves better."

"Maybe she wants to wait."

He smiled. "She was the one who got me thinking again, really thinking. It wasn't anything she said necessarily. It was just that I knew I could never have her unless there was some way that I could clean up my past. I had gotten to the point where I had accepted my situation, accepted the fact that I would never climb any higher. Cami made me want to climb higher. But she deserves someone who can take her. Now."

For sometime we talked. It was as though I had lost my brother, and he had finally returned. I wasn't aware of the passing of time until we heard a car drive up, doors open and close, and then the girls' voices.

"Are you expecting Susan?"

"Susan," I groaned. "I forgot the picnic."

Just then Susan and Cami came down the steps. From the doorway they could see JB but not me. Susan peered through the screen door. "You sure look relaxed," she said, laughing incredulously. "Here we all sit waiting for the picnic to begin while you've got all the stuff." She opened the door and both she and Cami stepped inside. "I thought…" She froze, as did Cami. Their startled gaze went from JB to me and then back to JB. "Who's who?" she stammered. Her gaze shifted to me. "You're Jacob, aren't you?" she asked, not at all positive.

Cami hadn't taken her eyes from JB. "You're JB. I know it."

Embarrassed and a bit awkward, JB pushed his chair back and stood. "Hello, Cami," he said simply. He pressed his lips together.

Cami walked toward him slowly. When she was finally in arm's reach, she stopped and peered over at me. "I do have the right one this time, don't I?" she questioned.

I smiled. "You've got the right one."

She looked back at JB and then studied his ear. "You're JB all right," she observed. Without hesitating more, she threw her arms around his neck and kissed him. It brought back memories, but I was glad this time she had the right guy.

I reached out and took Susan by the hand and pulled her next to me. "These two might want to be alone," I whispered huskily. "And the Hardaway picnic is probably going to go into a wild tail spin if we don't get over there with everything in the back of my car."

"Oh, the stuff!" Susan gasped, pulling me toward the door.

Cami and JB separated momentarily. "We'll be right there," Cami called out. Turning back to JB, she questioned, "You are coming, aren't you?"

"I haven't been invited."

"You're invited."

When Susan and I reached the park and climbed out of the car, she took me by the arm and we started the long walk across the grass to where the family was gathered around several picnic tables. The only ones who seemed to pay much attention to us were Susan's two brothers, Teresa and Denton. The others didn't know enough about who Susan was dating to think much about us.

As we reached the group, I took Susan's hand as she introduced me to her aunts and uncles and cousins. Several times she leaned against me or took my arm. It was obvious that we were good friends.

Teresa seemed in shock, as though she couldn't take her eyes off Susan and me. She hung back without speaking to anyone or commenting about our being together. As it got time to sit down, Denton spoke up and remarked that no one had brought the drinks from the back of his truck.

"Jacob and I will do that," Teresa piped up as though she were afraid someone else might volunteer and steal her opportunity. She looked at me, waiting to see if I would accept her invitation. "That is if Susan can let go of Jacob's arm long enough for him to get away."

Susan looked at Teresa quizzically and smiled. "Do you want me to help?" Susan offered with her arm still through mine.

"No," Teresa retorted, shaking her head and wagging her finger, "Jacob and I can handle this."

Teresa and I walked till we were out of earshot before either one of us said anything. "All right, Jacob," she began, not looking over at me as we headed for Denton's truck, "what is this with you and Susan?" Before I could answer, she fired off, "And don't give me a bunch of baloney."

"I got tired of coming to these Hardaway affairs without a date."

"Jacob," she muttered, "you're so totally dumb. Are you two just putting this whole thing on?" She looked over at me.

"What do you want me to say?" I smiled, tucking my shirt in as I walked.

"Try the truth. You're setting me up, aren't you? Admit it. Susan hasn't ever had any use for you and you haven't had much use for her." She paused. "Well, maybe you've been a little more friendly lately."

"We've been a lot more friendly," I said, stopping at the truck.

Teresa looked up at me. "You're just good friends and this hand holding and garbage is just a big show for me?"

I leaned my forearms on the back of the truck and looked out in the street. "Actually, we're a little more than good friends and..." I stopped. "And there's no show."

"I don't believe it," she grumbled, looking away. "Even if you can say it with a straight face. I've been watching your every move since you came to Huntsville."

"Not every move."

"What about Tyson?"

"What about him?"

"Where does he fit in?"

I shrugged. "Well, Teresa, I really didn't plan to reserve a spot for him. I'd kind of like to have Susan to myself."

"She likes Tyson. I know it." Her eyes narrowed. "That night she came in at two in the morning, all dreamy-eyed and dancing about like a dummy. That wasn't a show."

"Tyson brought her home at ten forty-five. I was the one who brought her in at two in the morning." She stared at me. I smiled faintly. "Honest, Teresa," I said, holding up my right hand. "You see," I joked, "I've been looking around for a really sharp sister-in-law. I told you once that you were too young for me to marry so I guess I'll have to take you as my sister-in-law."

"Jacob, get real. I'm not stupid."

"Teresa," I said seriously, "I think I love your sister."

She stared at me. "Have you even kissed?" she accused.

"That's a personal question."

"So I'm getting personal."

I smiled. "Yes, I've kissed her. I love her."

"Have you told her that?"

I hesitated. "Not exactly. Not in those words."

She heaved a sigh. "What you need is a good coach, someone that will help you…"

"No way," I cut in, shaking my head and pushing away from the truck. "The last time you coached me we almost had a disaster on our hands."

"You'll have to admit that if it weren't for my help, even though I was trying to get you lined up with Cami, you probably wouldn't have fallen for Susan. Isn't that true?"

"Do you two need some help with the drinks?" Susan called to us, walking across the grass.

Teresa and I stopped talking and stared at one another until Susan came up to us. She slipped her arm through mine and leaned against me. "You're not trying to cut in on me, are you?" Susan asked Teresa, reaching out and gently brushing Teresa's cheek with the back of her hand.

Teresa suddenly looked totally indifferent. "Nah, he's too old for me." Then she quickly jabbed, "And he's probably too young for you. But I kind of like him hanging around so…" She grinned broadly. "Forget what I said the other night. I was wrong. You're the one he's always loved. Not Cami. Hey, we'd better get these drinks over to the picnic," she burst out, pulling a case of canned soda from the back of the truck and starting across the lawn in the direction of the picnic tables.

"We're going to miss Daddy's announcement if we don't hurry," she flung over her shoulder. "If he ever gets up the nerve to make it. What he needs is a really good coach."

Susan looked up at me and smiled as Teresa headed across the grass. "Does she approve?"

"I believe she thinks we're moving too slow."

Susan laughed, jabbed me in the stomach with her fingers and responded, "I'd agree with her there."

Handing Susan a case of soda and taking one myself, I nodded and said, "You won't get any argument from me. And I don't even need a coach to tell me that." I smiled. "Let's go give your dad some encouragement."

Susan laughed as we started across the park.

ABOUT THE AUTHOR

Alma J. Yates was born and raised on a small farm outside Brigham City, Utah, and attended Box Elder High School. According to his recollection, he was not a great student, but he did ponder the possibility of one day becoming a writer. In the early 70's, he served in the West Mexican Mission. Later he graduated from Brigham Young University with a B.A. in English and an M.A. in educational administration.

Alma taught high school English for several years in Snowflake, Arizona. It was during these years that he wrote and published his first novel, *The Miracle of Miss Willie*. After teaching English six-and-a-half years, he moved into school administration. Now he works as the principal of Highland Primary School in Snowflake.

For years, writing had been one of Alma's loves. In addition to dozens of short stories and articles that have appeared in Church magazines, he has published six novels prior to *Double Take*: *The Miracle of Miss Wille*, *Horse Thieves*, *The Inner Storm*, *Ghosts in the Baker Mine*, *No More Strangers*, *Please* and *Nick*.

He and his wife, Nicki, are the parents of seven sons and one daughter.